Praise for the Noodle Shop mystery series

DIM SUM OF ALL FEARS

"Provides plenty of twists and turns and a perky, albeit conflicted, sleuth." —*Kirkus Reviews*

DEATH BY DUMPLING

"Vivien Chien serves up a delicious mystery with a side order of soy sauce and sass. A tasty start to a new mystery series!"

—Kylie Logan, bestselling author of *Gone with the Twins*

"*Death by Dumpling* is a fun and sassy debut with unique flavor, local flair, and heart."

—Amanda Flower, Agatha Award-winning author of *Lethal Licorice*

"A charming debut, with plenty of red herrings. The heroine's future looks bright." —*Kirkus Reviews*

WONTON

TERROR

VIVIEN CHIEN

St. Martin's Paperbacks

This is a work of fiction. All of the characters, organizations, and events portrayed in this novel are either products of the author's imagination or are used fictitiously.

Published in the United States by St. Martin's Paperbacks, an imprint of St. Martin's Publishing Group.

WONTON TERROR

Copyright © 2019 by Vivien Chien.
Excerpt from *Egg Drop Dead* copyright © 2019 by Vivien Chien.

All rights reserved.

For information, address St. Martin's Publishing Group, 120 Broadway, New York, NY 10271.

www.stmartins.com

ISBN: 978-1-250-22834-5

Our books may be purchased in bulk for promotional, educational, or business use. Please contact your local bookseller or the Macmillan Corporate and Premium Sales Department at 1-800-221-7945, ext. 5442, or by email at MacmillanSpecialMarkets@macmillan.com.

Printed in the United States of America

St. Martin's Paperbacks edition / September 2019

10 9 8 7 6 5 4 3 2 1

For my fellow daydream believers,
Keep on keepin' on.

ACKNOWLEDGMENTS

- - - - - - - - - - - - - - -

I am extremely grateful to the following:

My amazing agent, Gail Fortune, who continues to show me unwavering support and encouragement. Thank you for the pep-talks and reassurances! To my magnificent editors, Hannah Braaten and Nettie Finn, how I got so lucky to have both of you I'll never know, but I am thankful for you every day. To Allison Ziegler, Kayla Janas, and Mary Ann Asher for all you do to make the Noodle Shop series excel. You gals are the best! And as always, I thank St. Martin's Press for the incredible opportunity to be part of their author-ly family.

Thank you to Joshua Hood for answering my completely random questions on sneaky ways to blow things up. If anything, you are patient. And to Michael Boomhower for conversations over Mexican food, entertaining my queries on explosives, the occasional vampire, and everything in between. I appreciate you more than words can say.

To my wonderful dad, Paul Corrao, for just about everything under the sun. Your support means the world to me. Thank you from the bottom of my heart. To my mother, Chin Mei Chien and my sister, Shu-Hui Wills, thank you for wise words and life lessons. Much love to my soul sister, Rebecca Zandovskis, for keeping me afloat when the high tides roll in. I am fortunate to have you in my life.

Alyssa Danchuk, thank you so much for your continued support, your many years of friendship, and for being the familiar face at many of my book events. I appreciate you. To my gals, Mallory, Lindsey, and Holly who always have my back and keep up morale when I'm up to my eyeballs in edits. Thank you, thank you!

To the book bloggers, sellers, and librarians, a million thank yous not only for the support you give to my series and kind words along the way, but also for the services you perform every day. Go books! To my readers, you guys are freaking awesome! Many thanks to all of you for picking up my series and allowing me, Lana, and all the wacky characters of the Noodle Shop mysteries into your lives.

To the unnamed friends and family who have encouraged me along the way, I thank you always.

CHAPTER
1

"The Poconos or Put-in-Bay?" I waved two travel brochures in front of my good friend and restaurant chef, Peter Huang. My boyfriend, Adam, was planning a weekend getaway for my upcoming birthday and he'd left me in charge of location selection. The only problem was that I couldn't make up my mind.

Peter and I, including many others from the surrounding community, were standing in a parking lot on a blocked-off Rockwell Avenue in preparation for the first Asian Night Market of the summer. Rockwell, between the two intersecting streets of East Twenty-first and East Twenty-fourth, was barricaded from traffic to host the weekly outdoor event from sunset until 11 P.M. Every Friday evening during the summer months, local businesses—some Asian and some not—set up a booth to display their merchandise or food.

And as restaurant manager of the Ho-Lee Noodle House, I, Lana Lee, was tasked with the duty—by my mother—to accompany Peter to at least seventy-five percent of the events.

Not that I minded in the least. Would I take hanging around outside on beautiful summer nights over being cooped up in our family's restaurant? That would be a yes.

The evening was just beginning and the market wasn't yet open to the public. Peter was busy prepping our rented grill and workstation while my job was to handle cash flow and take orders. He had given me specific instructions to not touch his grill, and without a fight, I complied. Instead, I busied myself with the travel brochures that Adam had passed on to me the other day. When it came to stuff like this, I was never good at making a decision.

"I don't know, man, I've never been to either one before." He leaned over the grill, and the black baseball cap that he always wore sat low, covering his eyes. "Flip a coin or something. That's what I always do when I can't decide."

I grumbled at the colorful pamphlets in my hand. "I don't know why he can't pick where we're going. It was his idea to begin with."

Peter chuckled. "If you pick something lame, maybe he'll pick something else."

"Hmmm . . . not a bad idea . . ." I stuffed the brochures back in my purse underneath our workstation counter. As I stood up, a food truck pulled into the parking lot and maneuvered itself carefully near the fence adjacent to our location, next to two other trucks that had arrived earlier.

The truck nearest the stage sold bubble tea in

every flavor known to man, and would be sure to bring long lines, especially in this heat. The truck that would now be in the middle spot sold barbecued meat on sticks. They also pulled in a lot of business since their product was so easy to carry while walking around the night market.

The current vehicle pulling in, Wonton on Wheels, was owned by Sandra and Ronnie Chow, who had been friends of my parents since I could remember. Sandra and Ronnie were always starting one business venture or another, but they were new to the food service industry.

It was only a little over a year ago that they'd jumped on the food truck bandwagon and, so far, it seemed to be going pretty well for them. Even though the married couple had been friends with my parents since I was little, they'd become more distant over the years and we hardly saw them anymore. My mother used to drag me to their house to play with their son, Calvin, who was only a few years older than me. I remember him being something of a bully. My dad would try to convince me that Calvin teased me because he liked me, but at that age I couldn't have cared less. After all, boys were "yucky."

Sandra, a rail-thin woman with sunken cheekbones and a sharp nose, hopped out of the passenger seat and inspected her husband's parking job. After she'd made a loop around the vehicle, she stood near the driver's side window and gave him a thumbs-up.

"Good thing we didn't bother bringing any wontons with us," Peter said, watching as the couple worked to set up their truck. "They're totally going to steal the show."

As far as Asian food trucks go, Wonton on Wheels was a genius idea if I'd ever seen one. They prepared wontons in a variety of ways: on skewers, as salad cups, fried, steamed, and of course, in soup. I had sampled a couple varieties myself . . . you know, for research, and found that I was a fan of their steamed wontons in chili sauce. Thinking about them made my mouth water.

I decided to focus on our station instead of drooling over wontons. Maybe at some point later in the night, I'd get the chance to slip away and grab myself a couple.

After the register portion of the booth was set up just the way I wanted it, I checked the time and noted there was about ten minutes left before the general public would be allowed through the barricades.

Sandra had wandered off from the food truck and was now standing at a booth diagonal to both of our spots. She was chatting up a woman who appeared to be peddling handmade jewelry. The woman locked eyes on me and waved me over. Sandra turned around to see who the woman was waving at and smiled when she realized it was me.

I smiled in return and waved, letting Peter know that I would be right back.

When I approached the jewelry stand, the woman came around to the front of her table and grabbed both of my hands. She was a petite woman with chubby cheeks that reminded me of my mother. "Waaaa . . . Lana Lee!" She leaned back and gave me a once-over, nodding in approval. "You are so grown-up now!"

I kept the smile on my face, unsure of what to say. I didn't recognize this woman at all.

"You do not remember me, but I was good friends with your mother when you were a little girl. My name is Ruby."

I shook my head. "I'm sorry, but it's nice to meet you . . . again."

"That's okay." Her eyes darted back to the Ho-Lee Noodle House booth. "Is Anna May here too? I bet she is a beautiful woman now."

Anna May is my older sister and as far as I'm concerned she's okay looking. "No, she's working at the restaurant tonight, but I'll be sure to tell her you said hi."

Ruby pinched my cheek. "Your mother must be so proud of you."

"I hope so . . ."

She stepped aside so Sandra and I could say hello.

"It is so nice to see you, Lana." Sandra extended her hand. "It has been a very long time."

Most of the older generation of Asians are opposed to hugging, but I can't help it, I'm a hugger. I blame my dad for that one. So forgetting my manners, I wrapped my arms around Sandra. "Nice to see you too."

Sandra winced as my arms squeezed her shoulders.

I jumped back. "Oh, I'm sorry!"

"It's okay," she replied apologetically. "I hurt my back this week. It is nothing serious."

Ruby tsked. "You hurt your back . . . again?"

The two women exchanged a look that was lost on me.

"So . . ." I said, feeling slightly out of the loop. "Is this your first time at the night market?"

Both women nodded.

I inspected the table of jewelry Ruby had on display. "These are gorgeous."

Organized in velvet trays were cloisonné earrings, jade bracelets, rings and necklaces made with opals, mother-of-pearl, and turquoise. She even had a selection of Chinese hairpins and hair combs.

"Thank you." Ruby admired her table of accessories. "I make everything by hand."

"Wow, really?" I studied the intricate beadwork on a pair of pearl earrings and wished I possessed the skill and patience to create something that delicate. "You should talk to Esther Chin about carrying some of these in her shop. I bet these would sell like crazy at the Village."

Ruby and Sandra shared another unspoken message before she replied, "Perhaps I will talk with her."

"Speaking of crazy, get ready for tonight," I warned them. "It gets so jammed with people, they can barely get through. Last year we ran out of food within—"

"Sandy!" a gravelly voice shouted from behind us.

The three of us turned in the direction the voice was coming from and saw Ronnie Chow standing near the back of the food truck. He was short, chubby, and sweating like he'd just run a marathon. "Get over here now!" He waved his arms frantically at his wife. "Stop messing around! No gossiping. We have work to do!"

"Okay, I'll be right there," Sandra said in a sheepish tone. When she turned to face us, I noticed that her cheeks were pink with embarrassment. "I will talk with you later."

The two women exchanged a final look before Sandra walked off.

When she was out of earshot, I turned to Ruby. "Is everything okay?"

Ruby shook her head, disappointment etched in the soft lines of her face. Her eyes stayed on Sandra as she approached her husband. "This is how Ronnie behaves. I don't know how Sandra can handle him." With a heavy sigh, she turned away from the couple and walked back around her table.

I continued to watch the Chows while Ruby busied herself making the final preparations to her jewelry stand. I gathered that Sandra and Ronnie were speaking harshly to one another by their jerky body language and strained expressions. Ronnie pointed at their food truck and then pointed at the food truck next to them. I saw Sandra look around him, fold her arms across her chest and turn on her heel to head back inside their truck. When she turned away from him, I caught her profile and could see her lips moving as if she were mumbling something to herself. She disappeared on the other side of the vehicle and I turned my attention back to Ruby to wish her luck on her first evening at the night market.

I said good-bye to Ruby and made my way back to Peter who had been watching the exchange.

"What the heck was all that about?" Peter asked.

"Oh, I guess that lady at the jewelry stand was a friend of my mother's when I was a kid."

"No, I didn't mean that . . . I meant them." He tilted his head toward Wonton on Wheels.

"I have no idea, but I was wondering the same thing."

CHAPTER
2

To be clear, the path I ended up on isn't exactly how I imagined my late twenties would go. Less than a year ago, I was determined to turn myself into a corporate hot shot who wore stiletto heels and fancy suits. Never mind that I have yet to find a pair of stilettos I can wear longer than fifteen minutes without staggering in pain.

But an unforeseen turn of events that began with an ugly breakup and kept on spiraling led me down a road I couldn't have anticipated. That's life, right?

Before I knew what was happening, I was working at my parents' Chinese restaurant, Ho-Lee Noodle House, as their day-shift server, sporadically dyeing my hair unnatural colors—I'm currently rocking purple—and solving crimes in my search for truth and justice.

Now a handful of months later, I'm managing the family business while my mother enjoys an early semi-retirement, dating a detective with the Fairview

Park police department, and deliberating on what color to dye my hair next.

In short, I finally felt happy. And my life—though on a different track than intended—was starting to feel normal again. As the crowd began to enter the streets, I took a moment to appreciate my current plane of existence. It was good to be Lana Lee.

Rockwell Avenue was soon filled with masses of people moving from one tented booth to another in search of handmade goods, local services, or menu samplings from nearby restaurants.

Asia Village, the shopping plaza that housed my family's restaurant, was well represented on the busy street. Aside from Peter and me, Kimmy Tran from China Cinema and Song, an Asian entertainment store, was two tables away from us selling CDs and Chinese movies. Esther Chin, who owned Chin's Gifts, was somewhere down the street peddling her porcelain knickknacks, music boxes, and jade jewelry. Jasmine Ming, from Asian Accents hair salon, was showcasing a table of hair treatments, shampoos, and nail care products while Mr. Zhang, from Wild Sage herbal shop, was at the opposite end of the street enlightening people on proper usage of herbal remedies and elixirs.

Even Penny Cho from the Bamboo Lounge was present. She was handling the onstage entertainment that was set up at the end of the parking lot. As the night continued, dance numbers and musical acts would be performed on the main stage that sat in front of an eating area packed with picnic tables. Once the entertainment began, our little tent would have a long line of people waiting to purchase spring rolls, dumplings, and fried noodles.

The beginnings of a line had already formed in front of our stand, and before I had time to truly appreciate the event, Peter and I were slammed with food orders. While he worked to keep the food pans stocked with the most popular items, I filled plates with customer requests and cashed them out as quickly as possible.

It was humid for a night in June and the air felt stale around us. The heat coming from the grill and below the pans wasn't helping matters. I made a mental note to remember clip fans for the following week.

The performances began around 7 P.M. and opened with a group of women dressed as geishas that wowed the crowd with a traditional Japanese dance. It was so beautiful that most of the crowd in the surrounding area paused to watch, and Peter and I got a break from serving customers. When the act was finished, applause erupted all around us, and within seconds the hungry visitors lined back up in front of the food carts.

Peter inspected the inventory below the counter, opening lids and counting what we had left. He shook his head. "Dude, we're almost out of dumplings already. I thought the spring rolls would be first to go."

We were only halfway through the night. I pulled out the small notebook I kept in my purse and made notes on what items we would need to adjust for next week's market. "I wonder if anyone else is running out of food yet."

My eyes traveled over to Wonton on Wheels, which had a line that was at least ten deep. Sandra was manning the window by herself, and when I glanced over to the front of the truck, I noticed that their son, Calvin, had arrived and was having what seemed to be a very heated discussion with his father.

Despite the fact that I had not been a fan of Calvin's when we were kids, he'd turned into a decent-looking young man. He was tall, thin with a little bit of muscle, and kept his jet-black hair short and shaved on the sides.

His full lips were turned down in a frown and his arms were crossed over his chest in what looked like defiance of his father. From small snippets I'd heard around the plaza, Calvin was constantly butting heads with his father, who was dead set on turning him into an entrepreneur like himself. But Calvin wasn't having any of it.

At eighteen, he'd enlisted in the Navy to avoid his father's scrutiny. But he hadn't lasted long and ended up getting out after a couple of years. Since then he'd been filling his time by going back to school and picking up odd jobs. Last I'd heard, he was working as a food delivery truck driver and drove routes that took him through various states in the Midwest.

I lost sight of the argument and quickly forgot about it when our next wave of customers arrived, keeping us busy for the next hour. In that time, Peter's mom and our split-shift server, Nancy Huang, showed up to lend a hand. The three of us worked in harmony with Peter cooking, Nancy filling the plates, and me cashing out the customers.

The remainder of the night continued without incident, and I felt pretty chipper. It was going to be a great summer and Ho-Lee Noodle House was sure to gain tons of new business attending these weekly events. As a marketing tool, I'd had postcards made with a picture of our restaurant on the front and our menu on the back to pass out with each order.

As the night trickled to an end and the crowd started to thin out, Peter, Nancy, and I began closing up shop.

Nancy, who is one of my mother's best friends, is a dainty woman with soft features. Her voice at times is barely above a whisper and the beauty of her youth has carried well into middle age.

She and Esther Chin are my honorary aunts, and I wondered how things would go when my real aunt, Grace, came to visit this summer. It had been a long while since everyone was in the same place at the same time.

Nancy placed a gentle hand on my shoulder. "I see Sandra Chow talking with Ruby Lin at her booth. It's been a long while since I've seen Ruby. I think I will go say hello."

"Yeah, I talked with them earlier tonight. I don't remember her at all."

"It was a very long time ago. Everybody is always so busy."

"Were she and Mom close?" I asked. "She mentioned that they were good friends when I was little, but I don't remember Mom talking about her."

Nancy tilted her head in consideration. "For a short time, yes."

Momentarily, I wondered if there might be an interesting back story, since Nancy wasn't offering much information. But if there was anything to be told, I'm sure I'd hear about it through the grapevine sooner or later. "Okay, well, we're almost all packed up here. I'll come and get you when we're done and ready to go."

She nodded and turned to leave.

After she'd joined the other two women, I busied myself with straightening up the cash box and the slips containing our orders. The order forms had been another one of my ideas to help keep track of what sold best and what didn't. I gathered them with a rubber band and slipped them in the cash box before locking it up.

When I lifted my head, I saw Calvin ambling over to our booth.

"Well, if it isn't Lana Lee . . . all grown-up." He laughed as he extended a hand over the register.

"Calvin," I said, reaching for his hand. "It's been a while, how have you been?"

"Not too bad. Not too bad, at all." He glanced down at my hand. "Firm handshake you got there. You're not a delicate flower, that's for sure."

I smiled in return. "That I am not."

He nodded in approval. "Right, so you're working for your parents or somethin'?"

"Believe it or not, I actually manage the restaurant now. It was completely unexpected, but it's paying the bills so I can't complain. What are you up to these days?"

He gave Peter a quick eyeball before answering my question. They exchanged a head nod and then he turned his attention back to me. "I just quit my job as a trucker and started working in an auto repair shop. I got sick of being on the road all the time, ya know?"

"I can imagine that would be hard on you. How do you like working at the auto shop?"

He shrugged. "Like you said, it pays the bills."

A scraggly man in a dingy T-shirt and torn jeans came walking up to us from the direction of the food truck area. He stood behind Calvin and peered up at the makeshift sign we had hanging from the top of our tent. "Ha . . . Ho-Lee Noodle House . . . for real? That's the real name?"

I pursed my lips. "Yes, that's the real name. And we're closed now, sorry."

Calvin chuckled. "Easy there, Sunshine, that's my uncle Gene."

"Oh!" I blushed. "Sorry, I didn't realize . . ." I re-assessed him. He seemed kind of young to be the brother of either Sandra or Ronnie. I would guess there was at least a fifteen-year difference between him and Calvin's parents.

"No sweat . . . I don't believe we've had the plea-sure." Gene stepped up to the counter next to Calvin and gave me a goofy grin. "I'm Gene Tian. Nice to meet you."

As the words left his mouth, I could smell alcohol on his breath. Clearly he had taken advantage of the beer tent.

"Nice to meet you," I replied, not bothering to of-fer my hand.

"My apologies for interruptin' your conversation, but I need to exit stage left with my designated driver over here." He jerked a thumb in Calvin's direction. "Come on, little nephew, time to get out of here."

"Okay, cool, just one sec." Calvin turned his attention back to me. "So, I was thinkin' maybe—"

"Hey . . . C . . . we gotta go . . . ASAP!" Gene grabbed his nephew's arm and yanked hard. "I need to use the facilities and I ain't usin' those Port-A-Johns, ya feel me? There's a nice bar there on the corner, we can stop in for a drink and I can use the can."

Calvin rolled his eyes. "All right, let's go then." He waved a hand at me. "Maybe we can catch up another time, Lee. I'd sure like to hear how your mom roped you into taking over the family biz."

"Sure, stop by the restaurant sometime," I offered. "I'm there all week."

He winked and ran after his uncle who had already started hightailing it toward the exit.

"Interesting dudes," Peter said as he finished cleaning off the grill. "I don't remember the last time I saw Calvin Chow. And that one guy for sure had way too much to drink. Good thing Calvin is taking him home."

"Odd that I've never met or heard of Gene before," I said as I watched them disappear down the road. "Whose brother do you think he is?"

"No clue, maybe he's visiting from out of town for the summer or something," Peter suggested.

"Speaking of visiting relatives," I said, turning toward him. "My aunt Grace is going to be here in a few days . . . I want to prepare you for my mother's crazy behavior."

"Oh man, is she gonna be all micromanage-y at the restaurant? Because we've gotten into a nice flow since Mama Lee has been out of the picture. I mean, I love your mom and everything, but my chi is flowing so much better now."

I laughed. "You've been talking to Mr. Zhang again?"

Peter shrugged. "Guilty as charged."

I inspected our tent and was satisfied with our progress. All Peter had to do was pull up the trailer so we could haul away our grill and we'd be on our way home. I was already dreaming about slipping into my pajamas and basking in the comforts of air conditioning.

Peter seemed to come to the same conclusion and dug in his pocket for the keys. "I'm sure there's a line out of the lot, but I'm going to make my way over there anyway. If my mom wants to leave just tell her I'll call her tomorrow."

"Okay, I'll be here," I told him.

Right as Peter turned his back to me, he paused, his body straight as a rod.

"What's wrong?" I asked.

I heard a crackling sound, and Peter's head turned in the direction of Wonton on Wheels. "Oh sh—"

Before I could fully understand what was happening, Peter grabbed me and knocked me to the ground. A large boom and the sound of hail followed. From my place on the ground, I could see flames lighting up the parking lot. Wonton on Wheels was on fire.

CHAPTER
3

- - - - - - - - - - - - - - -

It felt like Peter and I had been lying on the ground for an eternity as screams erupted in the surrounding area, but in reality it had only been a matter of seconds. After Peter assessed that the danger had passed, he finally let me up. I noticed that my arm was scraped from shoulder to elbow and gravel from the pavement was sticking to the blood covering my arm. I resisted the urge to faint, telling myself it looked worse than it actually was.

Peter sprang to action and grabbed a dish towel and a bottle of spring water from one of our travel bags. "Here, let me clean this up a little bit."

While he tended to my wound, I surveyed the area from my position on the ground, trying to see what exactly had happened while we were down. Outside of our tent, the area was complete chaos. The few police officers that had already been on site tried desperately to corral anyone nearby to safer areas. Shrapnel from the explosion was scattered all over the place and smoke from the flames billowed into the night sky. Panic flooded my brain and I craned my neck to check Kimmy's tent. It appeared to be fine as far as I could tell.

Oh my God, *where* was Nancy? I turned to Peter who had just finished cleaning my arm. "Peter . . . where's your mom?"

Time seemed to stop as he processed my question. "Mom!" He shot up from his kneeling position and whipped around in the direction of the jewelry stand. "Mom!"

Kimmy came running over from her tent and squatted down near the side of my head. "Lana . . . are you okay? Peter—"

"My mom!" Peter yelled at Kimmy before sprinting over to the jewelry stand.

A pit formed in the bottom of my stomach.

Kimmy watched Peter while I tried to hoist myself up. The two had recently started dating, and though Kimmy often tried to hide behind her "don't care" attitude, I could tell by the worried expression on her face that she deeply cared for Peter.

"Are you okay?" Kimmy asked again, giving me her arm for balance. "Did you hit your head or anything?"

"I don't think so." I inspected the side of my head with the tips of my fingers. "I think Peter put his hand down so I wouldn't smack my head on the concrete. My hip is killing me though."

"I'm going to see what happened over there," Kimmy said, her attention drifting over to Peter. "I hope Nancy's okay."

With relief, I heard sirens in the distance. "I'll come with you."

I limped alongside Kimmy and she held out an arm in case I needed it. When we reached the jewelry station, we found Peter hunched over his mother who was lying on the ground in front of the stand. Ruby was at the side of the booth and appeared mostly unharmed. She patted Sandra on the face, trying to get her to wake up.

Peter noticed us approach and glanced up. "My mom is breathing but she passed out. When she saw me coming, she said my name and then . . . her eyes closed."

I leaned on the tent pole to alleviate some of the tension from my hip. "I'm sure she's going to be okay," I reassured him.

Kimmy gestured toward the burning food truck. "Hey . . . who is that over there?"

We all turned and saw Calvin pacing near the fire as if he were trying to see through the flames. "Dad!"

"Was Ronnie in the truck when this happened?" I asked. "Does anyone know?"

Peter and Kimmy shook their heads.

"I was leaning down when the explosion happened," Kimmy said. "Thankfully I was far enough away that nothing really came at me."

"I'll be right back," I said to them and began hobbling toward Calvin.

When I reached him, he was near the back of the truck, trying to find an entry point. It was too late and I think he must have known that. "Calvin, what are you doing here?" I asked, tugging on his shirt. "We have to get away from here." Every movie I've ever seen where a vehicle blows up played through my mind and I was anticipating a second explosion.

"Uncle Gene and I barely made it to the corner bar when we heard the explosion. I rushed back to see what happened . . ." Calvin kept his eyes on the burning vehicle. "I think my dad's still in there."

"We don't know for sure, but either way you can't run into a fire. You'd never make it out again. The firemen are almost here, they'll be able to help." I tugged on his shirt again, and this time, he let me lead him away.

"Mom!" Calvin yelled once he spotted his mom passed out on the ground by Ruby's booth. He ran to her side and knelt down next to her, where Ruby was already seated. "Is my mom okay?"

Ruby's eyes were filled with tears and she brushed them away while braving a smile for Calvin. "Yes, she is okay, but I think she hit her head."

While we all huddled near each other, others who had been down the street came to see what all the commotion was. Jasmine, Mr. Zhang, and Esther came rushing over when they spotted us.

"Laaa-na!" Esther yelled, her gold bangles shimmying up and down her wrist as she waved her arm. "Laaa-na! You okay?" She grabbed my arm and inspected my wound. "You need the hospital. Right away."

"I'm okay, Esther," I reassured her. "I'm more worried about Nancy."

Esther's eyes darted down to where Nancy lay. "Aiya! Nancy!" She lunged to the ground and put a hand on Nancy's shoulder. "Nancy . . . wake up, okay?"

More police began to arrive, along with the fire department. A team of officers busied themselves with creating access points to allow the emergency vehicles to get through. The sirens neared and soon we saw the red and white lights of the ambulance bouncing off the sides of the buildings, making their way to the picnic area.

Pandemonium ensued as various authorities tried to section off the crowd and clear space for gurneys and medical equipment. The fire department worked to extinguish the fire as Calvin stood off to the side, anxious to hear results. I hated to see the hopefulness on his face, since I was sure there was no way someone could have survived that blast.

A paramedic came over and inspected my arm before leading me to one of their vehicles. I was in a fog, kind of dizzy, and slightly nauseous. I began to wonder if I'd hit my head after all. My ears rang and the world around me sounded muffled and distant.

The paramedic, a stocky woman with a blond ponytail, instructed me to sit down in the back of the truck while she took care of me. I complied and watched everyone else move with urgency around me.

When the night began, I'd been so hopeful that this would be the start of a great season, but now as I looked around all I saw was despair.

After the paramedic finished tending my wound and wrapped my arm in gauze, she recommended that I get further attention at the hospital. She didn't think

I had any head trauma based on the tests she could perform there, but she also reminded me you could never be too cautious. I'm not a huge fan of hospitals, so I thanked her for her assistance and said I would consider it.

In the time I'd been with the paramedic, the others who needed more serious attention had been whisked away. Peter had just finished being checked out and he stood off to the side with Kimmy. I hobbled over to them, favoring my bruised hip. My dream of pajamas and air conditioning had mutated into ice bags and a stiff drink.

As I met up with Peter and Kimmy, he stepped in front of her, putting a hand on my good arm. "Lana, they found Calvin's dad . . ."

Oh no, not Ronnie! "And?" I already knew what he was going to tell me by the expression on his face, but part of me was in denial.

"He didn't make it. They took his body away a few minutes ago. I saw them leave while the paramedic was wrapping my hand." He held up his left hand to show me the bandages.

"Where's Calvin?" I asked, searching the crowd.

Kimmy sidled up next to Peter. "He went in the ambulance with his mother. I think that other woman went with them. Ruby, right?"

I nodded.

A tall man with broad shoulders and blond hair approached us. He was wearing a white dress shirt and navy dress pants. I noticed a police badge clipped to his belt.

"Detective O'Neil, Cleveland PD," he said, gesturing to his badge. "Have you been checked out by a paramedic yet?"

I answered for the group. "Yes, Detective, thanks."

"I'd like to get brief statements from everyone affected by the blast. I know you've been through a lot tonight, but maybe we can chat for a few minutes and then have you come down to the station in the morning for an official report."

Again I answered. "I'm sorry, I'm afraid none of us really saw much of anything."

"And you are?" He was about a foot taller than me, maybe close to Adam's height, and had to look down as he addressed me.

"Lana Lee."

"Lana Lee . . . why does that name sound familiar to me?" he asked.

"I'm not sure . . . I'm the manager of Ho-Lee Noodle House. Maybe you've eaten there before?" I replied with a shrug. "We have a tent right over there." I pointed past him at our now sad, disheveled tent. The front of our grill had been hit with shrapnel and it had a giant dent.

He turned around to see where I pointed. "I see. And where were you when the blast occurred?"

"Me and my cook, Peter, were behind the counter area. He pushed me to the ground right before the explosion happened."

He switched his attention to Peter. "I'm guessing that's you?"

"Yes, sir, my name is Peter Huang." He didn't offer more, and I knew it was because he hadn't had good experiences with cops in his recent past.

"I see . . ." He turned to Kimmy. "And what's your story, Miss . . . ?"

"Tran . . . I'm Kimmy Tran." She was assertive as she said it and lifted her chin. "I was right over there." She pointed to her booth. "I was packing up DVDs when I heard the boom. Thank God, I was bent down or who knows what would have happened to me. Look at all this stuff everywhere."

Detective O'Neil pulled a miniature steno notebook from his pants pocket and grabbed a pen from the breast pocket of his shirt. He jotted down notes in a furious scribble and it reminded me so much of the first time I'd met Adam.

I waited until he was finished writing. "Detective, we'd really like to leave. Is there any way we can pack up the rest of our things and head home?"

"Not just yet, ma'am. I'll get you out of here as quickly as possible, but there are a few things that need to be cleared up before we can let anyone go. We'd also like all of you to return to your respective areas. That would help a great deal."

We all nodded in compliance and walked back over to our tent. Peter dug out three fresh water bottles and passed one along to Kimmy before she headed back over to her own booth.

I pulled out my purse, which had been stuffed under the counter, and searched for my cell phone. I needed to call my parents, my sister, my best friend Megan, and Adam to let them know what happened and that I was okay. While I was being attended to by the paramedic, I noticed that some local news crews had sent vans to cover the explosion. Their trucks sat at the perimeters of the commotion and circles of light engulfed each reporter as they talked into their microphones.

Sure enough, I had ten missed calls from both of my parents' cell phones, missed calls and text messages from Adam, Megan, and Anna May telling me to call them as soon as possible. The explosion must have already made the news.

I dialed my parents' home number. My mother picked up on the first ring. "Lana! Is that you?"

"Yes, Mom, it's me. I'm okay."

I heard her take a deep breath of relief and then she screamed to my father that I was all right. I heard him say "Thank God" in the background.

After she'd given me her attention again, I filled her in on everything that had happened. I hated to have to be the one to inform my mother that Ronnie Chow had not made it out alive, but I guess it was better it was me and not some stranger on the news.

My mother instructed me to go to the hospital and have them look at my head before urging me to call my sister next. We hung up after I promised I would call her as soon as we got off the phone.

I quickly called my sister and relayed the same information that I'd told my mother. She wished me well and told me to call her should I need anything. Next I called Megan, who answered before the phone even finished its first ring.

"Lana, thank God!" Megan breathed heavily into the phone. "I have been going nuts waiting to hear from you. I saw the explosion on TV at work, and was worried sick. Are you okay?"

"Yeah, I'm okay. Peter slammed me down on the ground, though, so I'm a little banged up, but nothing horrible."

She sighed. "I'm glad to hear that's the worst that happened to you. I left work and I'm at the corner of Rockwell and East Twenty-fourth, standing with a bunch of nosy people. I thought I'd be able to see if you got wheeled away on a gurney."

"I'd come to you, but they won't let us leave yet. Why don't you go home and I'll see you there. Hopefully I won't be here much longer."

"Okay, if you're sure. Because I'll stay here as long as you need me," she replied. "Are you even okay to drive?"

"I should be . . . I think."

"Lana, don't be stubborn. You can leave your car there."

"No, really, I'm okay. Besides, Peter is here with me."

"All right, well, I'm going to stop back at work and wrap something up. Robin is covering for me. You want me to bring home any food?"

"Yeah, a big fat cheeseburger with extra pickles. Actually get two, Adam might want one too. And fries, don't forget lots and lots of fries."

When I hung up with her, I heard a husky voice from behind me say, "Here I am worried out of my mind about you and you're placing a takeout order."

I turned around and sank into the most gorgeous green eyes on this planet. Detective Adam Trudeau stood on the other side of the counter in a black T-shirt and jeans. His reddish-brown hair was tousled as if he'd just left the house and he wore a concerned expression on his face.

"Adam!" I hobbled around the counter and buried my face in his chest, inhaling the scent of fresh soap. I was so relieved to see him, and I felt my heart calm as I pressed myself against his body. "How did you get in here?"

"The head detective is a friend of mine," he informed me. He kissed the top of my head and held me close to him. "We went to the police academy together."

I peeked up at him. "Detective O'Neil?"

"Yep, that's Darren. He's a good guy . . . kinda stubborn, but a solid cop."

"Nice to know what you really think of me, Trudeau."

Adam released me from our embrace, and we both turned to see a smirking Detective O'Neil.

"Trudeau . . . good to see you, man." Darren held out a hand.

The two men shook hands and leaned in for what I like to call a "man hug."

"You too, O'Neil."

"I was surprised to hear from you, it's been a while. Any problems getting past my guys?"

"Not at all." Adam scooped an arm around my shoulder, careful not to put pressure on my wound. "I really appreciate you letting me in to see my girl. I've been in panic mode since I heard the call come over the radio."

Darren glanced at me and nodded slowly, a sly smile spreading over his lips. "Ah . . . that's why the name sounded familiar." He turned back to Adam, and chuckled. "*This* is the firecracker you were telling me about."

Adam's body vibrated with laughter. "Yup. This is her."

I blushed. I guess my reputation preceded me.

CHAPTER
4

- - - - - - - - - - - - - - -

We were released shortly after Adam showed up and he followed me home, insisting on staying the night. Since I'd declined the hospital checkup, he wanted to keep an eye on me. All I wanted was my bed and those pajamas I'd been thinking about since well before the incident.

Megan and my black pug, Kikkoman, were waiting for us with a round of cheeseburgers and French fries. We sat around the kitchen table partaking of our late dinner while the two of them expressed shock over the blast. My dog waited patiently at my feet, hoping for a fry or two to magically drop into her mouth.

I was still too shaken up to really participate in the conversation so I focused on the food in front of me instead. I didn't last long after cleaning my plate and excused myself for a hot shower and sleep. Kikko tagged along after me, sensing the pain I was feeling and stood guard outside the bathroom door until I came out.

Adam and I piled into bed with Kikko burrowed beneath the blanket by my feet. I passed out as soon as my head hit the pillow.

That night I dreamt of unstoppable fires and explosions that were too close for comfort. A few times I woke up sweating and grasping for the water glass I always kept on my nightstand. Each time Adam woke up with me, rubbing my back and assuring me that I was safe.

When I finally got up on Saturday morning, I felt stiff, achy, and my ears were still ringing. Thankfully I didn't have to work that morning, but I did have to stop in and check on things since I'd missed a majority of the prior day prepping for the night market. Anna May and our teenage helper, Vanessa Wen, would be working the dining room.

Slipping out of bed so I wouldn't wake Adam, I made my way into the kitchen and dug around for coffee. Kikko had snuck out of the room with me, and she circled around my ankles while I filled the coffeepot with water. I was going to need extra caffeine today.

While I waited for the coffee to brew, I walked Kikko around the complex, attempting to clear my head of the previous night's events. It was a peaceful stroll along the sidewalk that loops through the handful of buildings that made up our apartment community.

Megan and I had been living together for several years in a quaint two-bedroom, garden-style apartment in North Olmsted. The apartment itself was slightly on the small side and wasn't the most original design. We longed for something a little more personalized; so we had recently begun to take some liberties and were redecorating. Otherwise the spot was perfect. It was a convenient location for both of us with regard to work; we had easy access to the freeway, and there were lots of great places for us to eat and shop. Not to mention the rent was the right price for two young women in the service industry.

We'd met in college, becoming fast friends, and within the first year of our friendship made the decision to move in together. Megan was the type of friend you knew was a permanent fixture in your life. The kind you could trust with anything in the whole wide world and knew she'd be there no matter what. Whether things were good, went bad, or got ugly, she was family.

When I returned from my walk with Kikko, Megan was hanging out on the couch scrolling through her phone and drinking a cup of coffee. Her blond hair was swept back with a black headband and she was dressed in light gray yoga pants and a black tank top.

She glanced up from her phone as I unleashed the dog. "I'm heading to the gym in a little bit, do you want me to grab some breakfast while I'm out? How about some doughnuts?"

I headed straight for the coffeemaker and poured myself a cup. "No, that's okay, I'm heading to the plaza in a little bit. I can pick something up at the restaurant."

"You don't want doughnuts?"

I could feel her eyes boring into my back.

"Maybe later."

"Well, do you want me to take off work tonight?"

she asked, continuing to scrutinize me from across the room. "We could catch a movie or maybe grab some drinks. It's supposed to be a great night for patio drinking."

Filling my coffee with the necessary cream and sugar, I joined her on the couch. "I'm fine, you know? Worried about Nancy and Sandra, of course, but I'm okay. Really."

Although I was mainly telling her the truth, that I was "okay," there was part of me that was, of course, still rattled by the whole ordeal. However, I didn't want her to worry more than I already knew she did.

The skepticism on her face was clear, but she let it drop for the moment. "Have you heard anything new?"

I shook my head. "Nothing so far. I was gonna call Peter in a little bit and find out about Nancy's condition." Reaching for the remote, I turned on the TV and flipped to a local news station hoping to find more information on what happened. When we'd left, there was no clear explanation as to what actually caused the explosion.

After fifteen minutes of a detailed weather report on how heat wave records were coming our way and a few commercials, a story finally came on about the blast. The headline read "Night Market Nightmare."

A female reporter with jet-black hair turned a grave expression to the camera as she recited the basics of the situation from last night. She informed the viewers that there had been one fatality and five people, including the wife of the victim, were in critical condition at local hospitals. And while authorities originally assumed the explosion was caused by a faulty starter or a propane leak, they were currently investigating for signs of foul play.

"Foul play?" Megan spat. "They're considering foul play now?"

"I think they have to, don't they?"

"I don't know, I wouldn't think so unless something was odd about it," she said.

"Well, who are we to say? Could be standard procedure."

"So, this Calvin guy . . . you've never mentioned him before . . . or Sandra for that matter."

"Probably because Calvin and I were never actual friends. Our parents were and we were kinda forced to hang out together. We haven't seen them in ages though."

"Hopefully his mother is okay. Sure was lucky that she wasn't with him when the truck exploded. Otherwise Calvin would have lost both his parents last night."

I sipped my coffee, internally shuddering at Sandra's near miss. "I wonder how they're doing. I should check in with them after I go to the Village."

My bedroom door could be heard creaking open from down the hall. Kikko's ears perked up and she waddled away to greet Adam.

"I'm the last one up?" he mumbled as he entered the living room. "That's unusual."

"I couldn't sleep anymore. My arm was getting sore," I explained. "There's coffee made if you want some."

He grunted and went into the kitchen. "I have to run into the station today and wrap up a few things, but you can have me for the rest of the day after that."

"I'm fine," I said.

Megan jumped up from the couch. "Yes, will you please knock some sense into this girl? She doesn't even want doughnuts."

Adam froze with the coffee mug mid-sip. "What do you mean she doesn't want doughnuts? That's not an actual thing, right?"

I groaned. "You two are being ridiculous. There are plenty of times I haven't wanted doughnuts."

"Name one," Megan challenged.

Adam shuffled into the living room and took a sip of his coffee. "I don't think you should be alone today. What happened yesterday is definitely on the traumatic side."

"I don't need babysitters," I reminded them. "I'm a grown woman."

"Yes, we realize that," Megan chimed in. "But having some company after what happened yesterday isn't going to hurt anything, right?"

The two of them were making me anxious. What I needed was to get out of the house and get moving. Sitting still with all this time to think was making me feel worse. "How about this? How about we all go about our day like normal human beings, and then later, we'll meet up for drinks." I looked at Megan. "On a patio somewhere."

"Sounds great." Megan beamed with victory. "I'll see you two later tonight."

* * *

Dressed and ready to go, I parted ways with Adam and Megan and headed to Asia Village. The enclosed Asian shopping plaza, located in the neighboring city of Fairview Park, was about a fifteen-minute drive from my apartment. I turned off the street, driving through the red-arched gateway adorned with golden dragons slithering up the columns, and made my way through the lot that wrapped around the cluster of pagoda-style buildings to the employee parking area.

While the indoor shopping center had seen many renovations—the pagoda façades, the addition of a koi pond, cobblestone walkways inside the plaza, skylights in the ceiling, and Asian establishments that came and went—my family's restaurant had remained in the building, in the same spot, for over thirty years.

It was already 11 A.M. and though business slowed in the summer, the Saturday shopping crowd was in full swing. I blended into the stream of walkers as I made my way toward the noodle house. The salon, Asian Accents, was packed with boisterous women getting their hair dyed, nails done, and legs waxed. Asian pop music floated out into the enclosed plaza as the door opened and a happy customer bustled out.

Wild Sage, the herbal shop, wasn't quite as busy, but Mr. Zhang had his hands full with a couple of people that had stopped in to ask for his expertise.

I should add as a side note that my grandmother—who has only been in the United States for around two months—and Mr. Zhang are spending quite a bit of time together. I'd say they were "dating," but you can't use that word around my mother when it comes to the elderly pair. It seems to make her eye twitch. One time when I brought it up, she told me to mind my own business and that they were just "friends."

Additional side note: I am quite frequently told to my mind own business when it comes to family affairs that do not pertain to me.

China Cinema and Song was surprisingly filled with shoppers browsing the DVD racks. There was even a line at the register where I could see Kimmy hustling to get customers rung up and out the door. Their store had been struggling for several months, but with the recent surge in interest in Asian films in the media, people were starting to catch on to the trend, and movies and shows from China, Taiwan, and Japan were on many must-have lists.

Even Cindy Kwan, who ran the plaza's bookstore, the Modern Scroll, was having a hard time keeping titles like *Crazy Rich Asians*, *The Joy Luck Club*, and *Little Fires Everywhere* stocked on the shelves.

Next in the row of stores leading up to the noodle house was my new personal favorite, Shanghai Donuts. Ruth Wu and her husband had only joined the plaza a month ago, and business was booming for them. I waved to Ruth through the window and continued on to the restaurant.

Ho-Lee Noodle House with its double doors, picture windows, and brazen sign claiming that we were the #1 NOODLE HOUSE gleamed in the sun that came in through the skylights. A few months ago, I had dreaded the sight of the place, wanting to fulfill my life's mission with something else, but now, just looking at it brought me a sense of calm and familiarity.

I opened the door, and found that we were busier than I had anticipated. We often found ourselves scrambling for customers in the summertime, since most Clevelanders wanted to enjoy the nice weather while they could and we didn't have outdoor seating. We had limited months of actually nice weather so many spent it at outdoor festivals, in parks, or at outdoor shopping areas that might otherwise deter them during our snowy months.

It must have been the Village's involvement in the night market that was bringing in the extra business. So many people that had come through our lines last night were surprised they'd never heard of us, and a lot of people had taken an interest in my flyers.

Vanessa Wen, our only teenage help and a thorn in my side, was at the hostess booth flipping through the latest issue of *Vogue* magazine.

I dramatically cleared my throat as I neared the counter. "Shouldn't you be helping with tables?"

Vanessa jumped, dropping the magazine on the floor. She held a hand to her heart and took exaggerated deep breaths. "Lana! Don't do that to me! You scared me half to death!"

Pursing my lips, I placed a calculated hand on my hip, imitating my mother. "Sorry to disturb your reading."

Vanessa blushed, the color of her cheeks matching her bubblegum-pink nail polish. "My bad. I only came up here for a minute because I thought that these people were going to check out, but then they didn't get up, so I got bored and I thought I'd read a little bit until they paid their check."

"Is Anna May handling everything on her own?" I asked, skimming the packed dining room for my sister.

"I'll go check on people's tea," she said, picking her magazine up off the floor. "Sorry, boss."

I sighed. Sometimes I could be hard on Vanessa, and I hated to be that way, but—thanks to my mother—she was here to learn about work ethic, and reading magazines on the job wasn't part of the lesson. "Yes, I think that would help . . . thanks."

She nodded vigorously and her ponytail bobbed up and down. "Have you heard anything new about Nancy?"

"Not yet, I'm planning on calling Peter as soon as I get to the back office. I didn't want to bother him first thing in the morning," I said.

Vanessa cocked her head at me. "You don't have to call him, he's back in the kitchen if you want to talk to him. He didn't tell you he was coming in?"

My eyes widened. "What? No, he didn't mention it."

"Yeah, he showed up first thing this morning. He and Lou have been tearing it up in the kitchen all morning. I thought he would have told you."

Lou is our evening and alternate weekend chef. I gazed back at the double doors that led to the kitchen. "Well, okay then." I headed back without another word.

I passed Anna May on the way back to the kitchen.

She was taking an order, but caught sight of me out of the corner of her eye. She acknowledged me with a curt nod and then went back to writing on her order pad.

When I entered the kitchen, I saw the two men standing side by side at the grill. The clanking of their spatulas almost had a rhythm to it, and they were so involved in what they were doing, they didn't even notice me walk in.

I went to stand near the grill, and Lou happened to glance up and notice me. "Boss lady!" he yelled with an overabundance of pep. "Surprised to see you in the house today!" He saluted me with the spatula. His slicked-back hair was covered with a chef's hat that sat crookedly on his head and he adjusted it with his free hand. Lou is a middle-aged guy with puppy-dog eyes and an overexaggerated smile. The smiling thing had gotten under my skin a time or two, but I was trying to work on that.

Peter, who had one earbud in his ear—most likely jamming to heavy metal—noticed that Lou was flailing his arms. He followed Lou's gaze and stared at me as if I were a ghost. "Oh hey, dude," he mumbled before turning his attention back to the strips of steak he was browning.

"Peter . . . what are you doing here?" I asked. "Shouldn't you be at the hospital with your mom?"

His focus remained on the browning meat in front of him.

"Peter," I said more firmly.

Nothing.

"Lou would you mind taking over everything while I talk with Peter in my office, please?"

"No problem, boss."

Peter looked up, staring at the wall in front of him. He did not turn to acknowledge me.

"NOW . . ." I said, feeling like a parent scolding their child.

Peter huffed and set the spatula down on the edge of the grill and walked past me into the back room without ever making eye contact.

The back room past the kitchen is an employee lounge of sorts. I use the term "lounge" loosely. It's a near barren room with a beat-up couch and an old TV set. Both items have been there since I was a little kid. There was also a small table where I used to do my homework when I was too young to be home by myself.

Inside the room was a smaller room, which is now my office. I've seen walk-in closets that are bigger. There's just enough room for a desk, a filing cabinet, and a guest chair. My mother never needed more than that. I was in the process of making it my own, but with things as busy as they had been, there was hardly any time for redecorating.

Peter slumped into the guest chair and I shut the door before sitting in my own chair. I set my purse on the desktop. "What's going on with your mom?"

His eyes were focused on the plant I keep on top of the filing cabinet. I can't be trusted with plants that require a lot of care, so Megan had gotten me an aloe plant that needed minimal attention. "She's awake and stuff, but she's super weak. She's got pretty bad burns all over one arm. And she hit her head pretty hard so they're keeping her for observation."

"She's going to be okay, Peter," I said, trying to sound reassuring.

A few months ago, Peter had learned the true identity of his father, only for his father to die shortly afterward. He'd made peace with what had happened, but I knew it stung him to realize how close he'd been to finally getting to know his father only to have that chance ripped away.

His eyes finally met mine, and he resembled a little boy. I'd only seen him this vulnerable a couple of times and each time it threw me off balance. We had grown closer in recent months because of everything we'd faced together and I was happy to say that Peter had become one of my best friends.

"I just can't lose her. You know?" he whispered. "She's the only family I've got and this whole thing has made that fact so clear to me. Like, it wakes you up, you know?"

"I know . . . and you won't lose her. Your mom is a tough lady, she's going to be fine. She just needs a couple days to rest."

"I did have to leave, though," he admitted. "It's hard to see her that way and I'd been there all night. I slept in one of those crummy chairs. The nurse tried to kick me out at first but I think she felt sorry for me. My mom can barely lift her head and she's lying there totally worried about money and not working. I told her I'd get some extra hours in to help with bills. You don't mind, do you?"

"Of course not," I said. "We'll help however we can. I can pay her for a few of the days she's gone. Business has been pretty good because of the night market, so we can afford to pad her paycheck."

He looked at me skeptically. "Are you sure?"

"Yes, don't think anything of it. We're all family here and we take care of each other."

"Okay, thanks. I owe ya one." He stood up to leave.

"Like I said, Peter, we're family. You owe me nothing. Just make me a bowl of udon noodles and we'll call it even."

CHAPTER
5

With my freshly made bowl of noodles, I headed out into the dining room to eat and relax in one of the booths right outside of the kitchen. Normally I'd hide away in the back room, but today I needed the background noises of other people chatting and the clanking of plates and chopsticks to distract me.

While I slurped my noodles, I scrolled through my phone and opened Facebook. I typed in Calvin's name and searched for his profile. I didn't know another way to get hold of him. I sent a friend request and typed a quick message asking him about his mother and if he knew how Ruby was holding up.

The dining room began to thin out as customers left to continue their shopping adventures, and Anna May came over to my booth, sitting across from me. She flipped over the empty teacup at her place setting and poured herself some oolong tea.

"How are you doing, little sister?" she asked after

taking a sip of her tea. She leaned back in the booth and rolled her shoulders.

I set my phone down. "I'm hanging in there, I guess. My entire right side hurts and my ears are kinda weird still."

"I still can't believe what happened last night. This whole place was in an uproar today. You should have seen the Mahjong Matrons this morning. They're convinced this is a sign of things to come." Anna May rolled her eyes. "You know how they get."

And I did. The Mahjong Matrons were our most faithful customers and as reliable as the postal service. They were the first ones in every morning regardless of rain, heat, snow, or any other weather conditions that Mother Nature could conjure up.

The four women were also the eyes and ears of the Asian community, especially when it came to the goings-on at Asia Village. Nothing got past them. Nothing. They were also old-fashioned, superstitious, and not afraid to express their opinions to anyone who would listen.

"Well, let's hope they're wrong about that," I said. "We don't need any problems before Aunt Grace gets here."

"That's the truth." Anna May nodded, drumming her French-manicured nails on the table. "Mark my words, Mom and Aunt Grace will be arguing within fifteen minutes of seeing each other."

"Fifteen minutes?" I asked. "You give them too much credit."

We both shared a laugh before my sister got up to greet a new table of customers that had just been seated.

Anna May and I didn't always get along, but we had silently agreed to call a truce of sorts until my aunt Grace had come and gone. My mother was beside herself with the news that my aunt was coming on such short notice.

My sister and I had nothing on these two; truly, they put us to shame. My mother didn't approve of her sister's life in the least, and vice versa. They fought about everything under the sun, from cooking techniques to how children should be raised.

Before I could pick up my chopsticks again, Ian Sung, our property manager, stormed into the restaurant. He scanned the dining room and when his eyes fell on me, he threw his hands in the air and came rushing over.

"Lana, there you are!" He unbuttoned the jacket of his navy blue tailored suit and sat across from me, sliding his hand across the table.

I didn't reach for it. Since his arrival at our plaza, he had been trying to casually woo me from time to time. He wasn't making any progress and that drove him crazy. Based on the little that I knew about him, he was a man who always got what he wanted.

The fact that Adam and I were officially a couple drove him nuts, and he inserted himself into my life any chance that he got. Needless to say, Adam was not a fan.

"Hi, Ian." I didn't hide the exasperation from my voice.

His dark brown eyes studied me intently from across the table. "Are you all right? I heard about what happened and that you had been injured. I thought about calling," he said while adjusting his tie, "but I figured Detective Trudeau wouldn't take too kindly to that."

"Well, I appreciate your concern, but I'm fine," I told him. "I'm a little banged up, but it could have been much worse if Peter hadn't been there."

"And how is his mother?"

"She's going to be okay, but they're keeping her for observation right now. He's a mess."

"As is to be expected," Ian said with a nod. His focus drifted toward the kitchen door.

I finally picked up my chopsticks and poked at my noodles. By now, they were cold and I'd lost my appetite. "Is there anything else you needed?"

He turned his attention back to me. "Hm? No, nothing else. I just wanted to stop by and express my concern. You should take it easy. Why don't you take a break from the board meetings until you've had some time to rest?"

"Okay." Even though I didn't feel that bad, it was one less thing I had to deal with, so I wasn't going to argue.

He stood up from the booth, and buttoned his suit jacket. "If you need anything at all, you know where to find me."

"Thanks, Ian."

He gave me another once-over before exiting the restaurant.

I gave my noodles another stab before I decided to give up. I took my half-eaten bowl into the kitchen and cleaned up a little bit while I was in there. After that, I went back to my office and took care of some light paperwork, starting a list of things that needed to be handled on Monday. My brain needed a break and focusing on the mundane was helping me avoid thoughts of the previous day.

Business had picked up while I'd been stowed away in the back, and when I came out, my sister and Vanessa were zipping around the dining room. I jumped in to lend a hand since we were short a person, and helped keep the dining room under control until it slowed down again.

I ended up staying until the plaza closed at nine. Peter, who had only left once for about two hours to visit with his mom, was busy cleaning up the kitchen when I finally made my way into the back. He sulked around the appliances, putting away utensils and tidying up while Lou worked on some dirty dishes in the sink.

We'd sent Vanessa home once the rush died down. My sister handled cleaning up the dining area while I took care of the cash intake. Within forty-five minutes after closing we were all done with our respective duties. Lou thundered a cheerful good-bye before leaving. Anna May, Peter, and I locked up the doors and headed outside, where we saw Kimmy locking up her parents' store. The gate had been pulled down and she fiddled with the lock at the bottom.

Kimmy stood up, straightened herself, and came sauntering over to us, her eyes fixed on me. "Lana, what the heck are you doing here? Don't you go home anymore?"

I shrugged. "Guess I needed to work off some tension."

"Good thing she stayed," Anna May added. "I would have had to call Mom in to work and she and Dad were busy visiting people in the hospital."

Kimmy held up a hand. "Wait a minute. Where is Anna May Lee and what have you done with her?"

Anna May looked taken aback. "What is that supposed to mean?"

"I just mean that I have never heard you say you were glad that your sister was around. Aren't you guys supposed to be mortal enemies or something?"

Anna May snorted. "Kinda dramatic, don't you think?"

I glanced at my sister. "You have to admit—"

"Oh come on, we're not *that* bad."

Peter chuckled. "You guys can be downright nuclear at times."

Anna May scowled at Peter. "You're not helping, Huang."

I stifled a laugh. "Okay, how about let's just get going." I checked my phone and saw that I had a few missed text messages from Adam and Megan. I was hoping for a notification from Calvin, but there was none. "I'm supposed to head out with Megan and Adam tonight," I said to the group as we made our way to the main entrance.

"Don't forget we have dim sum with Mom, Dad, and A-ma tomorrow," Anna May said.

"How could I forget?" I turned to face my sister. "We go every week."

"Well, don't get all drunk tonight and be surprised that you're hungover tomorrow. You know Mom hates when you drink at all."

"Yeah, yeah." I waved her off. "I don't exactly feel much like drinking anyway. I'll be fine."

"You better be. Mom will have a fit if you show up all messed up in front of A-ma."

Kimmy pointed at my sister. "There she is. Anna May is still intact."

Anna May groaned. "Whatever . . . I'm heading home. I'll see you tomorrow, little sister." She bumped my arm with her own and hurried out the door.

"You know, teasing my sister isn't going to help the situation," I said to Kimmy. "We're trying to get along for the time being."

"Whatever, your sister is a total nag, and I know how to get under her skin." Kimmy shrugged with indifference. "What can I say? It amuses me."

Peter had grown quiet on our way to the parking lot, and as I opened the Village's main door, the stagnant summer heat smacked us in the face. It was unusual so early in the summer.

"Hey, why don't you guys join us tonight?" I suggested to the two of them. I felt like Peter could use a distraction of some kind and what better way to get his mind off his worries than to drag him and Kimmy out for a night on the town.

Peter shook his head. "Nah, man, that's cool. But you can go if you want," he said to Kimmy.

"Oh, I can go if I *want*?" Kimmy snapped at him. "Whatever. First of all, you know I do whatever I want anyway. And second of all, you're not going to sit around in your apartment and mope all night. You're coming out with us."

Peter started to say something but must have

thought better of it. We all knew Kimmy didn't take no for an answer. He sighed. "Okay . . . where are we headed then?"

I checked through the messages I had from Megan. "I guess we're heading to Punchbowl Social down in the Flats. She wants to go bowling."

Kimmy smiled. "Sounds like a plan to me. We'll meet you guys down there. I want to change into something Flats-worthy."

I said good-bye to the unlikely couple and made my own way home. I was excited to go bowling with the group, but I didn't know how I would fare with my recent injuries. Still, it would be nice to be out of the house and occupied with something other than these pesky thoughts.

That night, the five of us had a blast and for a few hours all our problems drifted away while we drank, bowled, and danced to silly songs from two decades ago. I was only able to bowl a few frames because of my shoulder, but I enjoyed just being with my friends and Adam, who surprised me with his lackluster bowling skills. Considering that he was someone who had great aim with a gun, it was a shock to discover he was more likely to throw a gutter ball than a strike.

Peter also seemed to let loose, and it was great to see him smile after the difficulties of the past twenty-four hours. As I watched Megan get another strike and do a victory dance, I couldn't believe that less than a full day ago, we'd been standing around on Rockwell Avenue suffering the aftermath of an unexpected explosion.

Little did I know that the next day our troubles wouldn't just return, they would multiply.

CHAPTER 6

"Wake up!"

I opened my eyes to find Megan standing over my bed, frantically waving the TV remote. Kikko rustled under the blankets, poking her head out to investigate the commotion.

Stretching my arms over my head, I reached for my pillow and plopped it over my face. "Not yet . . . half an hour. At least."

"Lana, this is serious . . . I just turned on the TV and you have got to see this." She flipped the blankets off me and grabbed my pillow, throwing it to the side. "It's about the explosion. Hurry. Up!"

"Fine," I grumbled, flung myself out of bed and followed her out into the living room. Kikko trailed behind me, snorting along the way.

A male news anchor with a stern face shared a split screen with a young male reporter who was standing in the parking lot where the food truck disaster had taken place. In the background, crime scene technicians worked through the rubble digging for evidence. Right as we entered the living room, the screen went back to the news anchor and in the top corner was a live video of Detective O'Neil giving a public statement. The news anchor's image shrank as the detective took over the screen, caught in mid-sentence.

"—confirmed to be signs of foul play and tampering with the vehicle in question. We're currently investigating some potential leads. If you know anything at all in reference to this case, please contact the Cleveland Police Department. Thank you." He held up a hand signaling to the crowd that he was finished, gave a respectful nod, and turned abruptly away from the camera, refusing further questions.

The news anchor returned with a grim expression and shook his head as he segued into the next headline. Megan turned the volume down and plopped down on the couch, keeping her eyes fixed on my reaction.

I hadn't moved from my spot in front of the TV. I just stood there, staring at the floor trying to formulate a linear thought. But all that came were flashbacks of the fire, the feel of blacktop digging into my arm, and the sounds of people screaming in terror.

"I knew this whole thing was odd," Megan finally said. By the look on her face, I could tell she'd been waiting to say that since she'd woken me up. "Didn't I say this whole thing was odd? I told you, Lana, these things don't just up and happen. Not like this."

"Okay, you were right," I mumbled.

"Do you think this was meant to be a murder? Or do you think that part was an accident? It could just have been someone wanting to ruin their business and damage the truck."

"Maybe, I don't know." As Megan posed the questions that I had already been thinking on my own, I wondered if attempting to solve the crime would be the best way to alleviate the anxiety I'd felt. As they say, there is nothing better than facing your fears head-on and taking action.

"Do you remember seeing anything strange? There had to be a sign that this was going to happen."

I thought back, reviewing the night from the moment I arrived to the time of the blast. "Well, Calvin and Ronnie had an argument earlier in the night. And then before the explosion, Calvin did take off in a hurry," I rambled, still staring at the floor. "His uncle was rushing him out of there . . . he had to use the bathroom or something and they were going to the corner bar."

"So they left the area, but not the night market itself?"

"Well, no. The corner bar across the street and maybe four or five businesses down from the picnic area."

"That little place with the red awning?" Megan asked.

"That's the one."

"Okay, so what do you know about this Calvin guy? Do you know anything about his uncle?"

Her questions were coming at me so rapidly I hardly had time to process them. I moved over to the couch, stepping over her legs, and sat down next to her. "Um, I don't know much about Calvin. I know next to nothing about his uncle . . . I'd never even met him before the other night. I know Calvin doesn't get along well with his dad. He was in the navy, and then he used to be a truck driver for a while . . . now he works for his uncle as a mechanic in his auto repair shop."

"Aha!" Megan yelled.

Kikko jumped off the couch, and scuttled into the other room.

"Aha what?" I asked.

"Come on, Lana. If anyone would know how to blow up a vehicle, it would be a mechanic."

"I don't think Calvin would murder his own dad though . . . right?" I asked. Did I even know that to be true? How bad was their feuding? I didn't know anything about Calvin anymore, not since we were kids. He could be a psycho for all I knew.

"Well, that's why I asked if you thought it was an intentional murder. It could have been an accident. Maybe he wanted to get back at his dad for something, and just meant to damage the food truck as payback. I mean, he's a mechanic . . . doesn't mean he's a good one."

My attention drifted to the coffeemaker. I needed fuel to think. I also needed to get dressed. I was supposed to meet my family for our weekly dim sum outing at Li Wah's in less than two hours.

Megan seemed to sense my thoughts as she sometimes did. "I'll make the coffee, you go do your thing." She shooed me away as she stood from the couch. "We can speculate more about this later."

I showered and dressed myself in sort of a haze that only made my morning routine more horrendous and lengthy. When it comes to getting ready, I can be a primper . . . and a scrutinizer.

Megan brought a cup of coffee to where I sat at my vanity. "You know, maybe you should talk with this Calvin guy. You could potentially find something out."

I set down my eyeliner and reached for the mug in her hand. "The thought crossed my mind while I was in the shower. I sent him a Facebook message yesterday, so when he responds maybe we could get together in person and I could ask some questions. But I don't know . . . it all started to seem a little farfetched the more thought I gave it. Our imaginations tend to get away from us. And I'm not entirely sure that I want to get involved with this one. To be honest with you, I keep going back and forth with the idea."

She stepped back to better assess me. "Are you kidding? First, how could you not want to get involved? Second, our imaginations are right on point. You heard what that detective said, there was foul play. *And,* like you said, Calvin was arguing with his dad . . . *and* . . . the uncle—"

"Because it could all be a coincidence. None of it necessarily means that Calvin or his uncle were involved in what happened." I took a sip of coffee and savored the first taste of caffeinated goodness. There was nothing better.

"Bagh!" Megan swatted the air. "You know as well as I do that a majority of crimes are committed by family members. Just because you've known this guy since he was little doesn't mean that he's not capable of doing something like this. Calvin Chow is number one on my suspect list."

Li Wah's is a Chinese restaurant on the east side of Cleveland in a plaza much like Asia Village. The restaurant serves dim sum daily and my family has been congregating and partaking of their delicious menu every Sunday since Anna May and I have moved out on our own. It's my parents' way of making sure that they see both of us at least once a week regardless of what's going on in our lives. Of course, I was currently working at the family business and seeing my parents several times a week whether I wanted to or not. Like I said, it wasn't part of my life plan.

I pulled into the parking lot and hurried into the restaurant where I knew that my family would already be waiting. I'm usually late to everything. I'd like to believe it's because I'm a free spirit and time is relative, but for whatever reason, people don't seem to buy that. As they say, everyone's a critic.

As suspected, I spotted my parents, my grandmother, and my sister seated at a table with two empty chairs. I rushed over, noticing the agitated look on my mother's face. The table was bare, except for teacups, which was unusual because they normally started ordering without me. The fact that there was no food in sight kind of worried me . . . and made my stomach gurgle. It felt as if my appetite were slowly coming back.

My mother, who is best described as a "little Asian woman," was sitting next to my father, whom

I lovingly call "a big ole white guy," and they were deep in discussion. They didn't even notice me walk up to the table. My sister was fiddling on her phone, clearly ignoring the conversation, and my grandmother appeared to be doodling on what looked like a Chinese newspaper.

"Hi, everyone," I said, a little out of breath. "Sorry I'm late."

My grandmother picked her head up and grinned at me, her silver front teeth sparkling. "Lana is here," she said in Hokkien. I couldn't really speak the language myself, but I could understand the bare minimum. I found myself recognizing more words the longer my grandmother was here, since she knew almost no English whatsoever. It made communication very difficult at times. There were a lot of hand gestures and mimicking involved in our conversations.

My family predominantly spoke the Taiwanese dialect of Hokkien, but they also mixed in Mandarin at times, and it was hard for me to keep up. My sister had a better understanding of it as she'd spent a lot of time studying the language with my mother. I hadn't had the same interest or patience so her knowledge surpassed mine by a long shot.

I sat down next to my grandmother, leaving the seat next to my sister empty. Smiling at my grandmother, I glanced down at what she was doing. She was drawing mustaches on everyone in the photos. When she caught me looking, we both started laughing.

With an exaggerated sigh, my sister put her cell phone down on the table, and rested her chin in her hand. "Welcome to crazy-people hour." She tapped a well-manicured, ruby-red nail on her nose and her eyes slid in the direction of my parents.

I looked among the three of them and lifted my shoulders in question. "What's going on?"

My father answered for the group. "Your mother is a little upset over this morning's developments with the Chow family," he explained. "And frankly, so am I."

"Upset?" my mother spat. "UPSET? I am mad!"

A few people turned around to gawk at our table. I smiled apologetically to the elderly couple sitting directly next to us. "Mother . . ."

"Lana," my mother returned with sarcasm.

"Okay . . . first, where is the food?" I asked, searching the room for the dim sum cart. "We should eat before everyone loses their minds."

"I think Mom scared away the staff with her *harsh whispers*," my sister quipped.

I saved my eye roll for better use. Spotting the man with the cart, I got his attention and signaled him over. He wheeled the cart over and stood in front of me, avoiding my mother.

I exaggerated a smile. "Hi, we'll start with some shrimp dumplings, a basket of spare ribs with black bean sauce, sticky rice with minced pork, spring rolls, and some turnip cakes."

Using a pair of tongs, he lifted the steamer baskets out of the heated cart and placed them gingerly on the table.

My grandmother's eyes brightened and she quickly speared a shrimp dumpling with her chopsticks.

After the server left and our table was filled with the variety of foods I'd chosen, everyone dug in, taking a sampling of each item for their plate.

When I'd polished off a spring roll—one of my very favorite food items—I reached for the teapot and filled my cup. "Now what's going on? I'm assuming that you guys are upset because the police said they're looking into foul play. But that's a good thing. Whoever did this needs to go down for it."

My mother looked at me with an impatience that confused me. I thought she would be happy that—for once—I was remaining levelheaded about the situation. Guess not.

"It's not that they're saying it was foul play, Goober," my dad answered. "It's that they're accusing Sandra Chow of the crime."

"What?" My mouth dropped. "They think Sandra Chow did it? But why?"

My mother's face turned a bright shade of red. "Yah. So stupid!" Her fist pounded the table.

"Bai-ling." My grandmother used my mother's real name in such a stern voice, you knew she meant business.

My mother sulked in her seat.

"I don't understand why they would think she did it," I said out loud. But in my head, I was thinking about the way I'd seen them communicate with one another at the night market. At best, they came off as business partners, not a happily married couple. At the time, I didn't think all that much of it, but now that it was being brought up, I had to consider it.

"Can't we just have a normal meal with normal conversation?" my sister asked. "Every time we sit down at a table, we're talking about some act of violence."

"Sure, let's talk about your criminal law class, Miss Lawyer," I said to her. "I'm sure you'll never have to talk about this kind of stuff once you pass the bar."

Anna May scowled at me as she bit into a pea pod.

"Sandra is a good person," my mother said, eyeballing my sister. "She does not deserve this. She has lost her husband."

"There has to be a reason why they think it's her," I said. I wondered to myself if Calvin was on the chopping block, as well. It was probably better if I didn't mention it, or my mother's hair might light on fire.

"Sandra and Ronnie were having some money problems and there's speculation that the explosion was used to get an insurance claim," my dad explained. "They think it's possible that it went horribly wrong and Ronnie got killed in the process. At least that's what they said to Sandra this morning when they interrogated her."

"That doesn't even make sense," I said. "Why would Ronnie be in the truck if they planned to blow it up together? And why would they do it at the night market and put other people in danger?"

"From what they said, it was a poorly made bomb. Their theory is that Ronnie somehow triggered it by accident or that it went off too early." My dad shook his head. "Totally unreal. I can't even imagine Ronnie being that kind of person . . . cheating the system that way. He's always been a hard worker. And then making a bomb on top of it?"

"Where did you hear all of this?" I asked.

"We spoke with Sandra shortly after her meeting with some detective," he said. "Your mother called her this morning to see how she was doing. She's still in the hospital with some burns, and I guess this jerk bag came to see her first thing this morning. They're not going to release any of this to the public, of course. So keep the details to yourself, okay?"

I assumed the jerk bag my father was speaking of would be Detective O'Neil. "Of course, Dad. I won't say anything."

"I need to see her," my mother said resolutely. "I need to see her right away. She will need someone to keep her company."

"How about Anna May and I go open the restaurant so you and Dad can visit with Sandra?" I offered.

My sister paused, chopsticks in midair. "Since when did you become the good daughter?"

I narrowed my eyes at her. "Don't get used to it. Limited-time offer."

CHAPTER
7

Anna May and I pulled into the parking lot of Asia Village one after the other and parked our cars next to each other.

When she got out of the car, she continued to tease me about my offer of giving my parents the day off. "Seriously, Lana, what has gotten into you? You're giving up your Sunday? It's your favorite lounging day."

The plaza was already open and bustling with customers, but our restaurant had shortened hours on Sunday.

"Mom needs to be with Sandra and I'd rather she just get it out of her system. You know she's already high-strung from the fact that Aunt Grace is coming to town."

My sister blew out a puff of air. "Yeah, you're telling me. And you know how it's going to go too. They're going to argue the entire time. One of them will bring up how they don't approve of the other, and then the other one will justify it and turn the whole thing around on whoever started the original argument. Blah, blah, same tune, different day."

It was odd to hear my sister react this way because, of the two of us, she was usually the good-natured one. But there was something about the ordeal of my mother getting together with her sister that brought me and Anna May together. My guess is that it was an us-versus-them situation.

We headed into the plaza and made a beeline for the restaurant. As we got closer, I noticed an attractive middle-aged woman sitting on the bench across from our restaurant. Her head was bent down as she scrolled through her phone, and long black hair covered her face from view. A large Prada bag sat at her side. She was dressed in a short-sleeved red silk blouse, a beige knee-length skirt and matching pumps. I didn't need to see any more of her to know who she was.

I grabbed Anna May's arm and stopped walking. "Oh my God, she's here . . . already?"

"Who?" Anna May asked, following my line of sight. She gasped. "What? She's a week earlier than she originally told us."

We shared a glance and then continued walking toward the woman.

"Aunt Grace!" I flashed my brightest smile as we approached her. "What are you doing here?"

"Girls!" Grace Richardson, my mother's extremely Americanized sister, stood up with outstretched arms. "Come here and give me a hug! It's so great to see you both!"

The three of us gathered together for a group hug,

and the minute we embraced, I could smell the Chanel No. 5 she was known to wear. Flashes of childhood memories with visits from Aunt Grace filled my head and suddenly I was six years old all over again.

"What are you doing here?" Anna May repeated as we stepped back from one another. "We weren't expecting you until late next week."

"Well, I was up at Martha's Vineyard with some friends, and found myself completely bored. It was me and two married couples, so you can imagine how I felt. I figured why not surprise all of you and come a week early. I rented a car and assumed everyone would be here." She gestured to the closed restaurant. "But then I saw you have different hours today, so I thought I'd sit and catch up on some work e-mails."

"We go to dim sum every Sunday morning before opening," I explained. "Usually Mom and Dad handle the Sunday hours, but they went to visit a family friend . . ." I trailed off. I knew my mother wouldn't want me to share any of the specifics just yet.

"Oh, that's right! I forgot you guys have that little family tradition. I was going to call your mother, but I thought it would be more fun to surprise her," Aunt Grace said with a sigh.

My sister gently brushed my arm with her elbow. "She is going to be so surprised, you have no idea. Shall we go inside?"

The three of us entered the restaurant and I went about flipping on lights while Anna May and Aunt Grace talked about my sister's law studies.

Don't get me wrong, I really like my aunt Grace. She's a great woman, but here's the thing: she turns my mother into a nightmare. The two women are as different as night and day. My aunt is more carefree while my mother is reserved. Aunt Grace never settles too long in one area though she does have a stable residence she keeps in California. Meanwhile, my mother hasn't left northeast Ohio since she came to this country.

Though our differences aren't the same as theirs, I often think that Anna May and I are also from two totally separate pea pods. I wonder from time to time how we'll be when we're their age, but honestly I don't think it will be this bad. At least I hope not.

"I'll get us some tea," I shouted from the back of the restaurant before disappearing into the kitchen.

On top of all that, my mother and aunt came to the United States for very different reasons. My mother came first as sort of an exploratory adventure. She wanted to study abroad and she ended up meeting my dad. Her original plan was not to stay, but love will set your life on a completely different path. But my aunt . . . well, she just wanted to get away from what she considered a mundane life in a country that—at the time—wasn't advancing to her liking. So she married an American man . . . hence the surname Richardson. She'd kept the American name and citizenship, but ditched the husband and moved on with her life, becoming the most freespirited person I'd ever met.

As a freelance writer for a popular travel magazine on the West Coast, she's able to spend a lot of her time jetting around the world and visiting one fabulous location after the next. Her trips' expenses are all business-related and she's compensated very nicely for uprooting herself most of the year. And from what we can tell, she has no intention of settling down. That drives my mother insane. She can't stand the lack of regimen in her sister's life and has begged her often to stay in one place, find a good man to marry. Sound familiar?

At my aunt's age, having children is a conversation of the past, so my mother has let that part of the equation go. But she will never approve of my aunt's carefree lifestyle.

I finished prepping the tea and brought a tray out into the dining area. My aunt and sister were seated comfortably at one of the front booths. Anna May scooted over so I could sit down next to her.

Aunt Grace grabbed for the pot and poured out three cups of tea. "Now, Lana, tell me . . . what's going on in your life?"

I took a sip of the hot tea, burning the tip of my tongue. "Nothing much, really. I manage the restaurant now, and that's about all my excitement these days. Dumplings, noodles, and paperwork all day long."

"Oh come now," Aunt Grace said, patting the table in front of me. "There must be something exciting going on. You're too young a girl to work so hard and have no fun. By the way, I'm absolutely in love with this hairstyle you've got. It's very in right now."

I smiled. "Mom doesn't like it, but she's starting to get used to it, I think."

Aunt Grace rolled her eyes. "Of course she doesn't

like it. Your mother has always been very traditional. A downright stick-in-the-mud sometimes."

"Lana is dating a police detective," Anna May chimed in.

I blushed.

"You have a *boyfriend*?" Aunt Grace cooed. "I bet he's handsome. When do I get to meet this man?"

"Soon, I'm sure."

"Ahhh." She leaned back in the booth and smiled to herself. "It has been too long since I last visited. You girls are growing up so fast. Ooh! Which reminds me, I have gifts for both of you. They're in the car with my luggage. I'll have to grab them before we're done here. Do you know when your mother is going to be home?"

I shook my head. "Not entirely sure. We just left them about a half hour ago. Why don't you call her and let her know you're here? She might shorten her visit if she knew you were here."

My aunt batted the idea away. "No, it's more fun this way. I love to see the look on your mother's face when she's surprised. It's priceless."

I could feel sweat gathering near my hairline. "Believe me, she is going to be so surprised."

I have kept many a secret from my mother. Some of them are for her own good, and some of them are for my own sanity. But it didn't seem right to keep this a secret. Call it growing up, but I didn't want my mother to suffer a surprise I knew she was dreading.

While my sister and aunt shared stories about recent happenings in both their lives, I slipped away into my office and called my mom. She picked up on the second ring.

"Laaa-na, I am very busy," she said. The agitation was thick in her voice and I hated to add to it.

"Mom . . . I thought you should know that when Anna May and I got to the restaurant, Aunt Grace was waiting for us."

Silence.

"Mom?" I pulled the phone away from my face to make sure we hadn't been disconnected. Nope. Still there. "Mom? Did you hear what I said?"

A string of swear words in Hokkien followed. I knew because those were some of the words I actually understood.

"You better not let A-ma hear you say those things," I warned.

"Why would she come so early? Ai-ya, I do not have time for these things." My mother huffed into the phone, and in my head, I could see her face scrunching up in dissatisfaction.

"She said she wanted to surprise you. I thought you might want to know, so I'm telling you. But you have to act surprised, Mom. I don't want to get dragged into any arguments over this."

"Okay, I'm coming there."

"Mom . . . *promise* me."

"Okay, yah, yah, I promise. I am coming there. Do not tell Anna May anything, either."

I chuckled to myself. Apparently I wasn't the only one who realized that my sister had a big mouth. "Hey Mom, is Calvin there?"

"No, I did not see him today. Why do you ask me this question?"

"Just curious is all. I figured he'd be there with Sandra. How about Calvin's uncle Gene . . . is he there?" I asked. "Or Ruby?"

"No, it is only me and your father. Everybody already went home."

"Is Gene Sandra's or Ronnie's brother?"

"Gene is Sandra's brother . . . why are you so nosy today?"

"No reason," I replied. I couldn't exactly tell my mother that if I decided to start looking into the case, I would need more information about the Chow family. "How is Sandra doing?"

"She is so-so. She is very upset about the police coming to speak with her. The nurse had to calm her down and gave her some pills. Her burns are also bad, and she has to stay for two more days, maybe. The doctor is coming tomorrow morning to see her again."

I could sense by the tone in her voice that she was mentally exhausted by the situation and the concern she had for her friend was evident. I chose to forgo any more questions. "Okay, well tell her I said hello."

We hung up after that, and I sat in my office chair spinning in circles while I thought about the Chow situation. Where the heck was Calvin hiding? Was he handling the funeral arrangements since his mother was still in the hospital? I still hadn't heard back from him on Facebook. I decided to try again. I left him a message with my cell phone number in it. Hopefully he would get back to me this time.

I knew next to nothing about these people except from way back when, and that certainly wasn't going to help me now. I had no idea where I would even begin and I hated to ask my mother too many questions for fear of her suspecting what I was up to. I had never shown any interest in being friends with Calvin even though my mother had asked me to keep in touch several times.

I rose from my chair, feeling frustrated and tense. As I headed out, turning the light off behind me, it dawned on me just how much I was irked by the whole situation. I couldn't stand to see how upset my mother was by all of this. And from what I could remember of Sandra, she had always been a pleasant and kind woman. Never had I felt unwelcome in her home as a child, and even though I would have rather done other things besides being carted around by my mother to visit with her friends, I always enjoyed seeing Sandra.

Yes, once I put my mother's reunion with my aunt behind me, I would have to deliberate with Megan again. Whether it was accidental or not, we had a murder to solve.

CHAPTER
8

Entering the kitchen, I found Lou prepping the kitchen appliances. My mother used to help cook on the weekends, but now that my grandmother was in the picture, she only came in on Sundays. Lou and Peter were carrying most of the weekend weight all by themselves. We were contemplating hiring another cook to fill in and do split shifts, but the problem was whether or not it would work with the budget.

"Hey boss!" Lou bellowed from the grill. He waved the grill brush he was using to clean in my direction. "Surprised to see you in on a Sunday!"

"My parents had some things to handle so I'm filling in."

"Great, great. Always good to see you." He gave me a thumbs-up before turning his attention back to the grill.

I left him to his preparations and went back out into the dining area where my aunt and sister were deep in conversation. I caught them in mid-laugh so it seemed that my sister hadn't spilled the beans about the recent food truck incident. It didn't have anything to do with us, but my aunt is quick to judge, and I was sure she would make some comments bound to aggravate my mother.

Instead of joining them, I went about preparing the dining room for our anticipated customers. The Mahjong Matrons—who were put off by our adjusted Sunday hours—would be in for their usual breakfast-turned-into-brunch.

Vanessa showed up ten minutes before her shift and bebopped all over the hostess station as she finished wiping down menus. She was caught offguard by my presence and I caught a glimpse of her stuffing a magazine back into her hobo bag.

The Mahjong Matrons filed in one by one a minute after I unlocked the doors, and marched like ducks to their usual booth. They took one look at my aunt sitting with my sister, and a flurry of whispers ensued. They recognized her from previous visits and knew what was coming. I think everyone knew what was coming. My mother and aunt had fought in public on more than one occasion. Talking in another language only saves you from those that don't know that particular language. In this environment, you really had to watch what you said in more ways than one.

I greeted the four elderly women with my customer service smile and a mischievous glint in my eye to let them know that I was on to them. They giggled in unison, and I told them I would be back with their tea.

In the kitchen, I readied their pot of oolong and told Lou to begin cooking their meals.

I arrived back in the dining area just in time to see my mother and grandmother walk through the front doors. A triumphant expression covered my mother's face. My father was nowhere to be seen.

Slowing my pace, I watched my mother in action. She neared the table and stopped abruptly, holding up a hand to her mouth. "Waaaa-saaaaaa! Big sister, you are here already?"

I almost wanted to put down the tray I was holding and give my mother a standing ovation. At times I think she missed her calling as an actress. I also said a silent thank-you for her actually keeping the secret between us.

Aunt Grace clasped her hands together. "Ai-yaaaaa . . . Bai-Ling . . . you are looking so young. It must be that cream I sent you in the mail."

My grandmother peeked around my mother, joyous laughter following as her eyes landed on her eldest daughter. She hugged my aunt Grace and then stepped back to inspect her. She nodded in approval and a tumble of Hokkien spilled from her lips as she squeezed my aunt's hands.

For a split second, I saw a glint of something in my mother's eye. I can't say for sure what it was, but perhaps a hint of jealousy.

Continuing on my path to the Matrons, I dropped off their tea and let them know their food would be out shortly. They barely heard me, as they were completely engrossed in the reunion happening a few feet away from their table.

I resolved to join my family, acting as if it were

just another day, and greeted my mother with a tap on the arm. "What are you doing here, Mom?" I asked, acting as surprised as I could, you know, for continuity.

"I was thinking I should check on you and Anna May to make sure everything was okay. And look what a surprise I got."

"How is Sandra doing?" my sister asked.

My mother scowled at my sister and my aunt caught the interaction. Immediately, she perked up.

"Sandra?" my aunt repeated. "Who is Sandra?" She glanced between my mother and my sister, waiting for an answer.

Neither of them responded, but not to worry, the Mahjong Matrons were on it. Helen, the oldest and most active gossip of the bunch, said, "Sandra Chow's husband was killed in a food truck accident this past Friday. But now they do not think it was an accident. They think someone did it on purpose."

My mother cringed.

Anna May quickly chimed in with the details of what had happened, including the proximity of the Ho-Lee Noodle House stand and my involvement in the explosion. My aunt eyed me with concern as my sister rattled on.

When Anna May was finished with the story, my aunt folded her arms across her chest and glared at my mother. "See? This is exactly what I'm talking about. This city is dangerous . . . you're lucky that Lana is okay. If they were my kids, I would have moved them out of here a long time ago."

My sister and I exchanged a look. It had begun.

* * *

When I got home that evening, Megan was sitting on the floor in front of the coffee table, legs crossed, with tiny glass squares spilled out in front of her. Her newest crafting endeavor was creating handmade magnets out of glass and cardstock or different images she found online. She was in the middle of gluing a magnet onto the back of a glass square as I walked in the door.

She did a double take. "Is that a Coach bag that you're holding in your hands?"

"My aunt Grace showed up today, and she brought gifts." She'd given my sister a similar Coach bag.

"And how is your mother taking it?" Megan set the glass piece down to dry.

Kikko shuffled to the door, sniffed my shoe, and then lifted her small head, eyeing the bag I was carrying. I put it down on the floor for her to fully investigate.

"Well, it wasn't too bad until Helen mentioned the food truck thing and then Aunt Grace insulted my parents' decision to live in Cleveland." Hanging my keys on the hook by the door, I left Kikko to her own devices and joined Megan, plopping on the couch behind her. I picked up one of the drying magnets and looked it over. "Then we had to hear all about Irvine, California, and how it's one of the safest places in the country."

"Eesh, and it's only the first day."

"Yeah, they went a whole five minutes without fighting. Anna May owes me money on that bet. She guessed they would go at least fifteen minutes."

Megan snorted a laugh. "How long is she staying?"

"Not entirely sure. She didn't say anything about when she would be leaving, but she doesn't stay in any one place that long anyhow. I give it maybe a week."

"Well, let's hope for your sake that it's a quick visit." Megan picked up another magnet, gluing one side of it before pressing it onto the back of a glass square. "You always get caught in the middle of their arguments and then you get all cranky."

"Tell me about it. Right now there are so many other things to focus on. Her visit couldn't have come at a worse time."

"Yeah, in your message you mentioned that you wanted to talk to me about the Chows . . . what's going on with them?"

"My dad told me there's an insurance-money angle involved. The police think there's a possibility that Ronnie and Sandra were trying to run some kind of scam and it went south."

Megan turned around to face me. "Oh really? That's interesting, don't you think?"

"I do, but . . ."

"But?"

"My mom thinks the whole thing is a mistake. She can't see them doing something like that. And if the police think Sandra was acting alone, she can't imagine Sandra would do anything to hurt Ronnie. And really, I can't see it either. But clearly someone is responsible if it wasn't an accident."

"Lana, I know you were wishy-washy about this the last time we discussed it, but I already told you, if you want to get to the bottom of this, I'm on board with you one hundred percent." She turned back around and focused on the glass square in her hand. "Just say the word."

"You really don't think I'm crazy for wanting to get involved?" I asked.

"Lana, I think you're crazy for a ton of reasons, but this doesn't happen to be one of them."

CHAPTER
9

I woke up that Monday morning determined and anxious to start my day. Which is an unusual occurrence considering I loathe Mondays almost as much as going to the dentist. But there was lots to do and no time to waste. Not only did I have a ton of paperwork to catch up on at the restaurant, but I needed to dig up information from the Mahjong Matrons and talk to Adam about whether or not he'd learned anything from his good ole buddy, Detective O'Neil.

It was a long shot that he would tell me anything, but it was worth a try.

I caffeinated myself to the best of my ability and dressed for work. It was going to be a warm day so I opted for a black skirt and wedged sandals. My mother had recently been making some noise about all of us wearing matching uniforms, but I'm guessing with my aunt's sooner-than-expected arrival, that idea would be put on hold. Small favors.

I prepared a fresh pot of coffee to brew for when Megan woke up, took Kikko for a quick tinkle time, and was on the road fifteen minutes earlier than I needed to be. I felt surprisingly put together considering everything that was going on around me.

When I arrived at the plaza, I ran into Kimmy in the parking lot. "Can you believe what's going on?" she asked without saying good morning.

She fell into step with me as I passed her car and we continued on to the entrance.

"Not really," I answered plainly. I found it was best not to indulge Kimmy's dramatics so early in the morning. If people thought Megan and I were bad at going on a tangent, it was only because they hadn't been formally introduced to Kimmy.

"I heard they think Sandra and Ronnie were trying to pull an insurance scam and it didn't go like they planned. *Then* I heard someone else say they think Sandra killed him on her own to keep the insurance money for herself. Isn't that totally nuts?"

"I doubt that's what actually happened," I said. "You know how these rumors fly around here. Someone says one thing, and then it turns into this awful game of telephone where the original context is lost. If anything the Chow family are victims, not suspects." I was proud of myself for saying it like I meant it.

"Yeah, maybe, but I think there might be some truth to this. I've heard they don't get along too well and the guy's a total jerk to his wife. Always yelling at her. I even saw them arguing at the night market in front of everyone. How embarrassing."

I let the conversation drop there and we said

our good-byes in front of the entertainment store. I walked on to the noodle house, taking a glimpse into Shanghai Donuts. I could see Mama Wu preparing the display cases. I caught sight of my favorite doughnuts and I immediately knew that I wouldn't make it a whole day without one. After I prepped the restaurant for opening, I'd have to pick up some sweets for myself and Peter.

I tidied up the dining area until Peter showed up thirty minutes later.

"How's your mom doing?" I asked, locking the door behind him. "Any progress?"

He shrugged his shoulders. "Better, I guess. The doctor is coming to check on her this afternoon and decide whether she can go home or not."

"Well, if you need to leave at any point during the day, just let me know. Maybe we can get Lou in here to cover you for a while."

"Right on." He sulked toward the kitchen before I could say anything else.

I knew this was weighing on him, but I didn't know what I could do to help. He wasn't really a "talk through his emotions" type of guy. The best I could do was be there for him in a show of support.

He busied himself with his morning preparations, and I went about mine. By nine, the dining room was immaculate and I was ready to greet the Mahjong Matrons. Not to disappoint, they all marched in with smiles on their faces.

After I situated them with tea and placed their order with Peter, I stood at the head of their table unsure of how to start my line of questioning.

Helen, the largest gossip of the four, broke the

silence. "Lana, what is it, my dear? You seem upset this morning."

"Well, I was wondering . . . what do you know about the Chow family?" I avoided eye contact while I said it. I felt like a busybody. Although, considering my audience, I had nothing to be ashamed of.

They all exchanged a knowing glance as if to say to each other that they knew exactly what I was up to. And that's exactly what I was afraid of. My only hope was that they would keep my inquiries to themselves.

Pearl, the eldest of the matrons replied, "The Chow family keeps many secrets. They do not come around like the others in the community."

"Why is that?" I asked.

It was Opal's turn to chime in. She was Pearl's younger sister and whispered rather than talked. "Because of Ronnie. We are almost certain he was the cause. He was a hard man and did not have many friends. He kept Sandra with him at all times."

The other Matrons nodded in agreement.

"Do you know how I would find out more about them?"

Wendy, who often acted as the sensible one, said, "Neighbors are always helpful people. They see many things. We do not know too much about them, but maybe someone else can help."

I thanked them and considered that option as I went back into the kitchen for their food. I supposed I could talk to their neighbors. But the only question was, how would I go about that? Wouldn't they find it a tad suspicious that I was asking them random questions about the Chow family? Especially considering one of them was just killed. I felt perplexed and slightly let down by the Matrons. I thought for sure they would have some gossip on the Chow family that would help with my investigation.

The rest of the morning went by at a steady pace. Anna May came in around eleven, covering Nancy's normal split shift. I sucked down some noodles before the lunch rush started. Anna May and I worked in sync until the crowd died back down.

The dining room had predominantly emptied, and our only customers left were two businessmen who sat near the window focused on a spill of papers they'd spread out on their table.

"Anna May . . ." I sidled up to my sister at the hostess booth.

She had a law book open and was highlighting the entire paragraph of a page. "Hmm?"

"Do you remember much about the Chow family?" I was hoping that my sister would remember some tiny nugget of information that could give me a little insight into what type of people they were. Maybe with her being a few years older than me, she had picked up on something I wouldn't have noticed.

She glanced at me from the corner of her eye. "Not really, why?"

"I thought you might know what happened. Mom used to take us over there all the time when we were little, and then all of a sudden it just stopped."

"No clue, little sister. You'd have to ask her about that. I think they had a falling-out or something. Or maybe they just grew apart. You know how things go in the adult world. Especially when families are involved. People get busy, they drift."

"How about Ruby Lin? Do you remember her?"

My sister capped her highlighter and put it down on the counter. "Okay, why are we playing Twenty Questions?"

"No reason, I was only wondering because Ruby asked about you at the night market, and it slipped my mind until today."

Anna May's shoulders sagged. "There isn't any other particular reason you're asking these questions, is there?"

I could feel my cheeks turning pink. "No, like I said, I'm curious is all. I mean, clearly she knew us as children."

"Uh-huh."

"Can you just answer the question and tell me if you remember her or not?"

"Sort of. I can't remember much though. I know she used to hang out at Esther's store a lot. The four of them would play mahjong sometimes."

"Four of them?"

"Yeah, Mom, Esther, Ruby, and Sandra. Then Ruby disappeared first and Nancy took her spot. Sometime shortly after that, Sandra stopped coming too. I think that's when they gave up on playing."

"Why don't I remember any of this? None of it sounds even the tiniest bit familiar to me. Where was I during the mahjong matches?"

She shrugged. "A lot of times you were with Kimmy at the Trans' store playing Barbies or whatever you guys did."

"And where were you during all of this?"

"Usually I was there with them, trying to learn

how to play mahjong. But I don't remember a lot of what they talked about. They'd waste a lot of time gossiping instead of playing the actual game, so I would end up finding a comfortable corner of the store and reading a book until it was time to go. I don't know if they ever actually finished their games."

"So what happened to Ruby and why did she stop coming around? How long after Ruby stopped coming did Sandra stop?"

My sister blew out a puff of air. "Why does it matter? I don't know, Lana. We were kids, I didn't care much about what was going on with the grownups."

"Okay, fine, geez." I sighed. "I guess I'll go in the back and finish some of this paperwork that's piled up. Come get me if it gets busy again."

She waved me away, already focused back on her textbook.

Once I was in my office, I checked my cell phone to see if there was any word from Calvin. Still nothing. How else was I going to get a hold of him?

I called Megan to tell her about the bust of a day I'd had so far.

"Well, Trudeau is still an option," Megan reminded me after I'd given her a play-by-play. "Maybe he'll tell you something worthwhile."

"Maybe. But what if he doesn't? What if he doesn't know anything either? He and that Darren guy don't talk all the time, so they might not have talked since the night of the explosion. Then I'm back to square one . . . although I don't feel I've ever really left square one to begin with."

"It won't hurt to bring it up anyway," she replied. "Still no word from Calvin?"

"Nope. As far as I can tell, he hasn't even read my message. I'm sure they have a lot going on with planning services and all that, but I thought he'd at least say something quick and short."

"You could always try his uncle's mechanic shop, right?"

"True . . ." I hadn't thought about going to where he worked. In a small way, it felt intrusive.

"Also, I think I have an idea. Do you still have the suit you bought for that interview a couple months ago?"

"Yeah . . . I already ripped off the tags, so I'm stuck with it. Why?"

"Maybe the Matrons are right. Maybe we should talk to the neighbors. And for that, I think we may need to go undercover."

Around three-thirty, Peter got a call from Nancy's doctor informing him that she was allowed to go home. Anna May agreed to cover the kitchen until Lou arrived, so I was back on dining-room duty until five.

Everyone had agreed to take extra shifts and work longer hours to compensate for Nancy's time away, including Vanessa.

There was only one table of two seated in the dining room, so I loitered in the kitchen watching my sister sauté shrimp, crab meat, and vegetables for a seafood lo mein dish. "How come no one ever bothered to teach me how to cook?" I asked.

"Because you've always been too impatient to learn the recipes," my sister responded. She kept her eyes on the food as she talked. "After a while, Mom got sick of trying to grab your attention."

What my sister was saying, unfortunately, was accurate. Growing up, I'd avoided the kitchen like the plague. I knew if I had too much knowledge in the cooking department, I'd be doomed to the servitude of restaurant work at the family business. Funny how things worked out.

"Well, there's no reason I can't learn now. Especially if I'm going to be running the place. Shouldn't I learn how to make everything on the menu?"

Anna May snorted. "You want to learn how to cook? *Now?*"

While the seafood cooked, she added steak strips and pea pods to the clean side of the flat-top grill.

"Yeah, why not?" I folded my arms across my chest. "Don't you think I could learn?"

She paused, thinking through her answer. "I think it's better if you stick to the business side of things, don't you?"

I glared at my sister, but I don't think she noticed. "I could probably cook better than you if I really tried. I happen to be excellent at picking up new things."

Anna May smirked. "Okay, little sister." She took lo mein noodles from the wok sitting on the stove, filled a plate with a generous portion, and topped them with the seafood and vegetables she'd just finished. She filled the next plate with the grilled steak and pea pods.

Still bitter, I took the hot plates of food and set them on my tray. I could learn to cook Asian food if I wanted. And maybe I would . . . when things finally settled down.

CHAPTER 10

That evening when I got home from work I found that Megan had already left for her shift. Feeling a bit lost and unsatisfied with my day, I pulled out my trusty investigator's notebook from under my mattress and settled on the floor next to my bed. I kept it hidden under there so no one would know what I was up to, and the only two who knew of its existence were Kikko and Megan. It was safe to say that my secret was secure.

I opened the notebook to a fresh page and scribbled some notes to myself about the explosion and listed the people who I thought could be involved. Obviously Sandra had to be listed because of the recent discoveries involving insurance fraud. I listed Calvin because of the negative relationship he was known to have with his father. Gene Tian, due to his odd behavior right before the incident. For good measure, I listed Ruby since she seemed to have some type of grudge against Ronnie and, from what I could tell, a deeper knowledge of the married couple's relationship than most people had. I also made a note about the possibility of a rival in the food industry. In the half page of scribbles I'd jotted without too much thought, I felt confident that my answer was there somewhere.

While I was writing out the details of the explosion and creating a timeline of sorts, my phone chirped and to my surprise it was Calvin calling me. My stomach fluttered as I reached to pick up my phone.

"Hello?" My voice sounded anxious and I leaned back against the bed, taking a deep breath.

"Hey Lana, sorry for not getting back to you sooner." Calvin paused. "Everything's been kind of crazy."

"No problem, I figured as much. Are you okay?"

"I've been trying to keep a low profile. We've got people all over us asking for interviews . . . it's super obnoxious considering I just lost my dad. These people have no respect."

He said it in such a matter-of-fact way that I couldn't tell if he wasn't upset about it or was trying to keep himself collected for my sake.

"I wanted to check in with you to see how things were and if you needed anything. I thought you might need a friend." I felt bad telling that white-ish lie, but I didn't think telling him that I was trying to rule him out as a suspect would go over very well.

"I appreciate it. I won't say that this whole thing hasn't been an ordeal because, without a doubt, it has. It's been just one thing after the next since Friday night."

Again, he sounded unaffected, almost as if he

were reading lines from a script. Had he said these same words to others?

"Why do you suppose they would automatically point the finger at your mother for this?"

"Isn't that what they always do? Blame the spouse?" Calvin asked. "Come up with some half-cocked theory on why the significant other wants the now-deceased party dead."

"Maybe," I replied. "I've heard a few rumors . . . is any of it true?"

"You mean about the financial stuff?"

"Yeah, were your parents struggling?"

"Well, they *were* having some financial problems . . . the food truck was doing pretty good, but they weren't making a whole lot of profit. I think they needed more time to build the business and that's why they thought the night market would be a good idea. My father had a lot of ideas on how to expand business opportunities."

I wanted to ask him if he thought his parents were capable of doing what they were being accused of. And I really wanted to ask him what he and his father were arguing about. But I didn't think any of it would come out the right way. I began to wonder if maybe Ruby would be more forthcoming with information.

"Lana? You still there?"

"Huh?" I snapped back to reality. "Yeah, sorry, I was just thinking."

"Anything worth sharing?" he asked with a chuckle.

"Who do you think would do this to your parents . . . I mean, knowing their situation, do you think anyone was upset enough with them to go this far?"

I could almost hear him shrug. "If they were having any other kinds of problems, I wouldn't know. Neither of my parents tell me much of anything."

Adam came over around 9 P.M. for a late dinner. It was the first time since we'd started dating that I offered to cook for him. Even though my Asian culinary skills were practically nonexistent, I wasn't too shabby with other types of recipes. On tonight's menu were Italian-seasoned chicken breasts, parmesan-lemon broccoli florets, and garlic and olive oil roasted potatoes. They were some of a handful of dishes that I felt confident making and thought it would be a good place for us to start. And by "us," I really meant me.

Since we'd met, Adam and I had been taking things fairly slow for both our sakes. Both of us had been in relationships that left us feeling less than stellar about jumping back into the dating world. But oddly enough it was working out for us since we were both in the same boat. I wasn't going to rush him and vice versa.

He showed up at my door about five minutes before the chicken was ready. When he walked in, he inhaled deeply. "It smells really good in here. I am starving."

I just hope it tastes as good as it smells, I thought.

While I finished preparing the meal, Adam entertained Kikko in the living room. I arranged the food on two plates and set them down on the dining room table. "Okay, dinner's ready."

Kikko, hearing the plates clink on the table, waddled into the dining area and planted her butt down next to my chair. Her tail wiggled as she watched my every move.

"Wow, look at this spread," Adam said, eyeing his plate with approval. "And here I thought you were going to warm up a pizza."

"Don't sound so surprised."

He chuckled. "Well, I didn't know you could cook. You never talk about it and you're never in the kitchen at the noodle house."

"That is a different story." I picked up my fork. "Deep below this mask of frivolousness, I do have a domestic side. Now hurry and eat before it gets cold."

I waited for what seemed like forever for him to take that first bite. I think cooking—or creating anything in general—is nerve-racking when you're sharing it for the first time with someone you genuinely care about.

Finally he took a bite of the chicken. He nodded with satisfaction, a smile spreading over his lips. "Lana, this is great. You've been holding out on me."

I laughed. "Wait until you try my lasagna."

He shook his head. "If you keep cooking like this for me, I'm going to gain a pant size."

While we finished eating, we kept the conversation light. We filled each other in on work, which was primarily me talking about the restaurant. He rarely tells me things going on at work besides "water-cooler" gossip. And then we talked a bit more about where we might vacation for my birthday.

After dinner, I cleared the table and put away the leftovers, making him a care package to take home. We moved to the couch, and I made coffee and dug some Biscoff cookies out of the pantry.

"So, I talked with Calvin Chow earlier tonight," I said as I handed him a coffee mug.

He took a sip of the steaming liquid, and observed me over the rim of the mug. "And?"

I settled onto the couch next to him. Kikko eyed the cookie in my hand. "And nothing, really. He told me that he's lying low because of reporters."

"I'm not surprised. It doesn't look good for them," Adam commented. "Especially his mother."

"You think so? I don't know, I have a hard time believing that Sandra and Ronnie were involved in some kind of insurance scam. My parents have known them forever and they're not that type of people."

"Desperate times, Lana . . . you never really know what someone is capable of when they're pushed into a bad spot. I see it a lot in my field."

He had a point there. I'd even seen it with my own eyes a few times. People usually seem innocent enough at first, but there are always those prover-bial skeletons in their closet. "So is Detective O'Neil looking into any other potential suspects . . . maybe someone set this whole thing up for a reason we're not aware of yet."

Adam slid a glance in my direction. I knew that look. It was the one he gave me when he caught on to my snooping. "Lana . . . why are you letting this whole thing bother you? This isn't your problem."

I blushed. "I know, but it's bugging me. It just doesn't seem plausible to me. And how would they even know what to do?"

"O'Neil said there were trace elements of chemicals used to create a homemade bomb. Nothing about the explosive was at all sophisticated. Whoever we're dealing with was definitely an amateur. Anyone can dig this stuff up online these days." He looked down at his mug. "Sadly, this isn't the first time some knucklehead has tried something like this."

"But do you really think that the intention was to kill?"

"Well, that's what needs to be found out. O'Neil mentioned there being a kitchen timer involved with the explosive. It's possible it was faulty or maybe it was set wrong. Ronnie could have wanted this to happen in public so it seemed more plausible. If it blew up somewhere less populated . . . well, who knows. Any way you look at it, the whole thing stinks."

I leaned back on the couch and considered Adam's input and the insurance-scam angle. I suppose it made sense to do something more public so it appeared real.

Adam wrapped an arm around my shoulders and pulled me close to him. "For once, this isn't my case, and I don't have to worry about anything. How about you don't, either? Let's enjoy the fact that things are quiet in our lives right now, and our weekend getaway will be uninterrupted."

I smiled, nodding in agreement, but in my head I was coming up with various scenarios for what I thought could have happened. Whether it was Sandra that had done this, or someone else, I was going to figure it out. One way or another.

CHAPTER
11

Late Tuesday morning when Anna May showed up to handle the split shift, I slipped over to see Esther at her store. From the little information I got out of Anna May, I knew that Ruby and Esther were acquainted well enough. Hopefully she could be my way in. My mother was sure to be suspicious the minute I brought it up.

Esther was behind her sales counter, which consisted of a row of glass showcases filled with delicate jewelry and hair accessories. On top of the showcase next to the wall was a miniature TV set that she used to watch her soap operas when there were no customers. Since she hated to be interrupted, I hoped she would give me quick answers without asking too many questions.

Her reading glasses were settled on the edge of her nose, and she lifted her chin, observing me through the rectangular lenses. "Lana." She tapped her own shoulders, giving them a shake.

I groaned, straightening my back as I approached the counter. You'd think by this stage in my life, I would have excellent posture with all this nagging she did. "I have to get back before the lunch rush, but I wanted to stop over and ask you about Ruby Lin."

She lowered the sound of the TV. "Ruby . . . why?"

I thought I heard the sound of disdain in her voice, but I continued anyway. "You know, she makes all that jewelry by hand."

Unimpressed, she replied, "Yah, I know."

"Well, I was thinking about buying some. Do you have her phone number so I can give her a call?"

Esther scrutinized me. "Why can you not wait until the next night market?"

I hadn't thought of that. Why couldn't I wait? "Oh, well, I wanted to get a gift for my aunt Grace and who knows how long she'll be in town. You know how she's always on the go." Yeah, that worked, right?

"Why not buy her a gift from here? I sell many nice things for you to buy your auntie." Esther tapped the top of the showcase in front of her.

"I saw something specific that Aunt Grace would like, and I want to get it before it's sold to someone else."

Esther stared at me, her eyes searching my face for signs of guilt.

Since I had begun my extracurricular activities solving some recent crimes, people were beginning to catch on when I started asking too many questions or did things they thought were out of character. It made things slightly difficult for me at times, like right now, but I always denied any involvement. Even if it wasn't believable at this point, I had to keep up appearances.

"So, can I have her phone number, *please*?" I begged.

Esther sighed as she reached underneath her counter and dug out a little address book. She flipped casually through the pages and found the number she was looking for, jotted it down on a notepad and tore off the page, thrusting it in my direction. "Do not tell your mommy that I gave you this. She will be very upset with me."

"Don't worry, I was never here." I took the paper from her hand and smiled.

She waved me away as she turned the sound back up on her TV, and I exited the store before any lectures could occur.

Once I returned to the noodle house, I hid in my office with my newly acquired phone number and gave Ruby a call. My plan was to meet up with her and look over her jewelry. I was going to purchase something from her so my story would check out, but my real motive was to get her talking without realizing that she was giving me any information. Ruby and Sandra appeared to be close judging by the unspoken words they exchanged with a mere glance. If I were a betting woman, I'd wager they were best friends. Megan and I often shared similar looks and the two older women had reminded me so much of us. And if they were anything like us, that would mean Ruby knew all of Sandra's deepest, darkest secrets.

* * *

As luck would have it, Ruby was able to meet with me after I got off work that evening. She'd given me directions to her house and said I could come by any time. The rest of the afternoon, I'd been anxious for the day to end and it probably showed in my movements. I tend to get a little scattered and fluttery when I'm anticipating doing something.

While I made my way into Mayfield Heights, I recited in my head what I planned on saying to Ruby. It would start off simple enough. I'd use the same story about buying something for my aunt that I'd told Esther. While she was showing her pieces from the night market, I would casually bring up Sandra and ask how she was doing. Then I'd go in for the harder questions. Talk about the rumors that were spreading about the Chow family. Maybe even act like Calvin had hinted at things being problematic.

I found the house with no difficulty, and pulled into the driveway, parking behind a black SUV that had definitely seen a lot of road.

The curtains were open in the large picture window in what I assumed to be the living room. I saw a figure stand up and walk to the front door. It was Ruby. When she saw me, she waved and opened the screen door.

"Hello, Lana." She held the door open for me and I stepped into her house taking in the scent of rice cooking.

"I hope I'm not disturbing dinnertime."

"Oh no, my husband is not home yet," she said, shutting the door behind me.

The house was spotless aside from the tools of her trade. A giant coffee table made of black lacquer sat in the center of the room and on top of it were all her velvet trays from the night market. Off to the side was a small folding table she had set up with a smattering of jewelry findings and tools necessary for clamping and bending wire.

The TV was on mute and it appeared to be a repeat episode of *Burn Notice*.

"Please sit down." Ruby gestured to the chair on the opposite side of the coffee table. "Would you like something to drink? Tea or coffee?"

"Some coffee would be nice, thank you," I said. Might as well get comfy while I probed her for answers.

Ruby disappeared into the kitchen, and I studied the particulars of her living room. She had a few pieces of Asian artwork hanging above the sofa. Three panels of black lacquer that matched the coffee table told a story made from ivory. Women in traditional robes gathered around a koi pond feeding fish while other women walked the countryside, parasols in hand.

When my host returned, she handed me one of the mugs she was carrying. It had already been lightened with cream. "I put a little bit of sugar in there for you too. Let me know if it's okay."

I sipped the coffee, burning the tip of my tongue. It was a little sweeter than I was used to, but I nodded in agreement anyway. "It's perfect, thank you."

She held her own mug in both hands, sitting on the edge of the sofa and leaning in toward her jewelry.

"You said you would like to buy some jewelry for your aunt?"

"Yes, she just came into town a few days ago and surprised my sister and me with some gifts. I thought I would return the favor."

She grinned. "I remember your aunt Grace. She is a very nice woman. Very high class too."

I chuckled. "That's a good word for it."

"What do you think she would like?"

I focused on the assorted jewelry. I really had no idea what to pick, and with what I actually wanted to talk about at the forefront of my mind, it was hard to concentrate on the sparkling objects.

To make life easier, I picked up a pair of black and gold cloisonné earrings that would match anything my aunt would wear.

"These are lovely," Ruby said, taking them from my hand. "I can put them in a nice bag for you." She rifled through her things on the folding table, plucking a bag made of sheer red organza from the pile. "Your aunt will be sure to like them. If I remember her correctly, these are just her style."

"Thank you for letting me come by on such short notice. I wasn't sure if you would be at the next night market after what happened with . . ." I made a production of looking away as if the topic made me uncomfortable. "Well, you know."

"Yes, what happened with Sandra and her husband is very terrible," Ruby replied in an even tone. "But I will still show up next Friday."

"It's a shame they're trying to blame this whole thing on Sandra, don't you think? I can't even imagine what this is like for her. First she loses her hus-band and now she's being accused of his murder."

She sat, eyes fixed on the TV for a moment. "Yes, this is quite a shame. Sandra would never be in-volved in something of this nature."

"Who do you think would do something like this to the Chow family? Do you think Ronnie's death was intentional? Or was someone just trying to ruin their business?"

"This is a difficult question to answer." She stopped, glancing down at her trays of jewelry. "Ron-nie did have many enemies, though. He tried to keep it secret, but there are many people who don't like him."

"Really? Like who?"

She regarded me with suspicion. "Can I ask what your interest is in this matter?"

"To make my mother feel better," I said. It was sort of the truth. "She was so upset when she heard they were blaming Sandra for what happened. She just couldn't believe it. I thought maybe if I could find some alternative reasons behind what happened, my mom could relax a little bit."

"Yes, I can understand your mother's concern. This was not expected to happen." Ruby picked up her cof-fee mug and took a sip. "If I were the police, I would consider those that did not like him. Sandra is an an-gel, she does not have any enemies that I can name, but Ronnie . . . he has made several people mad."

"Did you see anything strange that night?" I asked. "Maybe you saw something that you didn't think was important at the time."

An image of Calvin and his father fighting flashed into my mind along with the jumpy way his uncle had acted. Could have been the alcohol, but it seemed a little extra in my opinion.

"I saw him arguing with a couple of people . . . but this is nothing new. Ronnie is always arguing with someone. He has a very bad temper."

"Was there anybody specific there that night who would be capable of doing something bad to them? Maybe even to frame them?"

"I'm not sure, but perhaps the man who owns the barbecued-meat truck. I know that he was mad about something that night. I saw them arguing before the night market began."

Now that she mentioned it, I remembered Ronnie pointing with agitation at the other food truck and telling Sandra something in reference to it. I'd completely forgotten about that part of the night because I was so stuck on Calvin and his uncle.

"My mother told me that Gene Tian is Sandra's brother . . ."

"Yes, he came to . . ." She looked away. "He used to live in New York City, but he came back here to help Sandra with . . . her business."

"So he has experience with the food industry?"

"No, he is a mechanic," Ruby said. Abruptly she stood up. "Excuse me, I have to check the rice cooker."

Before I could say anything else, she had zipped into the other room. I leaned back in the chair. Gene kept popping into my head, mostly because of his behavior Friday night, but I didn't know if that was enough to go on. Maybe I could ask Ruby more questions about Sandra's brother when she came back from the kitchen.

She was gone for about five minutes and when she returned, she seemed a little less jittery than when she had gone in. "I must apologize, I really should finish preparing dinner for my husband. He will be home from work soon. Would you mind if we talked more about this some other time? Maybe at the night market if there's time."

"Oh sure, that's fine," I said, handing her my half-empty coffee mug. I was a little disappointed that I didn't get to finish my line of questioning, but I was grateful she'd met with me to begin with so I wasn't going to complain. "Sorry to have taken up so much of your time. I really appreciate it."

I quickly paid her for the earrings and she thanked me before walking me to the door. In my car, I took a deep breath and nodded resolutely. I had some digging to do when I got home.

CHAPTER
12

At home, I found a note from Megan stuck to the fridge telling me she'd be back around 9 P.M. She'd worked a split shift that day and was looking forward to coming home early so we could hang out a bit.

I walked Kikko around the apartment complex so she could handle her business before I got down to researching.

Back inside, I set myself up at the dining room table with my laptop and the notebook I hid under my mattress. I made a few notes while I waited for the computer to boot up.

Within minutes, I found the information I needed for the barbecued-meat food truck on the company's Web site. BBQ 2 Go was owned by Winston Leung. He offered his services by request for a flat fee to businesses who wanted him to occupy their parking lots during lunchtime, and included several photos of hungry patrons in business suits and dresses as they surrounded the truck. Another picture showed him standing in front of his food truck grinning with pride. He was tall, thin, and appeared to be somewhere in his early fifties. He had smiling eyes with several wrinkles showing that he laughed quite often. His demeanor was friendly and non-threatening. All in all, he looked like a nice man. But from experience, I knew that meant absolutely nothing.

I jotted down some more notes on Winston and ways that I could approach him. I thought asking him outright if he had issues with the Chow family might be a little too suspicious. I'd also have to come up with a way to actually have time to talk with him. The night market wasn't until Friday and I was anxious to question him before then. After all, we might not have time once the evening got started. Plus if Peter got wind of what I was doing, I already knew he wouldn't let me out of his sight.

My cell phone chirped next to me and Anna May's number filled the screen display. "Hello?"

"Hey, Mom wanted me to call and see if you wanted to join us for dinner with Aunt Grace. We're headed over to the east side."

"Siam Café?" I asked.

"Of course, it's Mom's favorite."

"I'm gonna pass tonight," I told my sister.

Even though I was hungry, I didn't think my brain could handle the conversations that would take place. I already knew what it would be like.

"Okayyyy . . ." Anna May replied. "But you know that Mom is going to call you herself when I tell her you're not coming."

"Just tell her I'm not feeling good."

My sister grumbled and we hung up. I went back

to my notes, attempting to orchestrate a plan to confront Winston. But before I could get too into it, my mother called.

"La-naaaaaa," my mother sang into the phone. "Anna May told me you do not feel good. What is wrong now?"

"My stomach feels weird," I fibbed. "I think I ate something funny."

"What did you eat today?" my mother inquired. "You are always eating junk."

"Um . . ." I had been at the restaurant all day and she knew that. To insinuate that I got sick at the restaurant would really set her off. "I had some leftover chicken wings when I got home from work . . . I think maybe the sauce was bad."

"Mommy tells you every day, you have to be careful eating spicy food. You are getting older now and your stomach is not the same. You cannot eat the same things as before."

Thankful to be on the phone so my mother couldn't see my eye roll, I agreed with her. "You're right, Mom. I should listen to you more often."

"Yah, I know," my mother said with triumph. "Are you sure you cannot come anyway? Your auntie will be sad that you could not make it tonight."

"I'll come next time, Mom. Right now, I think I need to lie down."

"Okay, okay. Mommy will check on you later."

She hung up and I stared at my phone for a few minutes in guilt. I hated to lie to my mother about why I didn't want to join them for dinner, but I didn't want to subject myself to telling her the truth, either.

Instead of torturing myself, I went back to my

notebook and concentrated on the other dilemma in my life . . . finding ways into this case. For the moment, I dropped the Winston angle since I was coming up with nothing in particular, and did a search on Calvin's uncle Gene.

Without much difficulty, I found Gene's auto repair shop, which was located on the east Side near Payne Avenue and East Thirty-third. Funny I had never noticed it before. Aside from that, there wasn't a whole lot of information to be found on him.

Kikko whined from her spot on the floor next to me and when I scanned her bowls, I noticed she was out of water. I got up and filled her water along with her food dish and paced the living room instead of sitting back down.

I felt lost, and unsure of myself. Nothing seemed to be taking shape. Nothing was sticking out at me. That in itself made part of me think that maybe Sandra really did do it. Then the question became, did she act alone or did someone help her? Or did Ronnie unknowingly have a hand in his own death?

I didn't know much about the Chows or what they'd been through as a family. The Matrons had told me they kept most of their business private and didn't associate extensively with the Asian community, so my normal go-tos were out of the question. It was all working against me.

I thought about how much trouble I'd had the first time I tried my hand at solving a mystery, and that's when it dawned on me. I scurried into my room and pulled a book off the packed shelves of paperbacks. A few months ago, Megan had gotten me a book about being a private investigator. Of course, it had more information than I needed since I had no intention of getting a PI license, but it did have helpful tips on how to conduct an investigation.

Flipping through the book, I stopped at a couple pages that seemed helpful, and that's when a lightbulb lit up in my head. I could check the county records to see if anything there might be helpful.

With renewed hope, I returned to my seat at the dining room table. I could have smacked myself for not thinking of it earlier. I typed in the appropriate information and before long I was on the page that I needed to conduct my search.

I typed in Ronnie's name first and found he had an impressive list of minor offenses—all of a semi-violent nature. But there was one in particular that caught my attention. It was related to his wife. I had a bit of trouble deciphering some of the coding that was meant to shorten the descriptions, but from what I gathered, there had been a domestic dispute, and charges were dropped in the end.

The most current entry in his file was from six months ago, and another man's name was listed as well. When I reviewed some of the details, it read as if a neighbor had gotten involved or the two men had gotten in a fight on their own. I couldn't tell, but I jotted it down in my notebook.

After that, I looked up Sandra's name and found similar listings under her file. So, I thought, sitting back in my seat, things had gotten physical between the couple. What could have happened? Had she been messing around with the neighbor mentioned in the report? Is that why another man was involved?

What if that was the real reason Winston the meat

truck owner and Ronnie were rivals? Could something have been going on between Winston and Sandra? What piece of information wasn't I seeing?

I must have lost track of time because Megan walked through the door as I was pondering what I'd found. It was a little past 9 P.M. and I hadn't even noticed. Kikko was dozing on the couch and Megan walking in with crinkling bags woke her from her nap. She sprang up from her spot and waddled over to try and catch a sniff of what Megan had brought home.

Megan held the bags up for me to see. "Thought I'd grab us some munchies. You hungry?"

"Oh good. Yes, I'm starving. I passed on dinner with my family tonight." I reached out for the bags. I could smell barbecue sauce and fried batter.

"Mozzarella sticks, chicken quesadillas, chicken wings, and French fries."

"Oddly enough, I told my mother I was sick from eating chicken wings so I could get out of meeting with them tonight."

"See? I'm turning you into an honest woman."

I faked a laugh and set the bags on the table while Megan went and grabbed a few things from the kitchen. She came back to the table with a two-liter bottle of Coke, two plates, and napkins.

"So what are you up to?" she asked, nodding toward the computer. "Digging into this case, I presume?"

"I went to see that woman Ruby from the night market after I got off work today."

"Oh, do tell." Megan opened the bags and pulled out the containers one at a time, organizing them on the table.

While we filled our plates and started eating, I

told her about my interaction with Ruby and the information I'd found online about Sandra, Ronnie, and the male neighbor.

"We need to find out what neighbor this was," Megan said, after finishing off a chicken wing. "Just like I said to you the other day, we'll go undercover and ask a couple questions. Maybe Sandra was having some private time with the neighbor and got busted by Ronnie."

"Do you think the neighbor could have had something to do with the explosion? Maybe his plan was to get back at Ronnie for something. And that would fit with why it happened at the night market. Assuming they kept the food truck at their house, a neighbor's involvement would be more plausible. But having it happen where it did might help give this guy some cover."

"Possibly. Or he did it to keep Sandra for himself," Megan offered. "Clearly she wasn't jumping at the chance to leave Ronnie."

"Unless she couldn't figure out a way and this was it?" I mulled the thought over in my head. "She must have been afraid of him?" My mind went digging back to the evening of the night market, working my way from the beginning of my interactions with Sandra. "That's it!" I yelled.

Kikko skittered away at the sound of my raised voice.

"That's it, what?" Megan asked.

"I hugged Sandra and she winced. She told me she'd hurt her back and I didn't think anything of it at the time, but maybe her injuries were caused by Ronnie."

Megan tilted her head back and forth while she weighed the scenario. "Okay, so it's become a pattern in their relationship since the incident six months ago. He doesn't trust her anymore, and they get into physical fights more frequently. Finally she can't put up with it anymore and decides to blow him up?"

"I hate to say it, but yeah." My eyes settled on the chicken quesadillas and I played the scenario out in my head, trying to see how she would put together this elaborate scheme. "How would an ordinary woman know how to blow up a food truck, though?"

"You can basically learn anything you want on the Internet."

"True, Adam said the same thing the other night. But it still seems odd to me." I tried to slow my thoughts, thinking over the details a little more carefully than before. "Or . . . she had someone help."

"But who? Do you think she involved Calvin in this?"

"I don't know. I keep going back and forth with that. He mentioned to me that he didn't know anything about what went on with his parents. Which might be true because I think his reaction to his father's death might have been a little different had he known what was going on behind closed doors."

"He could be faking it."

"Exactly, that's why I keep going back and forth. *But* I do know one person who keeps sticking out above everyone else."

"Who?"

"Sandra's brother Gene."

CHAPTER
13

"Looks like you found your starting point," Megan said. She leaned back from the table, and clutched her stomach. "And I think I just found my stopping point."

"It has to be her brother," I said, reassuring myself that the pieces fit. "Ruby said to me earlier tonight that Gene had moved back here from New York to help Sandra handle her business. Only she wasn't talking about the food truck business. Then she got flustered and left the room before I could say anything else, and when she came back, she rushed me out of the house. She must have realized she'd said too much."

"It does make sense," Megan agreed.

I smacked myself on the forehead. "Oh my God, and I wasn't thinking about this either. The two women exchanged weird glances with each other at the night market, kinda like how you and I do when we already know what the other is trying to say. Maybe she knew what was going to happen."

"But wait . . . do you think she actually knows what *really* happened? Maybe Sandra didn't tell her everything . . . if there is something for Sandra to tell, of course."

"If I were about to do something that major, I'd definitely tell you."

"Okay, that's true. But do we really think that Sandra is involved in this? Would Sandra really let her brother or possibly her own son go through with a plan this crazy? She'd be ruining her entire life in the process."

"If Sandra and Ronnie were struggling, maybe he convinced her that she'd do better with the insurance money. Maybe Ronnie had no involvement at all. And, it's very possible Gene didn't tell her the whole plan. He could have intended to kill Ronnie from the beginning but hidden that fact from Sandra because she would never agree to it." I paused. "Ugh, I can't believe how much this is all making sense now. Gene was in a big hurry to leave the night market that night, claiming he had to use the bathroom. He rushed Calvin out of the picnic area in the nick of time too. He had to have known that the truck was going to blow and didn't want to be anywhere near it."

"So now what do we do? And what about your theory involving the other food truck guy . . . Winston? There may be other motives here and we're just picking up the first one that's convenient."

She was right. It felt careless of me to dismiss the rival-food-truck angle altogether, but I couldn't help feeling that all these pieces fit so well. Then again, if

I was wrong, I could end up making things worse for the Chow family . . . especially Sandra.

"Okay, we scope out the neighbor situation and see what we can find out. Then we'll dig into this Winston guy and reassess what seems plausible."

"Sounds like a solid plan. But what about talking with Sandra herself?"

"She's still in the hospital for another day or two. I want to give her some time before approaching her. It's only been a couple of days since the accident. *If* she didn't know what her brother was up to, then she's actually grieving and I don't want to disrespect her feelings."

"You seem too sure about your theory, Lana," Megan pointed out. "We can't say for certain that her brother did it. Regardless of Sandra's involvement, we don't know that her brother was necessarily involved at all."

"True, true." I sighed. "It feels so right, though, doesn't it?"

"It does," Megan agreed. "And I wouldn't mind agreeing with you if there wasn't one glaring fact."

"Which is?"

"It came by us a little too easily. Which means the police are definitely thinking along these lines too, but they haven't found enough evidence to make any arrests. Don't you think we should be investigating the road less traveled?

"You're right. Okay, so we'll take our time and search through all the leads, but Gene is definitely going to the top of my list."

* * *

I fell asleep a bit more easily that night, and when I woke up, I felt more confident than the day before. One visit to Ruby and gathering a few minor pieces of the puzzle had brought me much farther along than I'd hoped. Of course, I was planning to heed Megan's warning, but I could feel it in my bones that I was on to something.

Maybe by talking with the others, I would be able to solidify the story as a whole. Of course, I'd present my theory to Adam when I finished looking into everything, and I would let him decide how to approach Detective O'Neil about it.

Once the restaurant was open and the Mahjong Matrons were settled into their favorite booth with tea, I decided to try a different set of questions on them. Maybe this time around, they'd have more interesting things to tell me.

Helen seemed to sense before the others that I had something I wanted to ask. She gave me the okay to interrupt their conversation.

I set their tea service on the table. "Do you happen to know much about Sandra Chow's brother Gene?"

"He owns an auto repair shop, right?" Opal asked. "He is the one who drinks too much?"

"Yeah, that's him," I said, watching the four ladies anxiously. "What do you know about him?"

"Not too much," Wendy added. "He has not lived here long. He was in the navy for many years, but something bad happened and then he moved to New York."

I hated to admit it, but I was kind of disappointed in the Matrons. Their lack of information on the

Chows and their extended family was disheartening. "Wait . . . did you just say he was in the navy?"

"Yes, that is what I said," Wendy replied.

"Is that why Calvin went into the navy?" I did think it was a little strange that he'd chosen that particular path considering what I knew of him at that age. He was nothing short of a degenerate.

"I think so," Pearl interjected. "I think that Gene was once a nice man, but then something happened to him while he was away. I think he and Calvin were close when Calvin was still a little boy."

"Yes, this sounds right to me," Opal said with a slow nod. "I am starting to remember too. Ronnie was always busy working, so Calvin spent time with Gene whenever possible."

Peter rang the food bell from the kitchen signaling that the Mahjong Matrons' food was ready. I hurried back into the kitchen, my mind stuck on the information the Matrons had just divulged. I didn't know if it meant anything, but it was potentially another angle I would have to consider.

What if Calvin idolized his uncle? He was always at odds with his father, and fighting against the grain. But, with his uncle . . . well, he joined the Navy, and though he failed, he still went through the motions. And instead of helping with the family business like his father wanted, Calvin had gone to work at his uncle's auto repair shop instead.

That led me to wonder if Calvin did indeed know what kind of man his father was. But that would imply that the abuse had started earlier than six months ago. What if he had abused Calvin too? While I did consider it a possibility that long-standing violence could be a large factor, there was no actual proof of it. There was no record of it except the one incident.

I tried thinking back to my childhood and the time that I spent with Calvin and his family. Most of it was a blur, but I didn't remember Ronnie being around a whole lot. It was always my mother and Sandra having tea and talking in Mandarin while Calvin and I played with his Transformers in the other room. Often it was already dark by the time we went home and Ronnie still hadn't returned from work.

Clearly there was more to this story than I realized and the new information about Gene's time in the navy spoke to that. Even though parts of today's theory felt a little on the thin side—I knew I was speculating wildly—I could see it developing if I just added a few more pieces.

The Matrons' food was placed on the tray and I stood staring into space as I worked out some of the different scenarios that could be additional possibilities. I reconstructed my original theory of Sandra and Gene plotting this together and substituted Calvin for his mother. Maybe Calvin was also sick of it all and asked his uncle for help.

It seemed likelier that this was the case rather than Sandra being involved. Perhaps Calvin wanted to protect his mother from his father and didn't have many people he could trust. He knew his uncle would back him up since Sandra was his sister. Or maybe he didn't mean to actually hurt his father, maybe he just wanted to scare him straight. I wondered what their argument was about the night that Ronnie was killed.

I made a mental note to talk with Calvin about the last conversation he'd had with his father.

Just then the food bell sounded again, jolting me out of my concentration. I jumped, nearly losing hold of the tray in my hands.

When I came back to the present, Peter was gawking at me. "Lana . . . don't even think about it." He waved his spatula at me.

"Think about what?" I asked.

"You're not fooling me, man. I know that look on your face. And whatever you're thinking about, stop it."

Over the course of the past few months, Peter had learned how to read me really well. I shrugged, pretending not to know what he meant, and rushed the food out to the Matrons.

CHAPTER
14

After work, I hurried home to meet Megan. She was dressed in a cream-colored button-down silk blouse with cap sleeves, a navy pencil skirt, and matching navy heels. Her hair was wrapped up in a loose bun and her makeup was conservative. She did a spin for me as I entered the apartment. "Well, what do you think? Do I look like an insurance agent?"

Setting my purse down on the table, I said, "Looks pretty convincing to me."

"Hurry up and get ready so we can head out. I have to be at work around eight," she said, shooing me off to my bedroom.

I took a quick shower and slipped on the suit I'd planned to wear on my last attempt at getting out of the restaurant business. But fate had stepped in, and I never had the chance to make the interview because my parents took an unexpected trip to Taiwan for my grandmother. I ended up running the restaurant while they were away and my mother was so impressed with how well I handled the last-minute pressure, she'd decided it was time for me to take over permanently.

The pinstripe knee-length skirt was a little snug as I put it on and I cursed the doughnuts that had made their way into my daily diet. After I threw on the cherry-red blouse that I bought to go with the jacket and skirt, I slipped on a pair of three-inch stilettos and gave myself a once-over in the mirror. Not too shabby, I thought.

We said good-bye to Kikko on our way out, and headed over to the east side where Sandra lived. They were still in the same house they'd lived in all those years ago, and since there had been no changes of address, it was easy to find them online.

I parked in the street, and we sat in the car assessing the two houses on either side of Sandra's home.

"Well." Megan turned to me. "Which one should we go to first? Or should we each take one?"

"Um no, I don't want to walk up to a stranger's house by myself," I told her. "This is already weird enough."

"Okay, let's try the left one," she suggested. "Who knows, maybe no one will be home."

We got out of the car and walked along the sidewalk to the house Megan indicated. The lawn was well kept and a few rosebushes lined the walkway up to the door. I stood off to the side while Megan rang the doorbell.

A tiny older woman opened the door a sliver and peeked out. All she exposed were eyes covered with thick-framed glasses and her nose. Her curly white hair was permed but not done, and appeared flat on one side as if she'd been lying down. "I'm not interested in whatever you're selling," she said, starting to shut the door.

Megan held up a hand. "No, ma'am, we're not here to sell anything. We just need to ask you a few questions."

"Are you here from the gas company? Because I told those yahoos on the phone yesterday that I already paid my bill. I can't help it that you folks take forever to process a damn check."

"We're not from the gas company," I said, inching a little closer to Megan. "We're insurance agents and we're here to investigate the situation next door."

"The situation next door?" The woman opened the door more, exposing the rest of her body. She was dressed in a pale pink housedress and had fuzzy slippers on her feet. It was apparent that she hadn't left the house all day. "I don't know anything about what's going on next door. I try to mind my business the best I can. We have enough busybodies in this neighborhood if you ask me."

Megan gave her a pleasant smile. "Any information could help us. We're looking into an insurance claim for the Chow family . . . and we were wondering if you could help us with some background on the family?"

"You mean that nice Asian lady that lives next door? I heard about her husband gettin' blown up, that's just a damn shame." The woman shook her head with disappointment. "I lost my Earl about three years ago. Cancer, though. Rare not to go from cancer these days."

"I'm sorry to hear that," I replied.

"Eh, thanks for the condolences, but I've come to terms with it now. Earl would have wanted me to live my life. I'm going on a cruise this summer. One of them all-inclusive numbers where they take you around the Caribbean."

"That sounds real nice," Megan said. "I hope you enjoy yourself. I've never been on a cruise."

"Yeah, they have all kinds of activities, too, but I'm really lookin' forward to the buffets. I heard they have some great food on them cruises." The woman slapped herself on the forehead. "Silly me, here I am yammerin' on about my circumstances when you came here to ask some official-like questions. Sometimes in my old age I drift from topic to topic without a care in the world."

"We don't mind," I said politely.

"Well, here's the scoop on that there Asian couple. The woman is pretty nice but she's kind of timid and keeps to herself. I've brought them holiday cookies and such, but we don't talk too often. One time that husband of hers shoveled my driveway for me. But then he realized that I wasn't drivin' anymore. I got an eye condition and I can't drive all that good."

"Were you aware of them having any problems?" I asked.

"Problems? What kind of problems?"

"Marital problems."

"Oh, them kinda problems. Well, dearie, who's married that doesn't have problems?" She chuckled to herself before continuing. "No, no kind of problems that I knew about. One time the police came by, but I wouldn't know anything about that. My hearin' ain't too good, either." She pointed to her ear, which was equipped with a hearing aid. "Most of the time, I can't hear anything going on, but I saw the lights goin' out there. Wondered what happened. That guy who lives on the other side . . . Chuck somethin' or other. He may know more. I think he's the street's top busybody. I always see him walkin' up and down the sidewalk talkin' to people. I don't care for him much, so I always turn my hearing aid down real low so I can't hear what he's sayin'. He gets tired of yellin' and scoots on to the next house."

Megan and I both laughed at that and the woman smiled in return. "Can't be too old for a sense of humor."

"Well, we appreciate your time," I said. "We'll let you get back to your evening."

"No problem, girls," she said good-naturedly. "Good luck with your investigation. And don't forget about Chuck. If anyone can tell you anything, it would be him." She waved to us before shutting the door.

Megan and I walked back down the drive and headed for the sidewalk leading to what would be Chuck's house.

Megan sighed. "She was a nice lady, but it's a shame she didn't know anything else."

"I know. I'm hoping this guy has something more for us. I think he must be the one from the police report."

Since Megan had done the honors at the previous house, I decided to step up for this one. I rang the bell and stood front and center, waiting for someone to answer. After a few minutes, the door slowly opened and a middle-aged man with a half-unbuttoned dress shirt and unbuttoned pants opened the door. He looked surprised to see us. "Oh, I'm sorry," he said, fumbling with the buttons of his khakis. "I thought you were someone else."

I blushed out of awkwardness. "Um, sorry to disturb you, we were hoping to take a moment of your time if that's all right."

"Are you from the IRS?" he asked, buttoning his shirt back up.

"No, we're from an insurance company," I said as confidently as possible. "We're here to ask about the Chow family."

He nodded in understanding. "Would you like to come in?"

Megan and I looked at each other, unsure of how to respond.

His attention turned toward the street, and he scanned the surrounding houses. "This is something we should probably talk about inside. You know how neighbors can be."

"Um . . . okay . . ." I felt uneasy about it, as I'm sure Megan did as well, but he had a point. You never knew who could be watching.

We stepped into the house, and stood uncomfortably by the door. He didn't make any attempt to shut the door behind us, and he didn't invite us to come farther in.

"I'm Charlie, by the way." He sat down on the arm of his easy chair and folded his arms across his chest. "People call me Chuck . . . Chucky sometimes. I hate that though."

Megan cleared her throat. "We won't keep you too long. What can you tell us about the Chow family?"

He leaned back, his arms remaining folded. "Well, I was sorry to hear about Ron, but man, that guy was a rotten SOB. Forgive my language."

"So, you weren't a fan?" Megan asked.

"Not in the least. I respect women, and that guy certainly did not. He knocked his wife around pretty hard. Don't know why, don't care. So, I got involved. I heard her yellin' from my backyard. I called the cops and warned them I was gonna go over there. I did."

I assessed Charlie from where I stood near the door. He was slightly muscular and maybe the same height as my dad, so he was tall. And definitely bigger than Ronnie. "Did this happen often?"

"Uh, I only knew about the one time," he said. "If I'd have known about more, I would have given that guy two black eyes."

"I see," Megan replied. "Are you aware of what's circulating in the news?"

"Sure am," he said with a nod. "Everybody on the block is talking about it."

"And what is your take on it?" Megan asked.

"If you ask me, I think someone killed that guy for sure . . . but it wasn't about no insurance money. That woman's got a brother . . . at least I think it's her brother from what I gather. I heard the two men exchanging words outside a couple times. And it wasn't pretty. I wouldn't put it past her brother to do something wacko."

"You really think so?" I asked. The pieces of my imagined scenario were clicking into place.

"I'll tell you ladies this," he said, leaning forward as if he were worried about being overheard. "If some jerk bag was takin' punches at my sister, he wouldn't live to tell the tale." He straightened up. "But don't put that part in your little report."

After we returned from our visit with Sandra's neighbors, Megan hurried to get ready for work and was back out the door within twenty minutes. I happily changed out of my suit and slipped into a tank top and capris. Pulling out my notebook, I headed into the living room and sat with Kikko on the couch. I needed to plot out my next moves.

Visiting with Sandra would have to be put on hold for a couple days. My next course of action should be to figure out whether or not Winston was someone I could absolutely add to the list or cross off. All I had to go on was what Ruby had told me. I thought it might help to give Calvin a call and see what his feelings were about the rival food truck owner. When we'd talked the first time, he said he didn't know of anything specific. But now that I had someone specific to focus on, maybe pieces would fit together for him.

I dialed his number. This time, I wanted to see him in person though. There's nothing better than questioning someone face-to-face. People take liberties on the phone. Eye contact is not an issue, facial expressions are not questioned, and at any minute the call could "drop."

"Hey Lana."

"Hi, Calvin, how are things?"

"The same. What's up?" He sounded slightly suspicious as he asked.

"Well, I wanted to see if you had any plans to-night. I thought maybe we could get together for some drinks and catch up like you wanted to. You know, to take your mind off everything going on."

He didn't respond right away and I thought maybe he suspected that I was snooping. When he finally answered, he said, "Sure, did you have a specific place in mind?"

"My best friend works at a bar called the Zodiac. Ever heard of it?"

"Yeah, that's over near your neck of the woods, right? I've never been."

"How about we meet there?" I asked. "She's a great bartender, and they have awesome food."

"Yeah, that sounds good. I'll meet you around nine-thirty?"

We hung up after finalizing our plans, and I gave myself a quick makeup refresher before heading out. Once I was finished, I had a little time left to kill before leaving, so I took Kikko out for another quick tinkle and then hopped online to do another, more thorough search on Winston. His Web site told me he'd be at Edgewater Live, a weekly event held at a local beach, on Thursday. I could try and get a hold of him then.

I made a couple notes to myself in my notebook before heading out to meet Calvin.

CHAPTER
15

- - - - - - - - - - - - - -

I arrived at the bar ten minutes early so I could get there before him and fill Megan in on my plan. She was stocking the beer cooler when I walked in.

"Hey woman," Megan said when I neared her. "I didn't expect to see you again so soon."

I settled onto a stool and told her about meeting with Calvin and what I planned to do about Winston.

She nodded in approval. "I can come with you on Thursday. I'll switch shifts with Robin. She's looking to make some extra cash anyway, and my shift is better than hers."

While I waited for Calvin to show, Megan brought me a drink and I placed an order for some fries.

Calvin arrived five minutes late, and stood at the entrance scanning the room. He was dressed in a plain, fitted white T-shirt and olive shorts. He propped his sunglasses on what appeared to be a fresh haircut as he made eye contact with me. He acknowledged me with a head nod and made his way over.

"Hey sorry, traffic was a nightmare on 271."

I snorted. "When isn't it?"

He pulled out the stool next to mine and sat down, focusing on the drink options behind the bar. Megan came by, introduced herself, and took his drink order, which was a gin and tonic.

Calvin drummed the bar nonchalantly as he assessed the room.

"I've been meaning to ask, how is your mother? I was thinking about stopping by to see her when she finally gets out of the hospital."

"With any luck, she can come home tomorrow. She'd like a visit from you, I'm sure. Aside from your mom, Ruby, and Uncle Gene, my mother hasn't had very many visitors. A lot of people are being weird with us since . . . well . . . you know."

I knew what it was like to be viewed a certain way. Not that long ago, Peter and myself, along with Ho-Lee Noodle House, were being given the stink eye. It wasn't a nice feeling and I tried to keep in mind that the Chows may not be guilty of anything at all. We certainly weren't. "You know, I've been giving it a lot of thought," I said, attempting to sound casual. "I know you said that your parents didn't fill you in on much, but did you happen to notice anything strange?"

Megan returned with Calvin's drink and rushed off to help another customer.

He removed the cocktail straw from the glass and took a sip. "Like what kind of strange?"

I shrugged. "Oh, I don't know. Maybe some type

of problems with another food truck owner. I know you said nothing specific stood out to you, but maybe there's something that didn't seem too important at the time. You know how people can be competitive for space. Even something small like that could turn into a larger argument over time."

He shook his head, "Nah, I don't think so."

"Do you know if your parents ever did anything at Edgewater Live?"

"Um, yeah, I think they did. Why would that matter though?"

"No reason, just curious. I hate to see you guys be put under the microscope by the police if there's someone else they should be looking at. Maybe they had a problem with someone at a different location and the feud followed over to the night market."

"Whoa," Calvin said plainly.

"Whoa what?"

"Do you really think that someone was targeting my parents on purpose?"

The sound of shock in his voice was almost enough to convince me that I was wrong about him having any involvement whatsoever. Yet there was something about his facial expression that left a tiny reason for doubt. His reaction was a little *too* surprised. Could the thought really have never crossed his mind that this wasn't a random act? Or was I really that conspiratorial in my thinking that I couldn't fathom the thought of it being a random act of terror? Then again, the local authorities had set their sights close to the Chow family as well.

"Well, yeah," I said. "But the police think—"

"Just because they think it was some conspiracy

doesn't mean it actually was," he replied. "Whoever did this could just as easily have decided to blow up one of the other trucks instead. Like BBQ 2 Go or something like that. I mean, maybe it was just a co-incidence that it was my parents' truck, you know?"

"True, but—"

"The cops are just trumping this up. Everybody wants to read into what happened like it's some big mystery to be solved. All I want is for them to catch the person who did this. Whoever it is." He sipped his drink, emptying the glass. He tapped the rim when Megan glanced our way.

I thought about his comment while we waited for Megan to return. *Like BBQ 2 Go.* Now why would he specifically bring up Winston's truck in this con-versation? Was I jumping to conclusions where there were none?

Armed with another drink, he took control of the conversation. "Enough about this doom-and-gloom stuff. Let's talk about regular life. Tell me what's going on with you. How did you get suckered into running the family business? If memory serves me right, you didn't want to have anything to do with it."

Disappointed that I hadn't gotten more informa-tion from Calvin, I gave in and told him a condensed version of what led me down my current path. When I was finished, I tilted my glass at him. "How about you?"

"Well, the Navy didn't cut it for me. I thought maybe it would give me some discipline, but I just don't fit that bill, you know?" He laughed to him-self. "Trying to fit a square peg into a round hole or whatever that old saying is. Then I kind of fumbled around for a while until my uncle came into town. I've been working for him at his mechanic shop for a little while now. It's whatever." He shrugged. "Other than that, nothing to tell really. No woman in the picture, no grand plans . . . just livin' life day by day."

Since he mentioned his uncle, I figured it was a good opportunity to learn a bit about him. "Oh yeah, your uncle Gene, I heard that he moved here from New York. Must be a big change for him going from living in a Chinatown of that size to something on a smaller scale."

Calvin laughed. "It's taken him some time to adjust, but he wanted to be close to my mother. Everyone's getting older and sentimental. You know how it is."

I thought about my mom and Aunt Grace. I didn't see Aunt Grace getting sentimental and moving to Cleveland any time soon. "So they're close then?"

"Yeah, for the most part. My uncle originally moved away because he couldn't stand my dad. They never really got along."

"Oh really?" I asked, curbing the urge to lean closer. I didn't want to appear too eager.

"Yeah, just typical alpha male stuff. My dad and uncle would always get into it and my mom started to get really mad at Uncle Gene. She'd always say that he was causing problems in their marriage. So, my uncle decided to leave and let them do their thing without interruption."

"So what made him come back?" I could feel my body bending forward and I readjusted myself on the stool.

Calvin drummed the bartop with his fingertips again, avoiding eye contact. I contemplated repeating the question in case he hadn't heard me, but I had a feeling he did. I didn't want to appear too pushy, and wanted to give him the opportunity to come around with an answer without any prompting from me. I finished my drink and excused myself to the restroom.

When I returned, he was seated and positioned exactly as I had left him, it was almost as if time had stopped. As I sat back down, he took a deep breath, his fingers finally still. "No one knows this minor detail . . . so can you not tell anybody?" he asked. The tone in his voice sounded pleading.

"Of course," I said. I wanted to cross my heart or pinkie swear, but that was probably overkill. "Your secret is safe with me."

"My mom was planning on leaving my dad a couple years ago. I don't know all the details . . . my uncle told me about it. I don't know if my dad was cheating or what, but my mom was ready to pack a bag. Only problem was, she didn't have anywhere to go, and nowhere to turn. I mean, I'm a mess, Lana. I can barely take care of myself. My mom knew I couldn't take care of her or anything. She didn't want to impose on Ruby, and she doesn't really have any other friends. So, she mentioned it to my uncle, and he decided to move back here so my mom would have some place to go."

My insides were screaming. It had to be Uncle Gene! Megan had replaced my empty glass with a fresh beverage while I'd been gone, so I took a sip of that and counted to five. I needed to keep it together.

"But clearly your mom never left your dad, so what changed?"

He sighed. "Your guess is as good as mine. Like I said, my parents didn't share a lot with me. If my uncle hadn't told me what was going on, I would never have known anything about it. They put on a good show for everyone. The model Chinese family. But they must have worked something out because my mother's attitude changed out of nowhere. She told my uncle to mind his business."

Yeah, like his mom found another way to get her husband out of the picture, I thought.

"Hey, where's the bathroom?" Calvin asked, craning his neck.

I pointed to the back where I'd just come from. "Past the pool tables on the left."

"Right on. I'll be right back."

When he was out of sight, I waved Megan over. She held up a finger signaling that she'd be over in a minute. I was practically bouncing on my stool. This little tidbit of information could hold the final answers to my questions.

I felt a gentle tap on my shoulder, and then a gravelly voice asked, "Excuse me, Nancy Drew, is this seat taken?"

I didn't have to turn around. I knew that voice by now. It was Adam.

Adam sat down on the empty stool on the other side of me, and wrapped an arm around my waist. Pulling me toward him, he kissed my cheek. His face was scruffy and he smelled of sandalwood and cinnamon. "I saw Calvin Chow headed back to the bathroom on my way in, so you can drop the innocent act. I know you have to be up to something."

I gently pushed away from him and looked him in the eye. "How do you know I'm not catching up with an old friend? Calvin and I go way back, you know."

His green eyes bored into mine, assessing my facial features. "Because I know when you're up to something. You get that look in your eye and you kind of chew on your bottom lip."

My hand flew up to my mouth. "No I don't."

Megan approached us with a beer bottle in one hand and my fries in the other. She slid the bottle across the bar to Adam. "Busted," she said, winking at me. She set my fries down, and pulled a bottle of ketchup out from somewhere under the counter.

"What are you doing here anyway?" I asked Adam.

He raised the beer bottle to his lips. "I figured you'd be here, so I thought I'd swing by and see what you were up to. You still haven't given me an answer about your birthday trip."

In the thick of things, I'd forgotten about the trip. I hadn't thought any more about it since he'd brought it up at dinner the other night. "I need more time to think," I said. "With everything going on—"

"Even more reason to focus your attention on something else . . . like a getaway. We could both use one at this point," he said. "I know I'm looking forward to getting out of this place."

"Can we talk about it tomorrow?" My eyes darted toward the restrooms.

"You mean when you're not interrogating Calvin Chow?" Adam raised an amused eyebrow at me.

"You can't get mad this time," I told him. "It's not your investigation, remember? And who was the one who said as long as I tell you things, you'd be understanding."

"No . . . but it's Darren's, and you really need to leave it to him. Besides, you didn't tell me, I—"

"Shhh . . ." Megan hissed, tapping the bar. "Here he comes."

Adam glanced over his shoulder, and I pretended to act natural, by salting my fries. Megan walked away casually as Calvin approached us.

Calvin noticed Adam's arm draped around the back of my stool and pursed his lips. "This guy bothering you or something?"

Adam snorted. "Hardly."

Calvin cocked his head at me.

"Oh, Calvin, I'm sorry, this is my boyfriend, Adam. He just happened to stop by unexpectedly." I winced. That sounded slightly unbelievable as I said it. "Adam, this is Calvin Chow . . . a family friend."

"Nice to meet you," Adam said with a head nod. No handshake was exchanged.

Calvin followed suit with a head nod and took his seat. "I didn't realize you were involved with someone."

Adam squeezed my arm playfully.

"Well, we didn't get that far yet. There's so much for us to catch up on."

"You guys been together long?" Calvin asked.

"A couple of months," I responded. I could feel my cheeks getting pink.

"Right on, how did you guys meet?"

"We, um . . ."

"I'm a police detective," Adam cut in. "And Lana here was under investigation . . ."

I thought I saw Calvin's eyes widen. He turned away, focusing on his drink. Finishing what was left in the glass, he set it down a little harshly on the counter and then drummed the edge of the bartop. "That's cool. Well hey, I don't want to be a third wheel or whatever, so I'm just going to exit stage left. Besides, I have somewhere I need to be." He pushed off his stool, and avoided eye contact as he got up. "Lana, we'll have to finish this another time."

Before I could say anything else, he rushed off toward the exit.

Adam chuckled. "Third wheel . . . uh-huh. I think someone has a crush on you, Lana."

I turned to Adam. "Me? Are you kidding? He flew out of here the minute you said you were a cop."

Adam and I stayed at the bar for another hour before I decided to call it a night. He had an early day so he headed home and said we would spend some time together the following evening as long as nothing crucial happened at work.

When I got home, I doodled in my notebook a little, making notes about Calvin's behavior and the things he'd told me about his mother's situation. Maybe he knew more about what was going on with his parents then he originally let on. Sure, maybe his mom and dad weren't telling him anything of use. But it sure seemed that Uncle Gene was sharing plenty.

Since I had to wait until Thursday to conveniently

run into Winston, I made a plan of action for the next day that would involve me visiting with Sandra Chow. Once Anna May showed up for work, I would take some food from the restaurant over to Sandra as a way to talk with her. I just had to keep my fingers crossed that business would be slow.

CHAPTER
16

Wednesday morning flew by, and before I knew it Anna May was strolling through the double doors of our family's restaurant. She seemed especially confident today and waltzed up to the hostess booth with a look of satisfaction. The restaurant was mostly empty except for a couple of tables finishing up a late breakfast.

"Ask me why I'm so chipper today," Anna May said as she walked up to the hostess booth. She smiled, showing all her teeth.

"Because it's another wondrous day at Ho-Lee Noodle House?" I asked, dramatically extending my arms.

She smirked. "No, little sister, because *I* ran into Henry Andrews today."

"Oh, that's great!" I clasped my hands together in mock excitement. "Remind me who that is again?"

Anna May huffed, crossing her arms over her chest. "You're going to ruin the story."

"Well, I can't help it if I don't know who Henry Andrews is . . . did you guys used to date or something? The name doesn't sound familiar at all."

She smacked her forehead. "No . . . Henry Andrews is a partner at Andrews, Filbert, and Childs law firm. He's a very prestigious lawyer in Cleveland. Geez, Lana, stop living in that cave of yours."

"Ohhh, *that* Henry Andrews."

With an icy glare, she replied, "I really hate you sometimes, you know that?"

I giggled. "Okay, sorry, sorry. Continue with your story."

Her face brightened again. "Well, I ran into him at the bank, and he recognized me from the time he came and spoke in one of my classes a few months ago. We started talking about my studies, and he suggested I apply to intern at their firm."

"What?"

"I know, right?" Anna May sashayed behind the counter, stuffing her purse in the cabinet underneath. "This is going to be amazing!"

"No, not right . . ." I said, rising from the stool. Mild panic setting in. "I need you here. What am I supposed to do without you? And Nancy is still out."

"Oh Lana, relax, will you? It's summertime, you can ask Vanessa to pick up a couple more shifts. I'm sure she'll want the money. I heard her tell someone she wants to start saving for some type of girls' trip to Cancún when she turns eighteen."

"I don't want to ask Vanessa, you know she drives me crazy." I pointed to my head. "Do you see these gray hairs? I think those are from her."

"Lana, you have to learn some patience."

I waved a hand at her. "My patience is fine."

"Well, you're just going to have to accept that I won't be able to help out as much. I really want this internship, and a partner told me to apply for it. A *partner,* Lana."

"Okay, okay," I said. "Fine, this is important, I know. When is this going to happen?"

"I'm submitting the paperwork in a few days, and then I have to be interviewed by all three partners. Hopefully as soon as possible."

I took a breath. Okay, I could deal with this. Nancy would definitely be back at work by then, and Vanessa would have to be my go-to for extra shifts. "Well, worst-case scenario, I put out a help wanted ad, I suppose."

"Try to live without me, little sister." Anna May winked as she stole my seat.

I groaned. "However will I manage?" I turned to head back into the kitchen.

"Where are you going?"

"It's been slow today so I'm going to drop off some food for Sandra Chow. She was released from the hospital this morning."

"Speaking of food," Anna May replied. "Mom is requiring a mandatory family dinner tonight. We're going to Bo Loong and you better be there . . . or else."

"Is the 'or else' from you or Mom?"

"Both of us."

I sighed. "When you become a hotshot lawyer, you better buy me a Mercedes."

* * *

Unable to decide what to bring Sandra, I went a little overboard. In a large paper bag with our logo printed on the side, I stuffed a container of vegetable lo mein, an order of Hunan beef, pork dumplings, three spring rolls, wonton soup, chicken teriyaki sticks, and enough rice to feed five people.

From the plaza, it would take me about forty minutes to get there. During my drive, I went over my line of questioning. Hopefully what I was trying to achieve wouldn't be too obvious.

About halfway there, my mother called. I pressed the speaker-phone option on my cell phone, which was propped up on my dashboard. "Hi, Mom."

"Laaaaa-na!" my mother yelled into the phone.

"Mom!" I yelled back. "I can hear you!"

"You are coming to dinner tonight," she stated matter-of-factly.

"Yes, Mother, I know. Anna May told me earlier today."

"Okay, you bring Adam with you. Okay? Auntie wants to meet him."

"I don't know if he's going to be able to make it. He might have to work."

"You tell him he has to come."

I knew there was no point in arguing. "I'll see what I can do," I told her.

"Where are you going? Are you driving somewhere?"

"Yeah, I'm taking some food over to Sandra Chow."

"Oh, that is very nice of you, Lana. She will be very happy. Okay, Mommy will let you go. Drive safely."

She hung up before I could say good-bye.

Once I reached Sandra's, I parked in the same spot I had the other day and hoped that neither one of her neighbors would notice that I'd returned. That was sure to raise some questions.

Before I got out of the car, I sent a quick text message to Adam letting him know that his presence was requested by both my mother and my aunt. He was going to love this.

With my carry-out bag in tow, I approached the house, and walked up the three steps to the front door. I rang the bell and heard a muffled chime go through the house. She lived in a modest brick bungalow similar to the ones around her. The exterior was white with blue shutters and minimal landscaping. The lawn was overgrown and desperate for a good mow.

A few minutes later, Sandra came to the door. Dark circles sat heavy underneath her eyes, and her skin looked sallow. A purple bruise ran down the entire left side of her face. And her left arm was covered in bruises and burns. Her long hair was drawn back in a sloppy ponytail that was tied at the base of her neck. She wore sweatpants and a long Cavs T-shirt.

"Oh Lana," she said. A hand went up to the side of her head where a lock of hair was sticking out from her ponytail. She patted it down self-consciously. "What are you doing here?"

I held up the food. "I thought you might need some comfort food. I know it can be a pain to cook for yourself, and since you're just getting home, this'll make it easier on you."

She gazed down at the bag and back up at me. "Thank you, that's so nice of you." She stepped to the side. "I'm sorry, please come in."

Her house was similar in style to Ruby's with the front door opening right into the living room. I entered her house and tried not to appear as if I were assessing the place, but I couldn't help it. It was completely trashed.

Styrofoam containers, wrappers, and pill bottles littered the coffee table. Blankets and pillows covered the couch, giving you the impression that she intended to sleep there. Shoes and flip-flops were scattered around the room, and in the corner next to the end table was a crumpled-up towel.

"Please excuse the mess," she said, shutting the door behind me. "I am not moving around so good. Ruby has offered to help clean up. She has been very sweet to me."

Here she'd only been home for a handful of hours, and she'd already turned her house into a disaster area. I smiled encouragingly. "That's okay. You don't have to explain. You should see my place. If you didn't know better, you'd think a tornado blew through."

She forced a laugh.

I stood awkwardly at the entrance while she hobbled around the room shoving things aside. There was a rocking chair off to the side of the couch that she cleaned off for me to sit in. "Would you like any tea? I have hot water ready."

"Sure," I said. I held out the bag in my hand. "What would you like for me to do with this?"

"Oh, follow me into the kitchen."

The eat-in kitchen was tiny, with an oak table meant to seat four. It sat next to a window that over-looked the backyard and seemed oversized for the area it occupied. She had the window open and a warm breeze flowed through the kitchen, fluttering the sheer white curtains.

"You can put the food over here," she said, pick-ing up a stack of mail on the kitchen counter. "I'll just put this in the other room."

While she went to take care of her mail, I set the bag on the counter. The sink was filled with dishes and I imagined they had been there since before the incident. I could smell the faintest odor of fried fish lingering from a previous dinner. I immediately felt bad for stopping by, and as I assessed the condition of her home, I wondered if this was a woman who was capable of murdering her husband. She was a complete mess.

When she returned, I noticed that she had combed her hair and adjusted the ponytail so she didn't look quite as disheveled. Her movements were jittery as she picked up the kettle and poured two cups of tea, hot water spilling onto the counter. "Would you like to sit in the other room? It's more comfortable in there."

"Sure, whatever's easiest," I said. The kitchen table was covered with random mail and paperwork. I didn't want to see her go to the trouble of moving everything into different spots.

I followed her back into the living room with my cup of tea, and sat down in the rocking chair. It creaked as I leaned back and I questioned whether or not it would hold me.

"I appreciate you bringing me some food from the restaurant. But you didn't have to go to any trouble." She set her teacup on the coffee table in front of her and leaned back into the couch. "I feel guilty already with Ruby making such a fuss. Do you know she was at the hospital every day as soon as visiting hours would start?"

"I'm sure that Ruby doesn't feel burdened. And neither do I. It was really no trouble at all," I told her. "We need to keep Peter busy anyhow. He's been so worried about his mother that he's a nervous wreck all day long. Cooking gives him something productive to do."

"How is Nancy?" Sandra gazed down at her hands, which were in her lap. She seemed so small sitting on the couch, like she'd sunken into the upholstery.

"She's better. Still very bruised and sore, but all in all, she's doing well."

Sandra nodded. "Good, I'm so glad to hear it. I've been meaning to contact her, but I don't feel much like talking to anybody."

I stared into my teacup. Was that a hint? "I know this must be so hard for you. Especially with everything that's involved with it."

Her eyes met mine. "What do you mean by that?"

"Well . . . just that . . ." I focused on my teacup again. "All the rumors . . . and the media . . ."

"None of it is true," Sandra said, lifting her chin. "I loved my husband very much. He could be a hard man sometimes, but he took care of me. I don't know who would do something like this."

I wanted to call her out, but I couldn't exactly

tell her that Calvin had told me about the pending divorce that she had planned not that long ago. I still wondered what made her change her mind in the end. Maybe she really did love him after all. "I didn't mean to imply anything. I just meant that I've heard what people have been saying, and I can imagine that would make things more difficult for you. Because you did love your husband."

Her shoulders sagged and she let out a deep breath. "I'm sorry, Lana. I didn't mean to snap at you. You have been so nice to bring me a care package, and this is how I treat you."

I leaned forward in my seat, the chair creaking with my movement. "Don't mention it. Really. I understand."

"I don't know what I'm going to do now. The investigation is holding things up, and I don't know how long it will take me to get the insurance money. Without the truck, I will have to start all over again."

"Do you think that your husband was murdered on purpose?" I asked.

"What?"

"Well, I just mean . . . do you think he was the target? Because maybe someone . . ."

Her eyes bulged. "How can you say this to me?"

I held up a hand. "Well, I just meant, is it possible this wasn't a random attack? I know that Calvin thinks it was, but if Ronnie—"

"No one murdered my husband on purpose," she replied firmly. A little too firmly, if you ask me.

"But it could be possible that—"

"No! Why would someone kill him?" Her voice rose. "What happened had nothing to do with him!"

"I'm sorry to upset you," I whispered.

"I think I should be by myself now," she said, rising from the couch. "Thank you for the food."

I took that as my cue to leave. I set my teacup on the coffee table and walked with my head down to the door. I felt embarrassed and about five years old right about then.

She opened the door, and stood rigid, refusing to make eye contact with me. "Good-bye, Lana."

"Bye, Sandra," I stopped on the threshold, hoping she would look at me, but she wouldn't. With a sigh, I headed out onto the stoop.

She slammed the door behind me, and I flinched. This had not gone as I planned at all.

CHAPTER
17

In the time I'd been inside, Adam had called and left a message telling me to call him back.

"Hey, beautiful," he said when he answered the phone. "What trouble are you getting into now?"

"Why do you always assume the worst about me?" I asked as I started the engine.

"I've found it's best to always think you're up to something. That way when you're not, I can be pleasantly surprised."

"Har-har." I checked for oncoming traffic and pulled out from the curb, making my way back to the freeway.

"So, dinner with your family, huh? That should be interesting."

"Tell me you can't make it. Tell me you have to work late. Save yourself from the impending tragedy that will be tonight's family dinner."

"Oh come on, it can't be that bad, can it?" he asked.

"Yes, and so much worse than you can possibly imagine."

"Well, as luck would have it, I'm available to-night. I'm excited to meet your aunt. And besides, I wouldn't want to disappoint Mama Lee. I'm still trying to win points with her."

"She's impressed with the fact that you want to take me on vacation. So that's something in your favor."

He chuckled. "And how's your father feel about it?"

"His eye twitches a little bit, but I think he'll be fine eventually," I joked.

"Oh good, so I'll pick you up at seven?"

"Sure, that sounds good," I said. "Hey, can I ask you something?"

"Anything."

"Do you think it's odd that neither Calvin nor his mother want to acknowledge that what happened to Ronnie might have been done intentionally?"

"Lana."

I could almost hear him shaking his head. "What? I just think it's weird that both of them were offended by it. Don't you?"

He groaned. "Not necessarily. I think the idea of your loved one being intentionally done in is more upsetting than it being a random act of violence. I mean, think about it. If it were me, would you rather me be murdered or die by circumstance? You know, wrong place, wrong time."

"Well, either one is horrible. But if there was the slightest possibility of you being murdered, I'd want to consider it and then if that's what happened,

I'd want my revenge on that person. Like that one movie with the guy who goes after everyone that killed his family."

"Oh, that one movie, huh?"

"Yeah . . . you know, that one . . . with the guy."

He sighed. "Our conversations are not like other couples', are they?"

"No, no, they're not."

"Okay, I'll pick you up at seven, babe. Try to do minimal damage until then."

We hung up as I merged onto I-271 South, heading back to the plaza. I'd been gone a shorter time than I originally intended and I'm sure Anna May would be relieved to see me back sooner than expected.

As I drove, I thought about what Adam said about Sandra's reaction. I guess I could see where he was coming from, and maybe I was just different. I've always been one to examine all the possibilities, even the outrageous ones. Although, in this case, it wasn't that outrageous considering what type of person Ronnie had been. But there was still a possibility that the murder might have been an accident and that damage was only meant to be done to the truck.

Still, with things the way they were, you would think that Sandra and Calvin would want to get to the bottom of it no matter what the answer might be. He was their husband and father. There was only one reason I could think of that would cause them to not entertain the idea at all. And that was if they already knew the answers.

* * *

When I made it back to the restaurant, I found it empty. Not a single customer occupied any of the tables. Anna May was up at the hostess counter with a law book open on the lectern, a highlighter poised and ready to weed out the important information.

"Let me ask you a question," I said as I approached her.

"If it's about getting out of tonight, you can forget about it. You're going to be there even if it kills you. I had to survive the last family dinner without you, and I'm not doing it again."

"No, it's not that. Adam and I will both be there tonight."

She glanced up from her book. "Detective Hottie Pants is actually coming? I'm impressed."

"Detective Hottie Pants? Have you been talking to Megan?"

"What's your question, Lana?"

"Say I was killed in a strange accident—"

"What kind of question is that?" My sister gawked at me.

"Just go along with it."

"Fine." She waved a hand at me. "Continue."

"Okay, say I was killed in an accident and no one was a hundred percent sure what happened. I could have either been murdered on purpose or by accident. Wouldn't you want to find out if I was murdered on purpose?"

"Of course I would," she replied.

"Thank you. That's what I said."

"I'd want to know, then I'd sue the pants off that person, and I'd buy everybody in the family a Mercedes in your honor."

I stared blankly at my sister. "You are such a b—"

"Hey, watch your mouth, young lady, this is a family restaurant." She snickered to herself and returned to her book.

"Can you just answer the question seriously?"

She huffed, setting her highlighter in the spine of her book. She folded her hands over the open pages and looked at me plainly. "Yes, Lana, I would want to know the truth. For better or worse, you're my sister. I'm not going to let someone get away with murder . . . especially if they killed you on purpose."

I nodded in satisfaction. "That's what I think too."

"But you can't expect everyone to feel that way, Lana. Death is a hard pill to swallow."

"I know, but shouldn't the truth be more important? So you can get closure? Wouldn't you want to know the why of everything?"

"Some people will never get that kind of closure, Lana. Sometimes, gone is just gone, and no matter what the circumstances were, it won't make it better."

"Yeah, I suppose you're right about that."

"I'm often right," she said with a smirk. "And if you're asking this because of the situation with the Chows, I would just drop it. Stay out of it and let the cops do their job. Something has always struck me as weird about that family, and the last thing I would want is for you to get involved."

If I'd been sitting down, I would have fallen off my chair. My sister rarely showed that kind of concern for me during our little chats. Usually she would harass me for being a busybody and that would be the end of it. "Well, thanks, big sister," I said, unsure of what else to say.

"To be honest with you, I wouldn't doubt it that Ronnie was killed on purpose. And who knows if whoever did it is done with their mission. I can't believe that no one has considered that maybe Sandra was meant to be in that truck too."

"Do you really think that could be a possibility?"

"Well, until they catch whoever did this, they're not going to know why anything happened. So far it seems that no one has gone after Sandra, but she did just get out of the hospital. Who knows what could happen next."

My mind started to drift with the thoughts of what could happen next.

"Now stop worrying about it and butting in. Go in the back and count the cash or whatever it is that you do. I want to finish studying since our night is going to be occupied with family time."

"Ugh, I can hardly wait," I replied.

"If there are any two people who can make you and me look like sisters of the year, it's definitely Mom and Aunt Grace."

CHAPTER
18

After work I rushed home and readied myself for dinner with my family, both mentally and physically. Anna May made me swear up and down that I would not be late—as I usually am—because she didn't want to get stuck in the middle of an argument should one arise before I got there.

Adam picked me up promptly at 7 P.M. and we made our way over to Bo Loong on St. Clair Avenue.

I noticed that my parents' and sister's cars were already in the parking lot. When we passed my sister's car on the way in, she opened the driver's side door so fast that the motion startled me.

"Anna May!" I yelled. "Give me a heart attack!"

"It's not my fault you're not observant," my sister said as she got out of the car and shut the door. "I told you I didn't want to go in unless you were here. It's safer in the parking lot."

Adam, who was standing behind me, squeezed

my shoulders. "Don't you two start . . . from what I'm gathering, you have enough to contend with."

"He's right," I said. "We can't be bickering too."

The three of us of trudged to the door.

My father was facing the door and not participating in whatever conversation was going on. He waved us over when he saw us coming in.

"Hi, Dad." I made my way around the table and gave him a quick hug.

My grandmother smiled at us, her silver teeth sparkling.

"Hi, girls," my aunt Grace said.

Her eyes landed on Adam and I swear I saw a glint of approval in her eye as she assessed him.

"Aunt Grace, this is my boyfriend, Adam," I said, squeezing his arm. "Adam, this is my aunt Grace."

My aunt smiled, extending a hand. "It's so nice to meet you, Adam, I've heard so many things about you."

He shook her hand and gave me a wink. "Hopefully my reputation is intact."

I eyed my mother who I knew was the culprit. She didn't know too much about Adam's and my relationship, but I'm sure that she threw in a lot of her own opinions.

My mother busied herself with filling teacups and set them at each of our place settings. "Come. Sit. We will eat soon."

My sister sat next to my father and I sat between her and Adam. Adam sat next to my grandmother who patted his arm in recognition.

My mother turned to me, her eyes narrowing ever so slightly. "Sandra Chow called me today."

"Oh yeah?" I asked innocently, grabbing one of the menus. It was a pointless endeavor. More often than not, when we ate as a group, my mother was the one who selected all the plates and we would eat family-style, sampling from all of the dishes.

"Do you know what she said to me?"

I could feel my mother's eyes boring into me. I lifted the menu higher, hoping the plastic menu would protect me from her interrogation.

My sister kicked me under the table. "What did you do now, Lana?"

"Nothing," I mumbled. "Look at your menu."

My mother tsked. "Why did you bother Sandra and ask her who killed her husband? This is not for you to worry about."

I heard Adam groan.

"Because," I said, setting the menu down, "I just wanted to know what she thought, is all. Am I not allowed to ask a simple question?"

"You need to mind your own business," my mother said firmly. "You are always causing trouble."

"I'm not *always* causing trouble," I said, feeling my cheeks getting warm. "I was only trying to help. Something isn't right, can't anybody else see that?"

My grandmother asked what was going on, and my aunt filled her in. My grandmother only nodded in return and sipped her tea.

"You are always too hard on the girls," my aunt Grace said nonchalantly. She leaned back in her chair, appearing casual. "Especially Lana."

My mother's eyes darted to her sister and she regarded her with a contemptuous glare. "I know how to talk to my daughter."

"Do you?" Aunt Grace asked in a challenging tone. "Look at this girl." She pointed at me. "She's doing wonderful. She's come from a hard time and now she's running the restaurant, has a handsome boyfriend, and is a smart girl who thinks on her feet. What more can you ask for? So she's a little curious at times. What's wrong with that?"

My sister snorted and this time it was my turn to kick her under the table.

Before my mother could respond, the server came over and asked to take our order.

My mother rattled off a variety of dishes, including sautéed watercress, Szechuan shrimp, beef with broccoli, pan-fried noodles with vegetables, egg drop soup, and pot stickers.

Once the server left, my mom turned back to her sister, pursing her lips. "You forget, you may be the older sister, but I *am* the mother. You do not tell me what to do."

"Yes, yes. We all know you're a mother," Aunt Grace spat. "But that doesn't mean you're wiser than me."

My mother scowled. Her expression was pure disgust and I could tell she was ready to blow up any minute.

"So," my dad interjected. "Lana, how was business at the restaurant today?"

I shrugged. "Actually it was kind of slow. Nothing out of the ordinary happened." For once, I wished I'd had a crazy day just so I could tell the story and take the attention away from the topic at hand.

He nodded and sipped his tea. Everyone sat in an awkward silence.

My aunt, who is never one to back down from a fight, acknowledged me with a tight-lipped smile. "Lana dear, do you think this woman is guilty of something and that's why you're getting involved?"

My mother clucked her tongue.

I hesitated to answer. I wasn't entirely sure I wanted to voice exactly how I felt in front of everyone, especially with Adam sitting right next to me.

"Not guilty . . . but I do think she's hiding something," I said quietly. "I just can't figure out what it would be."

My mother thumped her teacup on the table. "Sandra is not hiding anything. Stop being nosy."

"But Mom, she's being blamed for something she probably didn't do. And I think she could be covering up for someone because she knows who did do it."

"This is none of your business," my mother said. "How many times do I have to tell you to stop being nosy?"

I studied my mother's facial features. If there was one thing we had in common it was that our face often gave away our true emotions about something. It was hard to decipher what exactly had changed about my mother since the original conversation we'd had about Sandra's innocence, but something was amiss. Her demeanor now came across as defensive rather than justified and assertive. "Wait a minute, are you worried that she actually did it and that's why what I'm saying is bothering you?" I asked.

My father put an arm around my mother and pulled her close to him. She refused to make eye contact with me.

I gasped. "Mom, you *do* think she did it, don't you?"

"I did not say this," my mother replied, refusing to offer anything more.

Anna May whistled. "Well, well . . . isn't this an interesting turn of events?"

"Why do you think she did it?" I asked. "For the insurance money? Or maybe something else?" I was referring to the abuse, but I didn't want to say it out loud.

The food came and conversation halted while the plates were placed in the center of the table. My dad immediately grabbed the plate of watercress and began scooping some onto his dish.

"Boy, I'm starved," my dad said, attempting to change the subject. "Doesn't this food look great?"

My aunt would not let it drop. "Betty, if you know something, then you need to speak up."

I thought about how my mother had kept secrets for her friends in the past, and I wondered how many secrets she actually knew. "Mom . . ."

My dad huffed. "Listen, there are some things we don't discuss at dinner. And I think this is one of those issues."

Adam squeezed my shoulder. I'd forgotten all about him. I was so focused on my mother and her sudden desire to avoid answering questions about Sandra. "I think your father is right, Lana. Why don't we just enjoy dinner?"

"If you were trying to get points with the old man, you're not doing too bad," my father quipped.

I unwrapped my chopsticks while contemplating what my mother could know that wasn't public knowledge. I didn't feel like Sandra would tell my mother about a scheme that she had been cooking up recently because they weren't that close anymore. If Sandra was going to tell anything to anybody, it would be Ruby. So, if my mother knew something, it would have to be from a long time ago.

I didn't have much longer to think about it, because my aunt started a new argument.

As my aunt Grace spooned Szechuan shrimp onto her plate, she frowned at my mother and said, "This is just like you, Betty, always thinking you are better than everybody. You know what's best for everyone. This is why you always have problems."

And that's all it took. My mother lost the cool she had been attempting to keep and unleashed a string of profanities in Hokkien. My grandmother almost choked on a piece of broccoli.

It wouldn't have been such a big deal in any other setting, but we were in a Chinese restaurant with largely Chinese customers. And everyone turned around to gawk at us.

Anna May and I both sank in our seats, my father shook his head, and my aunt sat there with her mouth wide open in shock.

Adam leaned in. "What did she say?"

"You don't want to know."

The server came over and relayed to my father that another customer had complained.

I sank even further in my seat, my cheeks turning red.

Just another Lee family dinner.

* * *

Later that evening when Adam and I returned to my apartment, we took Kikko for a short walk around the apartment complex. Megan was working that night and wouldn't be home until after 2 A.M. Once we were settled back inside, I changed into some comfy pajama shorts and a tank top. We agreed to end the night with a movie.

As I flipped through the selections on Netflix, I could feel Adam staring at me out of the corner of my eye. "What?" I asked.

"You're not going to let this thing with the Chows go, are you?"

"Probably not."

He sighed. "That's what I figured."

I turned to him, my finger hovering on the play button. "Are you going to try and persuade me that I should give up?"

"No, actually, I'm going to tell you something that might make you reconsider it on your own."

"And what's that?" I set the remote down, giving him my full attention.

"I talked with Darren a couple of times in the past few days. We've been trying to set up a time to get drinks so we can catch up."

"Yeah . . ."

"He brought up the case, and I couldn't help but be curious about some of the details. I wanted to know why he was so focused on this woman being the guilty party. I asked about the Chows' financial history and tried to consider if this was at all plausible. I mean, typically women don't act out in this manner. It's possible, but rare . . ."

"And?"

"There's something that isn't really being talked about."

"What do you mean?"

"Sandra and her husband have a violent history," Adam stated. He assessed my face while he said it.

"I saw a little bit of that on their public record."

"Well, you didn't see the photos." Adam ran a hand through his hair, shaking his head. "They're pretty bad. And though it was only reported that one time, she hinted at the fact that it wasn't their first physical argument."

"So the abuse was pretty severe?"

"She's lucky to be alive. Honestly, if it hadn't been for that neighbor of hers that called it in, who knows if anyone would have known about it happening."

"But how could she have hidden—" And that's when it struck me. The distance that they had created with everyone else. It wasn't because everyone grew apart from busy families or because they moved to a new area or even due to the feud between Ruby and Esther that had caused the women to take sides. It was because she was hiding how she looked so people wouldn't know what was going on. Originally I had dismissed the thought because there had been no other record of it.

"I think that's why your mother is acting the way she is," Adam said. "I think deep down she knows that Sandra could be guilty . . . and maybe she has every right to be."

The whole thing sickened me and I was appalled by all that Sandra must have endured with a significant other who resorted to that type of violence. I leaned in toward Adam, wrapped my arm around his waist, kissed the edge of his jaw, and snuggled my face into his neck. I let out a contented sigh.

He smirked and tipped his head down. "What was that for?"

"Appreciation that you're not that kind of guy. There is still so much for us to learn about each other, but if there's one thing I know for sure, it's that you'd never hurt me like that."

He pulled me closer to his body, giving my arm a reassuring squeeze. "You're right about that, babe, it would never happen."

CHAPTER
19

Thursday morning, I woke up arguing with myself about whether or not checking out the supposed lead I had on Winston was necessary. Ruby had been the one to supply me with the information, and if what Adam told me was true—and I was sure it was— then that would mean Ruby might be covering for Sandra. And then I would be wasting time trying to get information out of a guy who had nothing to do with anything.

I went through the workday on autopilot, living inside my head and having argument after argument with myself. I felt turned around and I didn't know where I was going with this. Before I knew it, the workday was over and I was left with no choice but to make a quick decision. Did I go back to Ruby and pretend to know more than I did? It was possible that if I acted like I was on their side, she might tell me more than she had before. Or should I just go check out Winston? What would it hurt? Besides, I had been wanting to check out Edgewater Live for a few weeks.

I concluded that it wouldn't hurt anything, and I'd come up with the perfect scheme to question Winston. Why waste it?

At home, I found Megan in the kitchen, washing dishes and singing along to a Creedence Clearwater Revival song playing on the radio.

Kikko greeted me at the door, her squiggly tail going at full speed. I dropped down on my knee to give her a good back scratch.

"Do you ever wonder why they're always singing about the rain?" Megan asked without turning around.

"It has occurred to me a time or two," I replied.

"Are we still heading to Edgewater tonight?" she asked.

"Yeah, as long as you're still okay with that."

She shut the water off. "Of course. What time do you want to leave?"

I stood up and met her in the kitchen. "In a little bit. I just have to change out of these clothes and then we can go."

"How did dinner go last night?"

I made a face at her as I leaned against the refrigerator. "How do you think it went?"

"I can't wait to hear about this," Megan replied. "Especially since Adam got dragged into it."

"He said some interesting things last night that make me think that this adventure to see Winston may be a waste. But I think we need to do it anyway."

"Ah, so I see you're remembering my advice and broadening your suspicions."

"I really don't want to, but for different reasons now."

"Oh really?"

"Yeah, let me get ready and I'll tell you what Adam told me last night after dinner with my family."

"Well, don't skip the dinner story. I want to hear all that too."

"It's not a dull story, that's for sure."

After I'd taken a quick shower and changed my clothes, the two of us headed out in Megan's car to Edgewater Park. Traffic was heavy on the freeway so I had plenty of time to fill her in on both stories from the previous evening.

When I finished, she shook her head in amazement. "It looks bad for Sandra, I'm not going to lie."

"I know," I replied. "So you can see why this seems like a fruitless endeavor. Sandra definitely has a good motive. I don't want to believe that she would resort to these measures . . . but at the same time, she's been through hell and back. Who am I to say what she's capable of?"

"Well, still better safe than sorry. The detective is already focusing solely on Sandra and that angle. It's like he has tunnel vision. And isn't that what we're trying to avoid? We should see it through regardless. How awful would we feel if we didn't?"

"Yeah, I guess you're right about that. But I can see his point now. And I have to wonder if he's questioned Ruby and if she mentioned the interaction she saw between Ronnie and Winston. If she has, I wonder if Detective O'Neil will even take it seriously."

"Well, did you mention the Winston angle to Adam? Maybe he'd have some insight on that."

"No, maybe I should have though. It just seemed so pointless after he told me about Sandra's past. It took me all day to even decide whether or not we should actually go and talk to Winston."

By the time we arrived, the parking lot was full and we had to do a few laps before finding an open spot. The sun was just beginning to set and rested on the horizon of Lake Erie.

"Well, I'm glad you decided that we should. Because I really do think it's worth the effort. Plus, you'll have better clarity on making that decision once you talk with him."

"This is true."

"And, I can't believe your aunt . . . she really pushed your mom over the edge. I can't remember the last time she acted out like that in public."

"That would be the last time my aunt was in town. I thought for sure they were going to kick us out of there." I cringed at the memory. "I love that my aunt is here and we get a chance to visit, but at the same time, I'm anxious to know when she's going to head back. It's almost been a week and she hasn't made any mention of leaving."

"If she and your mother keep fighting this way, maybe it'll be sooner than you think."

"Let's hope so."

We got out of the car and stepped into the cool summer evening. We made our way over to the food truck area, which wasn't very crowded, and spotted Winston prepping to open.

Megan and I approached him as he wiped down

the thin counter that hung from the front of his truck. It held napkins, toothpick dispensers, and a tiny trash can.

"Hi Winston, what a small world. I didn't know you'd be here today!" I emphasized my surprise the best I could.

Megan snickered at my acting.

Winston turned around and it took him a few seconds to realize who I was. "Oh, Miss Lee, how nice it is to see you again!" He bowed his head in a jerky movement while he continued to wipe down his counter. "Are you here to enjoy the music?"

"A little bit of everything," I said. "Oh, by the way, this is my friend Megan."

He gave her a polite smile. "Nice to meet you."

"You too," she said. "I'm a big fan of barbecue."

"My food will be ready in about a half hour if you'd like to try some. I have competition tonight," he said, nodding his head toward another barbecue-themed truck. "But maybe Lana has told you how popular my barbecue sticks can be."

"They are pretty delicious," I told Megan. "I haven't found a better barbecue stick so far. It's too bad you didn't get a chance to try Wonton on Wheels though." Megan and I had gone over this part on the way here. She knew it was her cue.

"Ugh, I know. It's such a shame about what happened," Megan said, shaking her head. "Poor Ronnie. I'm just glad more people weren't hurt in the explosion."

Winston observed us, but did not say anything in return.

"It's a good thing you were already gone," I said

to Winston. "Your truck might have caught on fire too. Talk about lucky."

He glanced at his truck as if he were assessing the potential damage it might have suffered. "I am also grateful that no one else was hurt. And I am thankful that I was gone already." He pointed toward his own dual hundred-pound tanks. "Food trucks can be very dangerous. They can be a weapon on wheels."

My eyes shifted over to the tanks. "Have you seen what they're saying on the news about Sandra?" I knew that he had. Everybody in the city had. "Do you think this could be true?"

He shook his head adamantly. "I don't think a kind woman like Sandra could be guilty of something like this. Even if her husband was a creep."

"Oh, did you two not get along?" I asked, feigning surprise.

Winston shook his head. "No, not at all. Our last conversation was an argument. I feel a little bad about it now that he's gone. But he could be such a jerk sometimes."

"What did you two fight about, if you don't mind me asking?"

"The usual. He was always trying to steal my ideas and then park right next to my truck. I came up with the wonton idea first, but before I changed my menu, he took it from me. Wontons on a stick were my idea."

"I had no idea," I replied.

"And Sandra knew this. She apologized that night for his behavior. I had asked him not to sell that item at the night market while my truck was next to his, but he refused. It was a simple favor. Business owner to business owner. But he was always like this. I shouldn't be that surprised. It is very possible he pushed the wrong person too far."

"So you think this was an intentional attack against Ronnie?"

He nodded with resolution. "Absolutely. Look around this area. We are all fighting for the same business."

I needed time to think this new information through, but I couldn't do it while we were standing in front of Winston. "Well, we should let you get back to work now, we'll be back when you're open and get some barbecue."

"Okay, I will see you then," Winston said, turning to get back into his truck. "Enjoy the evening!"

Megan and I walked away and she refrained from saying anything right away because she knew my wheels were turning. After we made it down to the water, I stood as close as I could get without the tide touching my toes. I let out a long sigh.

"Well, what are you thinking?" Megan asked me.

"I remember seeing Ronnie gesturing toward BBQ 2 Go while he was arguing with Sandra. He must have been telling her about the confrontation, and then shortly after she went and talked with Winston."

"So you think he's telling the truth?"

"I do."

"Do you think it's possible that it was him after all? I mean, he was parked right next to Wonton on Wheels, and like he said, food trucks are a weapon on wheels. Maybe he slipped in between the two trucks and left Ronnie a surprise."

"Yeah, but did he hate him enough to actually go that far?" I asked. "He seemed pretty matter-of-fact about the whole thing."

"Well, Lana, a lot of crazy people are calm. They do think what they've done is justified for one reason or another. He probably doesn't feel any remorse," Megan replied.

"True, but how could he have been sure that Ronnie wouldn't be right behind him? Or that Ronnie would even be in the truck at the time it happened? And wasn't he worried that Sandra would be in it as well?"

"Maybe that was a risk he was willing to take. Sure, he likes Sandra well enough, but would he let that stand in the way of what he thought he needed to do?"

"All valid points," I said as I watched the lake. The setting sun sparkled on the caps of the waves, and I tried to lose myself in the beauty of summer for just a moment. But the mystery at hand kept me from fully appreciating the scenery. "Well, it seems like we can't dismiss him as a suspect after all. At least not yet."

Megan sighed. "I guess you're right about that. If only something would happen to give us a sign."

CHAPTER
20

- - - - - - - -

Friday came with a sense of dread. The first night market since the explosion last week was scheduled for tonight, and I wasn't excited about it anymore. For a brief moment, I thought that perhaps this week's market would be canceled due to the travesty of the previous week. But the crime scene unit had cleaned everything away and the area was back to normal. On top of that, too many people had invested time and money, permits had been paid for, and so the event would continue as planned.

During the week, the Mahjong Matrons told me they'd heard there would be more firefighters and policemen on patrol at the market, and a thorough inspection would be done on all food service trucks attending the event.

My mother was working at the restaurant so I could have the day off in return for the time I would be putting in that evening. She seemed really anxious about heading to the restaurant and mentioned something along the lines of keeping busy while Aunt Grace spent some one-on-one time with A-ma. Aside from that, my mother and I had barely spoken two words to each other since the night of the dinner. I wondered if it was because my aunt was taking my side or if my mom didn't want to be confronted about the situation with Sandra. Either way, it was best to give her some space.

I spent the majority of my day jotting down nonsense in my investigation journal, searching for information involving propane tank explosions, and pacing the perimeter of the apartment. When I got sick of that, I took Kikko on a leisurely walk around the complex, attempting to clear my head.

As I headed down the walk to our apartment, Megan pulled into the parking lot. She'd gone to the gym and stopped at the grocery store on the way home. I met her at her car and waited while she parked so I could help her bring in the groceries.

"How was the gym?" I asked, grabbing a couple bags from the back with my free hand. Kikko propped herself up on the edge of the backseat and sniffed around.

"Same old stuff," she said, grabbing the remaining bags. "What have you been up to all day?"

We walked back to the apartment together, Kikko leading the way.

"Nothing much really. Going over the Chow case."

Back in the apartment, Kikko waddled away to find a toy, and Megan and I set everything down on the kitchen table. She rummaged through the cupboards, making room for the things she'd just purchased.

Her eyes landed on my laptop, which sprang back to life as the table shook from the movement. "You're looking up how to blow up a food truck?" She pursed her lips. "Really, Lana?"

"Well, I don't know what else to do at this point," I said to her with a huff. "I thought maybe if I saw exactly what went into it, it would help me narrow down who would do it."

"We've been over this. Anybody can look up how to blow something up or make a bomb in this day and age. The FBI is going to show up at our house." She closed the Internet browser. "No sense in dragging us through the mud. Why don't you try talking to someone who knows things about cars, like—"

"A mechanic! I should talk to Calvin's uncle Gene!" I slapped myself on the forehead. "I don't know why I've been avoiding it. I keep trying to work around him when he's the one I should be gunning for."

"Okay, well, I was thinking you should be a little more discreet. You know, more along the lines of asking someone who isn't related to the guilty party," Megan said. "But if that's what you think is best."

"No, this is a good idea," I said, pacing around the table. "I've been thinking he's involved somehow anyway. Maybe I should just get it over with and question him. See what kind of feel I get for him."

"How are you going to do that without Calvin around?" Megan asked.

I stopped pacing. "What? Why do I need to worry about that?"

"Because you questioned him and he got weird about it. Then you questioned his mother and *she* got weird about it. You don't think it came up in conversation between the two of them? If you start talking to his uncle in front of him, he's going to know that something's up and you're nosing around where you shouldn't be."

"True," I said, thinking it over. "Okay, so how will I get to him without Calvin around?"

"I don't know," she said, putting some lettuce in the crisper drawer. "Maybe just stick to questioning other people who may know the same things until we can figure out a better plan."

"But then I won't know if I get a feel for his guilt or not. I'll just have to find out Calvin's schedule and talk to his uncle when he's not around."

"Okay, but if they tattle on you to your mother again, don't say I didn't try to warn you."

A few hours before the night market was set to begin, Peter and I met at our designated meeting spot on Rockwell Avenue. He appeared to be a little peppier than he'd been the last few days and I suspected that Nancy was starting to resemble her old self. I thought it best not to push for details and let him do his thing, so we worked in silence as we set up the workstation.

"Oh, by the way, I have the bill for the rental equipment," Peter told me as he worked on prepping the grill. "The rental guy was totally understanding and knocked a little bit off the cost since it wasn't our fault."

"Well, that's a small favor at least," I replied.

"Yeah, hopefully we can avoid any disasters tonight. People are talking about it all over the place, man. People tried asking me questions, but I just told them I don't know anything. No sense in adding to the drama."

"I think that's probably best."

Ruby showed up a few minutes later, and seeing us, came over to say hello.

"How is your mother?" she asked Peter. "I have been meaning to visit with her but have been so busy taking care of Sandra."

"She's doing okay," Peter responded. "Thanks for asking. I can tell her you said hello."

"That would be very nice of you." Ruby turned to me. "And how are you doing, Lana?"

I returned her question with an awkward smile. I assumed that Sandra had told her I'd been questioning her since Sandra had ratted me out to my mother. If she had any type of feelings about it, it didn't show. I thought it was best to keep my answer simple. "I'm doing all right," I replied.

"Good, good," she said, nodding her head. "Let us hope that this night market goes better than last week."

"Have you talked to Sandra?" I couldn't help myself after all. It was like a disorder.

She laughed in a way that insinuated she understood why I was asking. "Yes, I have, and do not worry so much about it. Sandra is very upset right now. She won't be mad for long. I know that your intentions are good." She snuck a glance at the area where Wonton on Wheels had been the previous week. "It will take Sandra some time to come to terms with what happened, maybe we can help her together?"

I followed her line of sight and it took me a moment to register that BBQ 2 Go was missing. Where was Winston?

"Lana?" Ruby leaned forward. "Is everything all right?"

I snapped back to the conversation at hand. "Oh yeah, sorry. I just realized that Winston isn't here yet. Normally he'd be here by now."

"Yes, that is most strange, isn't it?" Ruby turned to look again. "I noticed that myself."

The statement hung there for a moment, and I began to doubt whether I could actually trust this woman. There was something about her demeanor this evening that made me uneasy.

"I better tend to my booth. It is almost time to open." She waved to me and Peter as she walked back to her booth.

"She's a strange woman," I said to Peter. "I can't seem to figure her out."

"Don't worry, I can't figure out most women." He snickered. "Not being able to figure out one isn't that big of a deal."

Business was good right from the start of the night. We had a substantial line of people forming in front of our cart, and Peter and I worked as fast as we could to get everyone served and on their way. We were without Nancy's help that night, so catching a moment of relief was almost impossible.

The food truck area was short two trucks since Winston never showed, and of course Wonton on Wheels was gone. The open space felt foreboding somehow. I tried to keep my eyes away from that general area.

Kimmy's mother, Sue, had come along to help with their booth, while her husband Daniel minded the store. She was shaken up because of what happened last week, and didn't want Kimmy manning the table alone this time. They didn't have too much business, so Kimmy came by to lend us a hand for a few minutes so I could run to the restroom.

On my way back, I thought I saw Calvin's uncle Gene meandering around our food cart. I only caught a quick glimpse, so I wasn't sure that it was actually him. By the time I made it back to our cart, the man I thought I'd seen was gone and I couldn't catch sight of him again.

Kimmy went back to her booth and Peter and I fell back into step, working in a comfortable harmony.

Around eight-thirty, a local folk band got on stage and wowed everyone with an amazing acoustic guitar solo that kept most of the crowd occupied for at least ten minutes. Peter shoved a few dumplings in his mouth when no one was looking. Normally the two of us would get a snack break at some point in the evening, but that didn't seem to be a possibility tonight.

As the guitar player finished up the song, I heard

a fizzling sound and wondered if something was
wrong with the speaker system. No one seemed to
notice the noise except for me. When I turned to see
if Peter had reacted to the sound, I realized what I
heard was probably covered up by the sounds of the
grill.

What I didn't realize was that the sound was actually coming from a short distance away. Out of
the corner of my eye, I saw a spark and some smoke
before a rapid succession of pops went off, jolting
me and a few people who were in the near vicinity.

I am not ashamed to say that I screamed like a
woman being set on fire. Especially when the trash
can right next to our food cart burst into flames.

CHAPTER
21

Peter pulled me away and managed to get me a safe distance from the trash can before it erupted. The sound of sirens filled the area while police and firemen on site ushered the crowd out of the way.

The band had stopped playing and watched the chaos from their vantage point on stage. The fire itself was contained to the trash can and the flames licked upward toward the sky, but thankfully the evening air was still and didn't cause the fire to billow outward near the cloth tents, which, I assumed, were extremely flammable.

My heart was thudding with an alarming intensity, and I couldn't help staring at the trash can and noting exactly how close it was to our tent. A fireman ran over with an extinguisher and proceeded to put out the flames while the police kept people from getting too close.

Once the fire was out, the crowd applauded the fireman's efforts.

I recognized someone from the planning committee talking with a few police officers on the other side of the street. Peter and I still stood in the spot he'd moved us to as if we were frozen in place. I didn't want to go anywhere near our food cart anytime soon.

A tall police officer with short brown hair and broad shoulders approached us. The expression on his face was serious, but showed concern. "Are you two the ones who were working at that food cart over there?" He pointed at our abandoned station, which was surrounded by a thick cloud of smoke.

I nodded.

He observed me more carefully, scanning my face and assessing my body language with a skilled eye that was classic cop. "Are you okay, ma'am?"

"Yes," I said, my voice coming out as a squeak. I cleared my throat and repeated myself. "Yes, thank you."

"Did either of you notice anything strange right before it happened?" he asked. "Or see anybody lurking around?"

"I don't think so," I replied.

"No, everything seemed totally normal," Peter added. "It's been a good night so far."

Everything *seemed* normal, but was it? I thought about how I'd seen Gene in the crowd earlier that evening. Well, maybe. I wasn't completely sure it was actually him. But now that there'd been a small explosion near our food cart, I had to reconsider.

The police officer appeared to pick up on the fact that I was unsure of myself. "Ma'am, if you can think of anything at all . . . even if it seems like the smallest, most insignificant thing. It might help us figure out who's responsible for this."

I had no idea what to say. Was I supposed to say that I thought I saw someone who might be guilty of killing his brother-in-law, but I didn't actually have any proof of that? Or should I say that maybe I was being targeted because I'd been nosing around in places I shouldn't be?

I shook my head. "I can't think of anything at the moment, but if I do . . ."

"We'll get some quick statements from those of you that had a booth in the general area of the trash can. The fire department will take a closer look at what caused the explosion. If they have any questions, they'll follow up with you later."

Once the police officer had taken down our information and we gave him a brief description of how we'd seen the event take place, he thanked us for our time and told us that we could be on our way. Because of the upset, the planning committee for the night market had made the decision to end the evening early.

I hadn't noticed it, but the crowd had thinned out considerably and people were packing up their merchandise and food. Police lights flashed from the street corners where barricades were set up to keep traffic out.

Kimmy and her mother tugged their rolling plastic totes in our direction, stopping in front of our food cart.

Sue, a plump woman with an inviting smile and chubby cheeks, rushed over and squeezed my arms, looking me up and down. "Lana, are you all right? I called your parents to let them know you seemed to be okay. You need to call them as soon as possible. Your mother is very worried about you."

I nodded. "Yes, I'm okay, just a little shaken is all. At first I didn't know what was happening."

"A little shaken?" Kimmy said. "I'd be crappin' my pants right about now. You were only a few feet away from that trash can."

"Kimmy," Sue scolded. "Don't talk like that. Your language is terrible. You need to talk more like a lady."

She waved her mom off. "Peter, are you okay?" Her voice rose an octave as she addressed him.

"Yeah, just . . . ugh, man." Peter adjusted his hat. "It's like . . . you know?"

Kimmy snorted. "Absolutely. Just like . . . whatever."

Sue studied Kimmy and then turned to Peter and finally landed on me. "I don't understand what they are saying most of the time."

"I don't think most people do."

Kimmy glared at me. "Well, I'm glad you're okay enough to be making jokes."

I shrugged. I might have been making jokes, but I wasn't sure I was actually okay.

On the way home, I called my parents. My mother urged me to be more careful when I was out. As if I could have prevented a nearby trash can from exploding. When we got off the phone, I called Adam too to let him know that I was okay. I was almost sure he'd heard about it, which he had. He informed me that besides hearing about it over the scanner, it had been on the news already.

I tried desperately to remember seeing news crews there, but I hadn't noticed anything. Then again, I wasn't really with it at the time. Originally Peter wasn't going to let me drive home, but thankfully, with Kimmy's help in assuring him that I was a fully functional grown woman, he let me go.

Adam was working late, but promised to meet me at my apartment once he was done handling some things at the precinct.

When I pulled into my parking spot, Megan pulled in right behind me and parked in the open spot next to my car. She flew out of the car and rushed over to mine, opening my car door. "What the hell, Lana?" she fumed. "I've been trying to call you. You can't answer your damn phone?"

"I'm sorry, I was on the phone with my parents, and then I called Adam. I didn't realize—"

"Why don't you try calling your best friend," she said. "I saw what happened on the news. When I couldn't get a hold of you, I called Peter. He said you were on your way home, so I headed back this way as fast as I could. You shouldn't have been driving by yourself after a scare like that. Are you okay?"

"Yeah, I'm fine . . . just freaked out a little bit." I got out of the car and shut the door behind me. My legs did feel like Jell-O. "Let's go inside. I need to sit down for a minute."

We went inside, Kikko greeting us at the door. I patted her tiny head and flung myself on the couch.

Megan grabbed Kikko's leash from the hook by the door. "You sit and relax. I'll take Kikko out.

Do you want anything before I head out? A glass of water or something?"

"No, I'll be okay just sitting here."

The two disappeared out the door and I sank farther into the couch, leaning my head back against the arm. I took a deep breath and closed my eyes. Flashbacks of the evening played over in my mind like a broken record. As I tried to relax and focus on my breathing, I couldn't stop seeing Gene's face.

It had only been for a second and then some tall guy had gotten in the way. By the time he'd passed my line of sight, Gene was nowhere to be found, and I didn't see him again the rest of the time. Had my eyes been playing tricks on me?

A few minutes later, Megan and Kikko returned. Megan went into the kitchen and came back out with a bag of chips and two beers. "Eat. Drink," she said, thrusting a beer bottle and the bag of chips at me. "I ordered some pizza, and it's on the way."

I took the beer bottle from her hand and passed on the chips. "Thanks."

"What the heck happened tonight? Do you even know?"

Sitting up, I removed the beer cap and took a sip, the carbonation tickling my throat. "Honestly, I don't know for sure. There are a lot of small things that are coming to mind, but nothing concrete." I told her about thinking I'd seen Gene and also how Winston was nowhere to be found. I found both instances to be suspicious considering the outcome of the evening.

"Do you think it's possible that Winston was there after all? Maybe he knows the real reason why we were asking questions at Edgewater Live." Megan asked. "Maybe he canceled his spot so he could sneak around and plant explosives in the garbage can."

"Could be." I ran my thumb over the jagged edge of the beer cap. "It also could have been Gene. I swear he was there, Megan."

She leaned back, appearing unconvinced. "I don't know. I mean, I know that would probably make sense, but you're not even sure that you saw him. Your imagination could have been overreacting and gotten the best of you."

"I know, I've thought about that too. But both scenarios are equally doubtful though. It's not like I saw Winston lurking behind one of the stone zodiac statues. For all we know, he could have a logical explanation for not being at the night market tonight."

"Okay, true," Megan said. "But we just talked to Winston yesterday and he seemed perfectly fine. What could have happened from now until then to make him skip a Friday at the night market?"

"Well, that is a very good point. But I think there's something else I need to address first."

"What's that?"

"I need to talk with Gene Tian once and for all."

Adam arrived shortly after the pizza, and the three of us along with Kikko sat around the pizza box indulging ourselves with the greasy goodness. I even treated Kikko to a couple of pepperonis.

When we were finished eating, Megan excused herself, leaving me and Adam to our own devices.

"You don't remember seeing anything at all?" Adam asked.

He'd asked me four times since he'd shown up on my doorstep and my answer had been the same each time.

"No," I told him again. "There wasn't anything out of the ordinary. It was just a regular night."

I wanted to tell him about seeing Gene, but I felt even if I explained everything to him, it would still sound crazy and he'd dismiss the idea anyway.

Adam sighed. "I talked a little bit with Darren before I came over and he should have more information about what happened tomorrow. Whatever he knows now, he didn't want to say. But he definitely knows something."

"What do you think that means?"

He shrugged. "Could mean nothing. He knows you're my girl, so he might be holding back information since it's personal for me."

I felt goose bumps forming on my arms and at the nape of my neck. "Do you really think that I was the target?" All evening I had been hoping that it was just a coincidence. I didn't want to believe that someone had intentionally tried to blow me up . . . or set me on fire.

"I want to think it's happenstance, but truthfully, with you going around talking to these different people that may or may not be involved . . ." He paused, seemingly lost in thought.

I nudged his leg. "Yeah . . ."

He looked me in the eye. "Well, sweetheart, I think you may have ruffled the wrong feathers."

CHAPTER

22

- - - - - - - - - - - - -

Adam was already gone by the time I woke up on Saturday morning. Kikko was at the edge of the bed staring at me; her tail wiggled happily when she noticed my eyes were open.

I went about my morning routine and ran through a list of things that I needed to accomplish. I knew I should stop at the Noodle House, though I thought it would slow me down. Being at the night market instead of the restaurant on Fridays wasn't working out as well as I'd hoped. A couple of months ago, missing a day at work was not a big deal and I looked forward to it. But now, as the manager, I found myself becoming eager to know what was happening on a daily basis.

I needed to talk with Gene alone and I could only hope that Sandra had failed to mention my previous snooping around. I might have already lost my chance with Gene if she'd told him not to talk to me.

I also wanted to find out what had happened with

Winston and the reason for his absence from the night market. After walking Kikko, I turned on my laptop and pulled up Winston's Web site to find some type of schedule for his food truck. It said that he would be out in Westlake at Crocker Park. I could run out that way before backtracking to the plaza.

Next I looked up the hours listed for Gene's auto repair shop. He was open until 6 P.M. That gave me a little time, and I decided to save him for last.

I also wanted to make a point of talking to Ruby again. I didn't know if that was the best idea, but after the explosion last night, I had lost track of her.

Right as I was shutting down the computer, Megan poked her head out of her bedroom door. "Want to get breakfast? I'm starving."

"I think I'm going to skip it, I want to do a couple things today."

She took a step out of her bedroom. "Like what?"

I told her my plan.

"Well, are you going to invite me or do I have to invite myself?"

"Of course you're invited. But are you sure you want to run all over town with me? Don't you have to work later tonight?"

"I do," she said. "So what? Besides, I can eat at the plaza because I know you're not going to skip checking in at the restaurant today."

"Well, get dressed then, we're leaving for Crocker Park in an hour."

An hour and a half later, we were at the outdoor shopping mall searching for a decent parking spot.

It was always packed on the weekends and finding an open space could be quite the challenge.

When we arrived at the area set up for food trucks, it was obviously missing BBQ 2 Go, and I wondered where the heck Winston could be if he wasn't here. That was two events he'd missed out on along with a considerable chunk of money.

I saw someone walk by with a Barrio logo on their T-shirt. I stepped in front of the taco restaurant worker before he could pass me. "Excuse me."

The man turned in my direction. The aviator glasses covering his eyes were solid black and I couldn't tell if he was actually looking at me or not. "Yeah?"

"Do you know if the BBQ 2 Go guy is supposed to be here today?" I asked him. "I thought I saw him on the schedule."

He ran a hand through his shaggy blond hair that was hanging down over his eyebrows. "Uhhhh . . . not sure. I thought I heard someone else say that the guy got into an accident or his truck broke down or something."

"Oh okay, thanks," I said.

He nodded and continued on his way.

"That's odd, don't you think?" I asked Megan. When she didn't answer, I turned around. "Megan?"

Where the heck had she gone?

I scanned the crowd and found her in line at a food truck that specialized in breakfast foods. The side of the truck was covered in images of cartoon French toast and waffles.

I walked over and tapped her on the shoulder.

"Oh hey, sorry, I got sidetracked."

"The Barrio guy told me he thinks he heard Winston was in an accident . . . or that his truck broke down. He wasn't too sure on the specifics."

"How convenient that this would happen now, don't you think?"

"It is a little suspicious. But maybe there's another explanation."

Megan was next in line, and she held up a finger while she placed her order. When she was done, we stepped off to the side to wait. "Do you think that maybe he's a victim too? Maybe someone is going after his truck next?"

"I don't know. First, we have to find out what's actually happened to him. But the problem is, I have no idea how to get a hold of him directly. There's an e-mail address on his Web site, but who knows how often he checks that. It could be days before we get a response."

"Save it for a last resort. We're going to the plaza next, right? Maybe someone there knows how to get a hold of him."

I checked the time on my cell phone. It was too late for the Mahjong Matrons to be at the restaurant. Unless they were playing mahjong at the community center, I'd have to find someone else.

Megan's order was up. She grabbed the bag off the counter and we headed back toward the car. "I got you some French toast sticks."

"You're a peach."

"I know. So, now what?"

"Now we're going to Asian Accents." Whenever the Matrons weren't around, the hair salon was the next best place to get information.

* * *

The Asian hair salon was filled with women getting their hair done in preparation for the weekend. The place smelled like a mixture of hair dye chemicals, nail polish, and incense.

I spotted my own stylist, Jasmine Ming, putting highlights in someone's hair when we walked in.

Yuna, the receptionist, smiled brightly as we entered the shop. Her gold thunderbolt earrings sparkled as they swung back and forth like two pendulums. "Hey Lana!" Her hair was a mixture of black and lime green. She brushed aside a stray wisp before waving at Megan. "Hi, there."

Megan and I said hi in unison, and I stepped up to the sales counter, my eyes drifting back toward Jasmine. "Is there any way I could go back there and talk to her?" I nudged my chin in the direction of my stylist.

"Sure thing," Yuna replied. "I'm sure she won't mind." Leaning in, she said, "That's Mrs. Wong she's taking care of right now though. She's kind of a chatty lady, so look out."

"I'll stay up here," Megan offered. "I don't want to crowd the poor woman while she has her head in foil."

"Okay, I won't be long."

Yuna turned her attention toward Megan. "Say, you haven't thought about dyeing your hair lavender before, have you? Because we just got in this new shade that I think would be perfect on you."

I winked at Megan before walking away.

Jasmine caught sight of me out of the corner of

her eye, and paused with the tinting brush mid-stroke. "Lana! Hey, woman!"

As always, Jasmine's appearance was "on point." Her perfect, burgundy-highlighted hair was styled with giant curls that framed her heart-shaped face. Her winged eyeliner was never crooked, and the lipstick she always wore—a deep reddish-brown—never feathered or wore away. If I didn't know what an amazing person she was, I would have hated her out of pure jealousy.

I said hello to both women as I approached the styling chair.

Mrs. Wong was stuck facing forward and observed me through the mirror in front of her. She was a middle-aged woman with a wide face and freckles sprinkled across her nose and cheeks and seemed to be intrigued by my presence.

"What brings you by?" Jasmine turned her focus back to the section of hair she was working on. "It can't be your hair, I mean, your roots are coming in a little bit, but you've still got at least two weeks before you need a touch-up. Don't forget to schedule something with Yuna before you leave."

"I actually came by to ask if you or anyone here knows that guy Winston Leung who owns BBQ 2 Go."

"Winston . . . Winston . . ." Jasmine teetered her head back and forth. "I think I know who that is . . . but I don't know anything about him really. Why do you ask?"

"I'm trying to find him," I told her. "I need to talk with him about the night market."

"Yeah, what the heck happened last night? A

couple people here were talking about it first thing this morning, but I've been swamped with appointments so I didn't get to hear the full story."

Mrs. Wong's face instantly lit up. "You mean the giant explosion that happened near the food court area last night?"

I studied her face in the mirror. Giant? Who had she been talking to? I'll give you four guesses. "I wouldn't say it was giant . . ."

Jasmine froze. "Lana, weren't you there last night?"

"Unfortunately," I said, my shoulders slumping. "The explosion happened right near our food cart."

"Oh no! Are you okay? Was anybody hurt?"

"No, everyone is fine. The trash can contained most of it." I didn't know if that was intentional or the explosives hadn't gone off like they were intended to, but I wasn't going to tell her that. And with Mrs. Wong listening in, I wouldn't doubt that anything I said would be around the plaza in no time.

"Why are you looking for the man who runs BBQ 2 Go?" Mrs. Wong asked. "Was he involved in the explosion somehow?"

I could tell she was digging for tidbits to add to her story. "No, actually he wasn't there last night. I heard he was in some kind of accident and wanted to make sure he's okay."

"You know who would know?" Mrs. Wong snapped her fingers repeatedly. "That woman . . . what is her name . . . she's been in the news lately . . ."

"Sandra Chow?" I asked.

"Yes . . . her. That poor woman. Imagine losing

your husband that way. I couldn't even imagine how that must be. They'd probably have to put me in the crazy house. Anyway, her brother, that man that owns the repair shop, he might know. I've gone to him a couple of times to work on my car. And I've seen the barbecue food truck there before. They seem to be friendly."

My eyes widened. "Really? Gene and Winston are friends?"

"Yes, it would seem that way. He's a decent mechanic too, but he charges way too much and I told him if he doesn't lower his prices, he is going to lose all his business to Larry Chan." She pursed her lips. "Larry Chan takes longer, but his prices are the best. If I had another car, I would always take my business to Larry. But sometimes I can't wait a week to get my car back. He is very thorough."

Mrs. Wong looked as if she were going to tell me more about the perils of finding a good mechanic, so I quickly thanked her and told the two of them that I needed to be on my way.

Megan stood up from one of the chairs they had lined up against the wall. "Well . . ."

"Come on, let's go to the restaurant," I said to her as I pushed open the door and waved a quick good-bye to Yuna. "You're not going to believe this."

The Noodle House was fairly calm, and I found Vanessa stationed at the hostess booth, flipping through another fashion magazine. She threw it under the counter when I walked in.

"Hey boss," she said, smacking her gum.

I decided to let the magazine go. I had other things on my mind and I didn't feel like giving a lecture. "How's business?" I asked, assessing the dining room.

"It's been slow like this all morning."

"Where's Anna May?"

"She's covering in the kitchen today. Lou called in sick this morning. Some type of sinus thing."

"Okay, well, I'm not staying, just stopping by real quick." I signaled Megan to follow me to the back.

Anna May was bobbing her head to pop music and wrapping spring rolls. She turned as we walked in. "Little sister, what brings you by?" She nodded an acknowledgment to Megan.

"Wanted to check on a few things since I missed work yesterday."

"Yeah, what the heck is going on? Are you okay?" She wiped her hands on her apron. "I was going to call you this morning, but I figured you needed some sleep after a night like that. Mom filled me in on the minor details."

"Yeah, I'm fine," I told her. "I'm weirded out, but no damage was done."

"Oh, by the way, Calvin Chow stopped in today," Anna May said.

"Really?" Megan asked. She stepped up next to me. "What did he want?"

"Apparently to talk to you, Lana."

"Me?" I found it odd that he hadn't tried to call me instead. "What did he say?"

"Not a whole lot really. He had some food while he was here and asked if he could talk to you. I told him it was your day off, and he said it must have slipped his mind. Are you guys hanging out now? I told you to stay away from those people."

"No, we've hardly talked. I mean, we met for drinks the one time, but that was it." I avoided telling my sister what my intention was behind getting drinks with Calvin, but I assumed she had an idea after the recent conversations we'd had. "Did he say anything else?"

"No," Anna May said, agitation growing in her tone. "And I'm not your personal assistant, Lana. He can call you . . . which is what I told him to do."

"Okay, geez, sorry." I turned to head for the office. "I'm not going to be here long . . ."

"Somehow we'll muster the courage to soldier on without you, dear sister." My sister faked a smile and then turned back to her spring rolls.

Megan followed behind me. "That's weird, huh? Almost as if he were trying to figure out where you are. 'It slipped his mind'?"

"I know, that strikes me as odd too. It's not like he would know my schedule to begin with. The most I've told him is that I'm here throughout the week."

"Anyway, hurry up and do what you need to do so you can tell me what you learned at the salon. I'm dying of anticipation."

CHAPTER
23

Once Megan was filled in on what I'd learned at the salon and I finished handling a few minor things in preparation for work on Monday, we set out for the east side of Cleveland to pay a visit to Gene at his auto repair shop.

Tian's Auto Repair was located on Payne Avenue between two nondescript brick buildings that looked like they might be abandoned. Thankfully I found some street parking and we walked up to the door leading to a tiny reception area. Automotive-related posters hung on the wall and showed the inner workings of various engines and other parts that were not recognizable to me. There was nobody at the desk and the door into the garage was closed. There was a small wired window allowing you to see a small portion of the garage area.

I shrugged at Megan and walked up to the door, taking a peek into the garage to see if anyone was there. I stood on my tiptoes and scanned the room. "Holy . . ."

"What?" Megan asked from behind me. "Let me see."

On one of the lifts was the BBQ 2 Go food truck. It appeared to be in decent condition but I couldn't tell if the front end or the other side facing away from the door had any damage.

I took a step back so Megan could look. "Well, isn't that suspicious," she said when she saw the truck. "Of all the places for the missing truck to be . . ."

I twisted the door handle and pushed. It opened, so I took a step into the garage and peeked around the corner to see if anyone was there. No one. I decided to step farther in and inspect the truck for further damage.

The garage smelled strongly of gasoline and I resisted the urge to cover my nose. Trying to hold my breath, I walked around to the front of the truck, checking for signs of an accident. Nothing.

"Excuse me!" a voice bellowed from behind me. "You're not allowed in here!"

I whipped around to see an angry face staring back at me. It was Gene and he was not amused in the least.

I forced a smile. "Hi, Gene, I was just in the neighborhood and—"

"Wait a minute," he said, taking a step closer. "You're that noodle girl, aren't you?"

I straightened my back. "Yes, I'm the noodle girl." No sense in correcting him. By the slur in his words, I could tell he wasn't a hundred percent sober.

"What brings you by?" His stance shifted to a slightly relaxed position and he appeared to be a little friendlier now that he recognized me. "Are you looking for my nephew?"

"Yeah . . ." I said, thankful for the easy cover story. "Yeah, I thought I'd just stop by and say hi. See how he's holding up."

"See how he's holding? The man just lost his father. Even if he was a piece of garbage, it's still his father. How do you think he's holding up?"

"Sorry, I know it's a stupid thing to ask but—"

"No, hang on, I'm sorry," he replied. "I get a little heated when I talk about my brother-in-law. We didn't always see eye to eye on things."

"I can imagine that would make things hard between the two of you."

"You don't know the half of it. You married?" he asked.

"No."

"You have any siblings?"

"Just one sister," I said. "Older."

"She married?"

"No."

"Well, trust me when I say this. You better pray long and hard you get along with whoever she's married to and hope the same thing for her and your future husband, because in-laws can be a pain."

"I'll keep that in mind," I said.

"Well, I can tell Calvin you stopped by. But he's off today. Won't be back to work until Monday."

"Oh, no problem. I can just give him a call instead," I said. "By the way, what happened to Winston's food truck?" I pointed up at BBQ 2 Go.

"There was a situation," Gene said, not offering anything more. He shuffled over to a workbench and picked up an oversized crescent wrench.

"Was he in an accident of some kind? We missed him at the night market last night."

"I wouldn't say that," he said.

I took a step backward. "What do you mean? What happened, if you don't mind me asking?"

He turned his head toward me, venom in his stare. "Someone cut the fuel lines. Strange, isn't it?"

My breath caught in my throat, causing me to cough. "That *is* strange."

"Although I suppose it is awfully convenient it happened yesterday of all days, what with that second explosion at the night market."

"Oh, it happened yesterday?"

"Yup, couldn't have happened at a better time for him."

I took another step back. "Yeah, lucky break . . ."

"He was gettin' ready to leave for the night market when he found the problem. Called Calvin yellin' and screamin' to come out to his place and tow the damn thing. But Calvin was manning the shop alone when Winston called in. He had a customer in the shop at the time and was working on a tire rotation and oil change. I was off the clock and over at Sandra's house helping her with some yard work when I got the call from Calvin. Ruined my evening to tell you the truth. Here Sandra had made a big dinner as a thank-you for all my work in the yard and I couldn't even enjoy it.

"I'll tell ya, it's a shame all that's been going on over there," he said, his eyes sliding back to his crescent wrench. "You never know when these things are gonna happen to you."

Megan opened the door a crack and poked her head in. "Hey Lana, your sister just called, she needs you back at the restaurant, something about Lou calling in sick."

I sighed a breath of relief as our eyes met. "Oh, that Lou. He's always getting summer colds." I turned back to Gene. "Well, sorry to have wasted your time . . . you have a nice day."

As I walked away, I heard him drop the wrench on the table, and I jumped a little at the sound it made. "Be careful out there, young lady. Like I said, you never know when these things are going to sneak up on you. One day you're here, and then the next day . . . well, sometimes there isn't a next day, is there? Sure wasn't one for Ronnie."

"Thanks," I yelled over my shoulder. I sped up a little and Megan and I rushed through the tiny waiting room out onto the street. I inhaled the fresh air. The gas fumes had started to make me nauseous.

"What the heck was all that about?" Megan asked as we walked back to the car.

"I think he just threatened me," I told her.

She stopped. "What? Should we call the police?"

"No, just get in the car. Let's get the heck outta here."

Megan and I got home a little after two o'clock. We walked the dog and discussed theories. The popular one now was that Gene must have done it with Winston's help. Maybe Calvin was involved somehow and stopped by to see me in hopes of finding out what I knew. It was plausible that they were on to me.

"But what would be the purpose of damaging his own food truck?" Megan asked. "If Winston and Gene were working together, why would they cut his fuel lines? Couldn't he have just as easily not shown up at the night market? It's not like every single vendor is the same from week to week."

Kikko sniffed a patch of crabgrass, and I watched her smooshed snout wiggle back and forth with the urgency of a hound dog. "Well, for one thing, if the explosions are connected, and none of them were at this night market, the police would think they need to investigate elsewhere. And technically, we don't know the fuel lines were actually cut," I said. "He told us that they were, but would you know the difference? And if they were cut, it would make a more believable alibi should anyone look into it. Especially if Gene is willing to do the repair for free. Why wouldn't Winston go along with it?"

"Good point," she replied. "Okay, so they create this story for themselves. But who is the mastermind of the whole thing?"

"I don't know. They both have a reason to want Ronnie out of the picture. It could be either one of them, or both of them."

"So you think the damage done to his food truck is directly related to what happened at the night market?"

"It sure seems like it," I said, the wheels in my brain spinning faster with each word. "Think about it. Winston isn't at the night market, and neither are Gene, Sandra, or Calvin. And an explosion happens.

They all have an alibi that protects the other and who is going to disprove it? Winston's at home with a damaged truck and calls the shop, talks to Calvin who can't get away because of some customer, then Gene becomes involved by being the only one who can tow the food truck. And of course, he's at Sandra's house while she's cooking something up for him, thereby giving her an alibi."

"But that doesn't help us figure out which one of them cut the fuel lines to the truck . . . if any of them did at all," Megan reminded me. "It could have happened at any time earlier that day or even the night before."

"You're right about the timing of the cut fuel lines. Could have been at any time prior and could have been any one of them. But the main point is, they all have an alibi for the time of the explosion at the night market, and that's what really matters in the end."

"This is true. If they're all covering for each other and have the same story, then it's like you said and the police would start searching for new suspects. But how could they be sure that the police would tie the two explosions together?"

Kikko, finished with her thorough inspection of the crabgrass, headed back in the direction of the apartment.

I thought about Megan's question. "I think the only way they would connect the two situations is if there was a common denominator . . . like maybe the same materials were used in the making of the explosives or whatever."

"So now we just have to find out if that's what

happened," Megan said. "How are we going to find that out?"

"We're going to ask Adam, of course."

Megan had to work that night, and I didn't feel much like leaving the house, although I felt kind of bad about that when it was such a beautiful evening. But I had too much on my mind. I stayed in and scribbled ideas in my notebook, trying to make sense of my theories and the information I'd obtained that day. I checked to see if anything didn't fit in or if I'd missed a crucial element.

I did make note that Ruby had set me on the path to talk to Winston, and that she'd been strange about him not showing up at the night market last night. Maybe she suspected something as well. Or maybe she even knew more than she was letting on. I considered bringing that up during my next talk with her.

Adam was busy with work and didn't have a chance to respond to my text messages until several hours later. I'd just woken up from a short nap when the chime sounded on my phone.

It was Adam.

The text message I'd sent earlier in the afternoon had only asked if he knew anything new about the explosion, what caused it, and if it was similar to the chemicals found in the food truck aftermath. I didn't explain specifically why I wanted to know, but I assumed he would guess since we'd discussed whether the second bomb might be a present left for me.

His response was: *Yes, similar materials. Talk more later.*

The phone shook in my hand. They *were* similar, which meant that my theory of someone trying to link the two explosions and clear Sandra's name was plausible. The biggest problem I had with that was now I couldn't decide whether it made Sandra more or less guilty.

CHAPTER
24

Sunday morning I prepared for the traditional dim sum outing with my family. My mind was elsewhere, and I didn't feel much like going. But I knew that if I didn't, I would never hear the end of it from my mother . . . or my sister for that matter.

I'd toiled all night with the text that Adam had sent. Later in the evening, he called to tell me that similar components were used to make the second bomb, but it was definitely intended to be a smaller explosion. So, his guess based on proximity and my snooping was that someone wanted to scare me a little bit rather than cause any actual harm. Though it relieved me somewhat to know that it wasn't meant to kill me, my nerves were still rattled by the ordeal.

I questioned Adam about whether the fact the two explosives were of similar materials would cause the police to connect it to the investigation of the first bomb. He said he imagined that it would but that

Detective O'Neil hadn't mentioned what the police department's next steps would be.

While we were on the phone, I thought I should tell him about my encounter with Gene, but I knew how he'd react and I wasn't in a state of mind to handle it. I did have to tell him at some point since Gene had basically threatened me, but I needed time to think, to calm down, and to figure out what my next move was going to be.

I also reminded myself that this *was* Cleveland's case and not Adam's. What reaction would Detective O'Neil have to my meddling in his business? Would it cause problems between him and Adam? And more importantly, could I get in some kind of trouble? I mean, the second explosion could potentially be my fault. If I hadn't been snooping around, maybe nothing would have happened. Unknowingly, I could have caused the bomber to up their game. I was only thankful that no one was hurt in the process. Anything could have gone wrong.

I arrived at Li Wah's on time and found my sister lingering in the parking lot. Despite everything going on, I had to laugh. "You know, if you're going to be a big-shot lawyer, you're going to have to work on your confrontation skills," I teased.

"Ugh, I can deal with all kinds of chaos, Lana," she replied. "But this stuff with Mom and Aunt Grace is just too much for me to handle. Especially after the last get-together we had. How embarrassing."

We walked into the restaurant and found that the rest of our family was already seated. Two seats between my grandmother and father were open. I took the open seat next to my grandmother.

"Laaa-na," my grandmother sang.

I smiled at her, and she patted my cheek as I sat down.

Anna May and I exchanged our hellos with the rest of the table and got ourselves situated.

My mother looked exceptionally agitated today. I could tell by how she was scrunching her face at the menu as if she were deep in concentration. I knew she was only pretending to read it since she knew the whole thing by heart.

"Mom, you look nice today," I said.

She was dressed in a silver satin top with a ruffled V-neck. Both her arms were adorned with gold bracelets and she had her favorite gold necklace on with her matching earrings. I could tell she had taken extra care to dress herself for today's family gathering.

She returned the compliment with a wide smile, her round cheeks brightened with blush raised high. "Thank you, honey."

Honey? Uh-oh, she was really laying it on thick today. She never called me honey.

My sister tapped my leg under the table and we exchanged a brief glance.

"So," Anna May said. "I have some great news to share with everyone."

"Lord knows we could use some," my dad said. "Let's hear it."

"My internship application was accepted at the law firm, and I'm going to be starting there in two weeks!"

"Oh, darling!" Aunt Grace clasped her hands together. "That's marvelous news! I'm so proud of you!"

I caught my mother's eye twitch, but she was quick to hide it and she beamed at my sister. "Anna May, Mommy is so proud of you! You are such a smart girl."

"Well, that is great news," my dad said, patting my sister on the shoulder. "Things are really getting started for you now."

"Yeah, good job, sis," I said, nudging her with my elbow playfully. "We're one step closer to that Mercedes we discussed."

When she turned to scowl at me, I winked.

My grandmother was completely lost, so my aunt filled her in, and when she'd been properly informed, she clapped with amusement. "A-ma is happy!" She gave Anna May a thumbs-up.

"*Xie xie,* A-ma," my sister said, thanking her.

The server came around with the dim sum cart and my mother selected a variety of foods for the table. I immediately went for the shrimp noodle rolls, which were one of my favorites. Everything was going better than expected. Maybe we'd avoid a fight today. I was just beginning to relax when things took a turn for the worse.

"You know, Anna May," Aunt Grace said. "This internship can open a lot of doors for you. They're a pretty well-known firm, and I think a lot of places in California would love to have you work for them."

My mother slammed her chopsticks on her plate. "Why California? What's wrong with Anna May staying here with her family?"

"Ai-ya, Bai-ling, must you always make such a fuss," Aunt Grace clucked. "I'm only suggesting that this will open many opportunities for Anna

May. Maybe she would like to live somewhere else. It doesn't have to be anywhere in California . . . it could be New York . . . Chicago . . . Miami."

My sister and I shared another glance. No one else at the table spoke. My father pretended to be preoccupied with his shrimp dumpling.

"She is happy here," my mother said. "Is Mommy right, Anna May?"

Anna May picked up her teacup and took a long sip. "I haven't given it much thought, really."

My mother flared her nostrils.

I tried to think of a topic to bring up that would completely change the subject, but I was drawing a blank. The only thing that came to mind was my pending situation with Gene, Winston, and the whole Chow case. But, considering the circumstances, I didn't see that as a good idea for a topic change. I racked my brain while the two women began bickering in Hokkien.

"I decided on the Poconos!" I yelled over their voices.

Everyone stopped and stared at me.

My grandmother giggled. "Po-co-nos."

My dad seemed to pick up on my cue. "The Poconos sounds great for your birthday, Goober. Your mother and I have never been there, but I'm sure it's going to be a great trip for you and Adam. Do you think two rooms will be expensive?"

"Dad!"

"What?" He chuckled. "A father can dream, can't he?"

Aunt Grace tsked. "Both of you are too protective of these girls, they are both grown women."

I cringed. "It's okay, Aunt Grace, he's just making a joke."

"Why must you come here and insult us every time you visit?" my mother asked. Her face was turning red, and I knew she was ready to explode. "We are a good family, and we are happy with things the way they are."

My grandmother asked what was going on and my aunt quickly responded. However, my mother was not entirely happy with the response she gave and started talking over my aunt Grace, assumedly in defense of herself.

My sister put her head in her hands. "I just want to eat and go already. This is a nightmare." She said it out of the corner of her mouth so only I could hear. "And here I thought we were going to make it out of this one without an argument."

So much for my great idea of changing the subject. Who knew that the Poconos could be so controversial?

With quiet reserve, my grandmother spoke, and most of what she said was lost on me, but I did catch something about the value of family and appreciating people while they were still around. I imagined it was something similar to what my mother often told my sister and me.

After my grandmother's lecture, both women remained silent and focused on their food. The rest of us did the same.

Needless to say, the rest of dim sum was awkward, and I was anxious for the check to arrive. When it did, it was paid quickly and we all rose to leave.

The four of them had driven together, and I couldn't imagine the tension the car would be filled with and was immediately thankful that I had driven alone.

My sister and I separated from the group as we went out into the parking lot.

"Another awkward family gathering for the books," Anna May said, digging for her keys. "I don't know how many more of these I can take."

"Promise me something."

Anna May huffed. "I'm not buying you a Mercedes, Lana."

"No, not that. Promise me that when we have families and we get together, no matter how much we can't stand each other, we'll always get along for their sake."

My sister contemplated my request for a minute, and then nodded in agreement, extending her hand. "Okay, deal."

I took her hand and gave it a firm shake. "And yes, you are buying me that Mercedes."

Because dim sum had been so mentally draining, I thought I'd return home and lie on the couch with a cup of coffee to relax. It had been a while since I'd had a lazy afternoon with a good book. But instead I found myself sitting outside of Ruby's house. I needed to talk with her and I didn't want to delay it any longer than I had to. I needed to figure out what she knew, if anything. And I also needed to make a decision about what to tell Adam in regard to Gene and his not entirely veiled threats.

I wasn't sure Ruby would be home since I hadn't bothered to call, but it was worth a shot and I had nowhere in particular to be.

I rang the doorbell and stood outside for a few minutes, waiting for someone to answer. There was no awning on their front steps and the early afternoon sun was shining down on me.

Finally, I heard the lock turning and the door slowly opened. Ruby peeked her head out before fully opening the door. "Oh hello, Lana, I am surprised to see you. Is everything okay?"

"Yeah, everything's fine. Could I talk to you about something if you're not busy?" I asked.

She opened the screen door, inviting me in. "No, I'm not busy. I am working on some jewelry, but it is nothing I can't do while talking with you. My husband is out so you can keep me company."

I stepped into the air-conditioned home, my arms covering with goosebumps. "I won't take up much of your time, I just wanted to ask you a couple of questions."

She shut the door behind me, and gestured for me to follow her into the sitting area. "Would you like something to drink?"

"I'm okay right now, thank you."

"Have a seat."

I returned to the chair I had sat in during my previous visit.

The TV was on and a repeat of *CSI:NY* was playing. She turned the volume down before sitting down on the couch. "What can I help you with? How did your aunt like her new earrings? I meant to ask you the other night and it slipped my mind."

"Huh? Oh, I haven't given them to her yet," I said, completely forgetting I had gotten my aunt earrings to begin with.

"Well, do let me know how she likes them. I am always happy to hear when a customer is satisfied."

"I will. So . . . do you remember the other evening at the night market, you said we should try and help Sandra any way that we can?"

She nodded. "Yes, I do. Is that why you've come by?"

"Well, I may know who could have actually killed Ronnie."

Her eyes widened. "Please, tell me who."

"It's been right in front of our faces this entire time." I paused, taking a deep breath. She was either going to agree with me or assume I was a total basket case. "I believe . . . it was Sandra's brother, Gene." I took another pause to gauge her reaction, but there was none, so I continued. "I think maybe he and Winston could have done it together. You were right to send me in his direction."

She inhaled deeply and nodded in a slow, rhythmic motion as if she were processing the information with each bob of her head. "I see."

I thought I should justify my thinking. "It makes the most sense. They both had a plausible reason to want Ronnie out of the picture."

I told her about my encounter with Gene, the food truck situation, and things that didn't add up. When I was finished with everything I had to say, I let out an exaggerated sigh. "So, do you think I'm completely crazy? I know it's possible that I'm off base with this whole thing. But it just seems right."

"No, I don't think you're crazy at all, Lana," she said, shaking her head. "I believe you have thought this through and it is clear to me that you want to help Sandra just as much as I do. But I have known Gene for many years, and this situation does not seem likely to me. Though he can be a rough man at times, I don't see him doing anything to hurt Sandra's husband in such a way. You must be one hundred percent sure that her brother is involved. If you are wrong, this could make things worse."

"That's true," I said.

She smiled gently and rose from the couch. "If you would excuse me, I think I'll make some tea. Are you sure that you wouldn't like something to drink?"

I shook my head and she disappeared into the kitchen.

While she was gone, I thought about what she'd said, how unlikely Gene's involvement was, and how if I was wrong, it could create more issues for Sandra. I knew this was a delicate subject, and I needed to tread lightly and, most importantly, be a hundred percent sure I knew what I was talking about. There was still a lot I didn't know about Gene, and was it fair for me to assume the worst about someone I hardly knew even if some of the pieces did conveniently fit together?

Well, really, it was a double-edged sword. Either way it would cause issues for Sandra. I mean, how horrible would it be if your own brother killed your husband and put your life in danger as well. Not only did it turn out that *she* was being accused of the murder, but she could also have been in the truck. How could he have guaranteed that she wouldn't be anywhere near the blast if he'd already left the area? Something about that seemed off to me, but I couldn't quite place my finger on it.

In the event it was her brother, and despite the turmoil it would cause in their family dynamic, it didn't give him a right to go unconfronted and get away with murder. *Or* for his own sister to take the fall.

I still had a lot of thinking to do. Maybe my visit to Ruby was a little premature after all.

When she returned to the living room, she appeared a little preoccupied and sat down without acknowledging me. I wondered what was going on in her head. Maybe she did think I was a little crazy after giving it some thought.

"I've been thinking," she said finally. "The information you've found is really good, but you should look deeper into Winston acting alone. I have a strong feeling that he is the one behind all of this. As you said, his truck was conveniently damaged. Perhaps he damaged the truck himself to create an alibi? That would be a possibility, yes?"

I tapped the arm of the chair with my index finger, re-creating the scenario of events for the hundredth time in my head. "I suppose it's possible. It would also give him the perfect opportunity to use Gene as his witness. Maybe that's Gene's only involvement."

Ruby nodded her head in affirmation. "Yes, this all makes much more sense. Though Winston was not at the night market this past Friday, he could have easily planted another bomb in an attempt to take suspicion away from him."

She was right about that. And it would explain the crude construction of the bomb. Someone like Gene or Calvin would have more experience and could have produced something a little more sophisticated. Maybe I had misinterpreted what Gene was saying and he hadn't actually been threatening me. It was possible he'd been telling me to be safe.

"You're right, I should look into Winston a little bit more. There must be something that I'm missing." I wasn't going to tell her that I still had my sights on Gene as well. I knew she didn't want me to suspect him because he was Sandra's brother and this would cause her more pain, but I wasn't going to let him completely off the hook just yet either.

The front door opened, and a small Asian man walked in. He was thin with a full head of floppy hair, and wearing aviator glasses that were too large for his face. His khaki pants and a white button-down shirt were also too big for him. He looked surprised to see me and froze in the entryway.

"Oh hello," he said, bowing his head in short bursts. "I did not realize we had company."

"I was just leaving," I said, standing up from the chair. "I'm Lana Lee, Betty's daughter."

He turned to Ruby and cocked his head.

She let out a laugh. "Oh no, Lana, this is my second husband, Don. He never met your mother."

"Oh, I'm sorry for the mistake. It's nice to meet you, Don," I said.

"You as well." He bowed his head in short bursts

again. "Please excuse me, I must use the restroom."
He scurried through the living room, and I waved a
good-bye, but he was already gone.

I headed for the door, Ruby a few steps behind
me.

"Thanks for taking some time to talk with me
today, I really appreciate it. I'm going to take your
advice and see what else I can come up with."

"I wish you much luck, Lana," she said, standing
near the door. "Perhaps you can tell your boyfriend
about this as well. I'm sure he can help find information on Winston's past."

As I got into my car, I groaned in frustration. I
felt like I was on a merry-go-round that would not
stop.

CHAPTER

25

"Why would she assume that this guy Winston even has a past to begin with?" Megan asked, after I filled her in on my visit with Ruby.

I'd only been home for fifteen minutes, but the moment I walked in the door, I accosted Megan with my news hoping she could help me suss it out.

I rolled my neck, trying to release some of the tension that had accumulated throughout the day. My neck and shoulders felt stiff and I sensed the beginnings of a headache coming on. "I don't know, but she's definitely got a feeling about this guy. She brings him up quite a bit. I can't help but think she knows more than she's telling."

Megan already had her laptop on. She'd been shopping online when I walked through the door. Kikko was sprawled on the living room carpet gnawing on her bone, too busy to be bothered with what we were doing.

She tapped a few keys. "Why don't we look into him a little more then? Have you yet?"

"Nope, it kind of slipped my mind. I've been meaning to." I got up from my seat and went to the coffeemaker to brew a fresh pot. "But I really thought it was Gene this whole time. Now I'm not entirely sure anymore."

"Why? Just because this lady Ruby said so?" Megan asked. "Just because she doesn't want Gene to have any involvement with what happened, doesn't make him innocent. I know it makes everything a little more awful for Sandra, but it might just be the ugly truth."

I pulled a fresh filter out of the cupboard, measured out some coffee and set the pot to brew. "No, it's not just that. It's the more I think about it . . . well, okay, why would he risk accidentally blowing up his sister in the process? There's no way that he would know where she'd be at the time of the explosion. He was in a huge rush to get out of there, and it's not like he tried to make her come with him. All he was concerned about was him and Calvin getting away."

Megan was studying the computer screen. "Unless we go back to the idea that Sandra was in on it and she knew that it was going to happen so she made sure to be nowhere near the truck."

"That doesn't feel right either. I don't see Sandra being a part of this. She could have left her husband and she chose not to. Also, why would she stay close enough to the truck to get injured?"

"We've had this argument already, Lana. She could have easily decided this was the only way out.

Plus, you thought you saw Gene at the night market shortly before the second explosion. He could have been planting the bomb to clear his sister's name. As far as her getting hurt in the process, maybe that was so it would look more believable."

"I know, but we both agree that I'm not entirely sure that I saw him. You were the one who said that my mind could have been playing tricks on me, remember?"

"Whoa," Megan said, leaning in closer to the laptop screen. "Check this out."

I crouched behind her so my face was level with the screen and read where she pointed. "Domestic dispute . . ." I skimmed over the condensed information that the county public record page showed. "There are a couple of these on here."

"Yeah, and one of them is only a year and a half ago. Seems Winston got handsy with his wife? For some reason, it never occurred to me that he was married. I don't remember him wearing a ring, do you?"

"I'm not sure, I wasn't paying attention to that. Can I navigate for a minute?" I asked. She released her hand from the mouse, and I took over, selecting another option. "Divorce records . . ." I hovered the cursor over the line I read. "Shortly after the last domestic dispute charge."

"Well, that answers the married question. Okay . . . so these two men . . . Ronnie and Winston . . . they both have a heavy hand," Megan said, anger evident in her voice. "Do you think that whoever went after Ronnie is the one who tried to go after Winston? Someone trying to seek justice?"

"We're going on the assumption that Winston is the guilty party though," I reminded her. "This could just be a coincidence. There has to be another angle here."

"Yeah, but that's not what we're finding. So far it looks like someone really is going after him too."

"Or that could be the way he wants it to look," I suggested. "If it seemed like he was being targeted next, the police wouldn't look into him as a suspect."

"Do you think he cut his own fuel lines after all?" Megan asked. "I know you said it didn't really matter which one of them cut the fuel lines because it gave them all an alibi, but maybe it does matter. Especially if we're considering that Winston was acting alone."

"It's very possible." I took a sip of my coffee and pondered the idea. "But again, we have no way of knowing for sure who did what and when. And maybe you're right and I'm letting what Ruby said get to me. My original thought was that Gene has some type of involvement in this whole thing. If we take him out of the equation completely, does it make as much sense? Especially with the way he was behaving when we saw him at the auto shop. What do you do when everyone is covering for one another?"

"I don't know. It all seems too thin to me," Megan said, picking up the coffee mug I had placed on the table for her. "This is the most indecisive you've been in a long time. You don't sound sure of yourself at all."

I smirked. "That's because I'm not."

"I feel like all I'm doing is saying, 'now what?'" She sighed. "But I'll ask again . . ."

"Tomorrow's Monday. I think the best next step is to have another go at the Mahjong Matrons."

"But they didn't have anything useful to offer the other times you talked with them. What's going to make this time any different?"

"This time, I know what questions I need to ask."

The fact that this was the second Monday I found myself excited for the day to begin was a tad concerning. But I felt I was close to something and it made me anxious for things to get moving.

As patiently as possible, I waited for the Matrons to arrive for their breakfast. I went over the dining area twice, straightening place settings and adjusting teacups. At 9 A.M. sharp, they pushed through the double doors and headed for their table, Helen regarding me with a head nod.

I zipped into the kitchen and prepared their tea while I rattled off to Peter that he would need to prepare their order.

"Whoa, dude," he said, watching me put together a tray of tea. "What's the hurry today?"

"No hurry," I said, avoiding eye contact.

Before he could question me further, I rushed back into the dining area, careful not to disturb the teapot.

At their table, I set the teapot down. As usual Helen reached for the kettle and poured tea for all four ladies.

"You know," I said. "I was wondering if you ladies could help me with some information I'm trying to gather."

"Oh?" Helen could barely hide her interest. "You need help from us?"

"Yes, I had some questions about Ruby Lin." During my chat with Megan, one thing that I hadn't considered before crossed my mind. And that was Ruby's behavior. I knew that she wasn't a fan of Ronnie. And I also knew that she was guiding me along, but taking a backseat in pursuing an investigation herself. I found that odd. If something like this were to happen to me, would Megan sit idly by while others scurried to come up with answers? I think not.

Opal and Pearl straightened up. "Ruby Lin, you say?"

"Do any of you happen to know much about her?"

The two sisters looked at each other and smirked.

"She is an interesting woman," Opal said. "Perhaps a little on the strange side."

Helen and Wendy nodded in agreement.

"She was married a time before," Wendy began. "She had a lot of trouble with that husband."

"She did?" I asked. "What kind of trouble?"

Opal leaned back, a look of disdain on her face. "Some men think it is okay to raise a hand to their wife."

The four women remained silent after that comment and only nodded in agreement to one another.

"So, how are things with her new husband?" I asked. "I met him the other day . . ."

"They are good from what we know," Pearl said. "He is a quiet, nervous man. I think this is what she likes now."

I found it upsetting to learn that Ruby had suffered from domestic abuse as well. I hadn't known about it and I had a newfound sympathy for what she'd been through. I also felt a little shocked to realize that in all my searches through county records, I had never bothered once to look through hers. But I had been right to want to check her out now. "What can you tell me about her first husband?"

"He is very rich," Helen said. "I believe he was an investment banker. When they divorced, she was taken care of very nicely. He paid her a lot of money to keep quiet about their situation. That is why she does not have to work and can stay home making jewelry."

"What's his name?" I asked.

"David Yang," Opal replied.

The bell sounded from the kitchen, signaling their food was done, and I excused myself to get their order.

When I returned with their food, Wendy tilted her head up in question. "Lana, why do you ask these questions? Is there something wrong with Ruby?"

"No, nothing like that. Just curiosity, I suppose." I set down a plate of pickled cucumbers in front of her. "I don't remember her from my childhood, and when I met her second husband, I didn't realize she'd been married before."

"Of course, you would not remember her," Pearl said, laughing. The way she acted was as if this information were supposed to be common knowledge. "She and your mother stopped being friends when you were still very young."

I looked among the four women. "Wait, do you ladies know why they stopped talking to each other?"

Helen nodded. "Yes, of course, we all know this."

"Well, what happened?"

"The problem was not with your mother, but with Esther."

"Esther? What does any of this have to do with Esther?"

"Ruby wanted to sell the jewelry she made at Esther's store, but Esther would not allow this. She said that she did not wish to work with friends. Ruby did not take kindly to this and made many comments about Chin's Gifts selling only junk," Helen said.

Opal continued the story for her. "She caused Esther a lot of problems and, as you know, your mother is very protective of her. She told Ruby that she was not welcome at Asia Village any longer. After that, only Sandra came by."

Well, that made sense as to why the mahjong circle had been my mother, Nancy, Esther, and Sandra in the end. "But why didn't anyone tell me this? Why didn't Esther mention it?"

"It was a very long time ago," Pearl said. "All things have been forgiven. Their friendships will never be the same, but there are no hard feelings anymore."

Finding myself slightly disappointed with the details of the story, I left the four women to their breakfast. There were no other customers in the restaurant, so I wandered up front and sat down at the hostess station to stare out into the plaza.

I could ask my mother about Ruby, but would she give me a fair assessment? From the way that Esther told the story when I visited with her the other day, it sounded like my mother hadn't let go of her previous grudge with Ruby. Surprisingly, Esther seemed to be more levelheaded about the situation even though Ruby's behavior back then had been directed at her. She might end up being my best source for information. After all, I doubted Sandra would have a bad word to say against Ruby. On top of that, I was fairly certain any chances of contact with the Chow family would be nearly impossible.

That's when Calvin Chow walked in.

CHAPTER
26

Calvin was dressed in what I would consider a standard-issue mechanic's outfit. He had on a blue-gray button-down work shirt with a sewn-on patch that spelled his name in white cursive. And if I had to guess, his dark blue pants were more than likely a pair of Dickies.

Though he didn't appear unfriendly as he approached the hostess station, he didn't smile either. His eyes skimmed the restaurant before he spoke. Even though it was empty except for the Mahjong Matrons, he kept his voice low. "We need to talk, Lana," he said.

There was something in his voice that made the emotion hard to describe. He sounded concerned, angry, and sad all at the same time.

"Okay," I said. "I'm the only one here besides Peter right now. I can't exactly leave the dining area unattended."

He chewed on his lip. "I have to be at work in an hour, I don't have a lot of time. Do you think Peter could come up here and man the fort? It's not like people are breaking the door down to get in here."

By the way he spoke, I felt like what he needed to say was pretty important, so I agreed and went into the back to ask Peter if he would mind keeping an eye on the front for a couple of minutes. He gave me a strange look when I explained to him that Calvin was here to see me, but with a shrug, he complied and followed me up front.

I signaled to Calvin to follow me into the back room and I led him to my office, shutting the door behind us.

"So what's this about?" I asked, sitting behind my desk. I noticed that my hands were clammy and I wiped them on my pants. *No reason to be nervous, Lana, Peter is just a yell away*, I told myself.

"I've been trying to get a hold of you," he said, shifting awkwardly in the guest chair. "I stopped by the other day . . . I don't know if your sister told you. She hasn't changed much, that's for sure."

I laughed. "Not really, no. Why didn't you call me? You have my number."

"Why didn't *you*?" he replied. "My uncle told me that you stopped by the shop."

I grabbed a pen off my desk and twisted the cap off and back on. "I meant to, but it just slipped my mind. There's been a lot going on lately."

His eyes focused on my hand twisting the pen cap. "I know what you're up to, Lana."

"What do you mean?" I did my best to play dumb. As I suspected, they were on to me.

"Why are you going around asking questions? You're not a cop. Is it because you're a cop's girl-friend or something? You feel the need to get involved?"

"No . . . I—"

"It's none of your business what happened with my father. And we're not good friends or anything. So I can't understand why you're snooping around asking my family questions. It seems like an awful lot of trouble to go through for someone who isn't involved."

"Because—"

"I read about you, you know," he said. His tone was accusatory, as if he'd caught me in the middle of a great big scheme. "After we saw each other, I Googled you, and I saw the articles from the *Plain Dealer*. You think you're some great big detective, don't you? Do you think you're the Asian community protector or some stupid crap?"

"No—"

"My family isn't some game for you to—"

I slapped the pen on my desk. "Shut up! Geez, would you let me talk for one freakin' minute?"

He sat back in his seat, most likely caught off guard because I'd raised my voice at him. Did he think he was going to come to my restaurant and bully *me*?

"Now," I said, standing up and placing my hands on the desk so I could lean forward. "First of all, I don't think I'm some great big detective as you put it. I haven't asked to be a part of the things that happened. They occurred and I dealt with them. Each instance has affected me one way or another."

"But—"

I held up a finger. "I'm not finished yet."

He closed his mouth and turned away sulking, as if he were being scolded by a parent.

"The only reason I've been going around asking questions about your situation is because *our* parents used to be really good friends, specifically our mothers. And *my* mother is extremely upset by this whole thing. *And* even though my mother and I don't have the best track record, I hate to see her upset when she hears that her friend is suspected of being a murderer."

He started to say something and I held up my finger again.

"For the record, I think that your mother is innocent. But I'm not so sure about the people around you, and frankly, I'm starting to have more questions about you now too," I said, tapping my finger on the desk. No sense in telling him that I had been dabbling with the idea of him being a guilty party anyway. "Maybe the real question should be, why are *you* so upset with me asking questions? What are *you* hiding, Calvin Chow?"

His eyes widened. "Me? You think I would kill my father? After all these years, you would think that I'm capable of something like that? Murder?"

"Well, I don't know you . . . and as you said, we're not good friends."

"I haven't done anything wrong. I don't have anything to hide."

"Then tell me what you and your father were arguing about that day. I saw you two going at it during the night market."

He slumped in his seat, resting his chin in his hand. "It's the stupidest thing, and it kind of makes me look guilty. I don't know, maybe you're right, maybe I do have something to hide."

I sat back down in my chair, unsure what can of worms I'd unintentionally opened. But I had to know either way. I reminded myself again that Peter was just a yell away . . . given that I would have time to scream, that is. "Tell me what happened. I'm not going to judge you."

He sighed. "My father and I fought all the time. Since I was young . . . but his current problem was that he didn't want me to work for my uncle Gene. He hated that I was a mechanic and wanted me to join the family business instead. But I really didn't want to. Like I really want to work with my parents every single day of my life?"

I laughed, trying to lighten the tension that filled the room. "You're preaching to the choir."

He smirked. "Well, my dad's grand plan was to get another food truck going. He wanted to have Wonton on Wheels at more than one location, but that meant he needed someone else to run the second truck, and he wanted that person to be me."

"Okay . . ."

"But I didn't want to. I didn't want to run a food truck. I like working on cars, and I like working with my uncle Gene. He's a solid guy. I mean sure, he drinks a little too much, but he's had a rough life. He still gets done what needs to be done, so whatever. It's not my problem, you know?"

"You don't have to defend your uncle's drinking problem to me. Honestly, that's not my concern."

"Right," he said with a nod. "Anyway, when I stopped by the night market to see my mom, my dad pulled me aside to tell me that he was in the process of buying the other truck. He was waiting on some paperwork to clear with his credit but it was only going to be another day or two. And he demanded that I quit my job at the repair shop right away so I could get started on running this second truck for him."

"Then what happened?"

"I turned him down," Calvin said, his chin dropping to his chest. "I told my dad to go to hell . . . that was the last thing I said to him before walking away."

I felt my insides tighten. And now that I knew the story, I could understand why Calvin would think this would make him appear guilty. He and his father get into an argument a second truck, then tragedy strikes, and there's now zero reason to buy a second truck. There's no longer a first truck, and the man pushing for a new truck is dead.

But what if Calvin's motive was only to damage the first truck? Maybe he didn't mean to harm his father in the process. It had all been an accident after all. But would the authorities see it that way? And furthermore, would a jury see it that way?

Calvin watched me while I thought through everything he'd said. "See? Now you think I'm guilty too."

"Truthfully, I don't know what to think," I told him. "I don't see you going through all of this and then telling me about it if you were actually guilty." *Would he?* I thought. Was he even telling me the truth to begin with? No one would know otherwise. I suppose I could find out about the second truck and see if that checked out. But I would never know if that's what he and his father were actually fighting about the last time they spoke.

"Are you going to tell on me?" he asked. "I'm sure the cops would love to hear this story."

It was a fair question, and I wondered about that myself. Instead, I thought for the time being I could use my position as leverage. I looked him square in the eye. "No . . . if you agree to let me ask you a couple of things then I will keep your secret for the time being."

"Okay, that's fair. Shoot."

"Did you know that your father got physical with your mother? In a bad way, I mean."

His eyes bulged. "What? No!"

I hated to be the one to tell him, but it was important for me to know what exactly Calvin was aware of. "I did some digging on the county public records site and there was an instance where they got into a domestic dispute. Apparently, it happened more than once, but she never reported it. He also had a couple other offenses on his record that had to do with violence, but they didn't involve your mother."

He closed his eyes. "No, I didn't know. She did have some bruises on her arms and chin a few months ago, but she told me she fell out of the back of the food truck. I didn't have a reason to not believe her so I let it drop. She can occasionally be clumsy."

I leaned back in my chair. "What can you tell me about Ruby Lin?"

Calvin cocked his head at me. "Ruby? My mom's friend?"

"Yeah, do you know anything about her?"

He shook his head. "Not really. I mean, they're like totally best friends. Ruby is always around, helping my mother with stuff. She seems like a solid lady, but I couldn't tell you much about her personally. It's not like I sit around with the two of them."

"I figured as much." I paused for a minute because I really didn't want to ask my next question. However, it was the first thing that came to mind after he told me about his father wanting him to quit his job.

Calvin seemed to sense that I wanted to say something else, and he leaned forward, resting his elbows on his knees and clasping his hands together as if he were bracing himself.

I straightened my shoulders. "Calvin, this whole situation with your father . . . the new food truck, him wanting you to quit your job . . . did your uncle Gene know about all of this?" I held my breath while I waited for his answer.

"Yeah . . . he knew. I was so mad when my dad told me about it the first time, I went to blow off some steam with my uncle. We went out drinkin' and played some pool. We talked about what a jerk my dad is and then we laughed it off. My uncle knew I would never go for this food truck idea in a million years, so he didn't really care."

"I wouldn't be so sure of that," I said.

A line etched itself between his brows. "Wait . . . what are you trying to say?"

"I don't want to go in that direction. I know how much your uncle means to you. But I think we have to face the possibility that your uncle Gene was involved in your father's murder."

CHAPTER
27

Before Calvin left for work, I gave him a few brief details on what I thought happened concerning Winston, and that he might actually have played a part. I felt so bad about accusing his uncle who I knew he admired that I turned the tables and said maybe his uncle was covering for Winston in some way.

I tried my best to find out if Calvin knew anything about the relationship between his father and Winston, but he wasn't much help in that department.

We both swore each other to secrecy, and though it felt legit with a handshake and all, I still had my reservations about trusting Calvin. The thought had crossed my mind that he could be playing me to keep me quiet.

He did promise to look into the whole Winston angle though, and find out what really happened with the truck. I suppose he was doing it more for his own benefit than mine, with the goal of clearing his uncle of any suspicions.

The restaurant had remained calm while I was gone but Peter was glad to go back to the kitchen. The Matrons had finished their breakfast just as Calvin was leaving, and I cashed out their check.

On their way out, Helen warned me to be careful.

After I cleaned off their table, I returned to the hostess booth to wait for my next customers. The plaza itself was slow, and I found myself bored after a few minutes of watching a trickle of early-morning customers walk by.

There was a chance that Megan might be awake, so I pulled out my cell phone and gave her a call.

"Hello?" she mumbled into the phone.

"Did I wake you up?"

"Maybe just a little bit." She yawned. "What's up?"

"Calvin Chow just stopped by."

"Now I'm awake. What happened?"

I relayed the story, adding my own commentary on what I thought it all meant. I also told her about the information I'd gathered from the Matrons about Ruby and her first husband.

"Sounds like you've had a busy morning," she replied when I was finished. "So are you going to talk to this David Yang guy?"

"No . . ." I said. "I don't know if he would be all that credible."

"This is true. What could you hope to get out of the conversation anyway?"

"I know, I just have this weird feeling about Ruby. I mean, given the relationship between her and Sandra, and now learning about her past, it makes me question whether she's involved somehow. I mean, suppose it was you and me. How would you deal with me being physically abused?"

"I see your point," she replied. "So who is left to talk with?"

"Not Sandra that's for sure. I can't ask my mother anything. Maybe I'll talk to Esther again."

"If you ask me, it's a shot in the dark. Anyone you have access to will most likely tell you negative things. She is not a fan favorite in this crowd."

"True." I huffed. "Ugh, this is so frustrating. I'm ready for the whole thing to be over with. Adam's right. We are in desperate need of a weekend getaway."

"I know, but you'll figure it out one way or another. It's like we're just missing one piece. Once that's figured out, it'll be smooth sailing."

My aunt walked into the restaurant with a sad smile on her face.

"Hey Megan, Aunt Grace is here. Can I call you back later?"

"Give me an hour, I'm going back to sleep," she said before hanging up.

I set my phone down and stood to hug my aunt Grace. "Hi, what brings you by today? Want me to have Peter make you something?"

She hugged me and squeezed. "No, dear, I only wanted to stop by and let you know that I'm going to be leaving the day after tomorrow."

"Why so soon?" I asked. It felt obligatory to say that. Of course, I knew why she was leaving.

"I think your mother and I have bickered enough,

don't you?" She sighed, walking farther into the restaurant. After looking over the tables, she finally chose the booth closest to the hostess station and sat down. "I always hope that our visits are going to turn out better, but they never do."

I sat down across from her. "I don't want this to come out the wrong way, but why do you give her such a hard time about her decisions?"

She chuckled. "Your mother is a great woman, and she has always been a good sister to me. But I hate that she thinks her way is the only way to live. Her type of lifestyle is not for everyone, and she will never recognize that."

I took a deep breath. Maybe now was the time to finally be honest with my aunt—she seemed like she might be willing to listen. "Well, maybe instead of fighting against her, consider things from her point of view."

My aunt looked taken aback by my answer. "What do you mean?"

"The same applies to you, Aunt Grace. Your lifestyle doesn't necessarily fit everyone either. Did it ever occur to you that we're all happy living here just the way we are? Sure, traveling all over the world is great, but there's also something nice about having roots."

She looked down at her hands. "What you're saying is that I'm just as bad as your mother."

"Well, I wouldn't actually say it . . ." I smiled.

She glanced up at me and started laughing. "I suppose you're right, Lana. I think I've been so busy trying to prove to your mother that my life is worthy of her approval that I lost myself and the entire point of the argument. Truth is, I don't disapprove of your mother's choices as much as I seem to. I guess I just wanted to even the score a little bit."

"Maybe explain to her that you want her to accept your life even though it's different from hers . . . see what happens."

"I think I will," my aunt said with renewed confidence. "By the way," she said as she stood up from her seat. "We'll be having one last family dinner tomorrow night, and of course, you and Anna May are both invited to join us."

I stood up with her. "Required, you mean."

She laughed. "Would your mother have it any other way?"

"I'll be there," I said, as we walked back to the lobby. "Just let us know the time and place."

Aunt Grace gave me another hug. "You know, Lana, I really am proud of you. You're so grown-up now."

I hugged her and gave her a squeeze. "Thanks, Aunt Grace. Just don't tell anyone else that. They'll expect me to be mature all the time."

When I left work that evening, I was in a state of flux. I felt surrounded by loose ends and I didn't know what to do with myself. I didn't know if I could trust Calvin and thought I had made a mistake by confiding my theories to him. If Calvin were involved in some way or wanted to protect his uncle, things could get difficult for me. I was beginning to regret my decision to tell him so much.

Though he had told me where his father planned

to buy the food truck: at a used commercial truck dealer on Brookpark Road.

With no plans in mind for the evening, I found myself heading toward the dealer to see if Calvin's story checked out.

Twenty-five minutes later, I sat in the guest parking area of the dealership. I turned the engine off and got out, bypassing the showroom. A few salesmen watched me from the window and I pretended not to notice them.

I passed a row of vans and saw a used food truck sitting at the end. Okay, so the food truck existed at this dealership. At least that part checked out.

Before I could head back to the showroom to talk with someone, a salesman in a light blue dress shirt and khaki pants came sprinting toward me. "Well, hello there, miss." He stretched out a hand.

I did the same and he gave me a hearty shake that shook my entire body. "Hi."

"I see you're interested in this food truck," he said, releasing my hand. "As luck would have it, it's back on the market."

"Oh, is that so?"

"Yes, ma'am," he said with exaggerated enthusiasm. "And it's ready to be driven right off the lot. You'll of course have to do some superficial repairs, but there isn't a lick of rust on this thing."

"What happened to the previous buyer?" I asked.

The salesman glanced around to see if anyone had come out onto the lot. "I probably shouldn't be telling you this, but he passed away before the sale could be finalized . . . if you can believe it," he said. "His wife called to tell me about it, and I'll tell ya, that was an awkward conversation if I've ever had one."

"I can imagine," I said, looking the truck over and pretending that I was interested. I noted the price sticker on the window. "This thing isn't cheap."

"I'm sure we can make you a great deal," he said, rushing to stand next to me. "How's your credit?"

"Mediocre to fair," I said noncommittally, continuing my investigation of the truck. "And what about these propane tanks?" I pointed at the large tanks on the back of the truck. I wanted to sound like I knew what I was talking about.

"They are up to code, I can assure you of that. I've got all the appropriate paperwork."

I nodded as if the information were satisfactory. "Well, I have to discuss it with my business partner. You see, I'm just here to do a bit of scouting for us. I can't make any decisions without her present."

"Completely understandable," he said, pulling a business card out of his pocket. "Here's my card, don't hesitate to call with any questions you may have. I'm here six days a week."

I took the card and gave it a quick glance before sticking it in the side pocket of my purse. "I'll be in touch," I said, beginning to walk away.

"I wouldn't wait too long," he said, falling into step next to me. "There is another potentially interested party. I don't want you to lose out on this deal if they happen to come back before you make your decision. Try finding a truck in this condition at the same price. Won't happen in this town."

"Oh?" I stopped and turned to face him. "Another interested party?"

"Yeah, they stopped by a few weeks ago, but I was already in the process of selling it so I couldn't help them with this particular vehicle, but I never give up on a customer. I assured them I'd find them a truck in no time. But now that this one went back on the market, I gave them first dibs on it if the price is right. They were having a hard time deciding between a concession stand and a food truck . . . these damn propane tanks have everyone on edge these days. So I could understand their hesitation . . . but you're here now, so if you make me an offer, I guess it's their loss for not responding faster."

"I'm sorry? What's that you said about understanding their hesitation?"

"Oh, the propane tanks . . . my customer was worried about them. Much like you are, I'm guessing. They had all kinds of questions about what would happen if they exploded. If it would be like what you see on TV and all that jazz. Which come to think of it is kind of a bizarre coincidence considering what happened the following week." He snorted. "Although I suppose that explosion validated their concern."

"Yeah, I suppose it would . . ." Part of me had mentally left the conversation. He kept saying "they." Who was "they"?

The salesman was still yammering on about the propane tanks and I cut him off, "'They' . . . you said 'they' . . . is it more than one person interested in the truck?"

"What?" he asked, looking at me in confusion. "Oh no, for privacy. I can't very well tell you who's interested in the truck, now can I? I could get in serious trouble if I said the wrong thing."

"Gender wouldn't hurt, right?" I asked, shrugging my shoulders. "Besides, you already told me what happened with the previous buyer. What would be the harm in sharing another secret with a potential buyer?"

"Uhhh, I can't do that, ma'am, sorry." He rubbed the back of his head and smiled at me awkwardly. His eyes scanned the lot again. He appeared a little paranoid, and I began to wonder if he thought I was a secret shopper. "But you let me know as soon as possible if you're interested, okay? I'll see what I can do about making you a great deal."

Dissatisfied with his unwillingness to tell me more, I shook his hand in thanks and hopped back into my car.

In my mind, I imagined two puzzle pieces trying to work themselves together, but they didn't quite fit. What the heck was I missing?

CHAPTER
28

The next morning, while I readied myself for work, I caught myself tuning out from the present several times. The answer was there, I had it. My problem was the Winston angle. I didn't know how to get at him, and my only option was to wait for Calvin. Once I got to work, I'd give him a call and see if he'd learned anything new that could help. He had promised to call if he learned anything crucial, but again, I didn't know that he could be trusted.

When I arrived at the plaza, I hurried to the restaurant without stopping to say hello to Kimmy or any of the other shop owners like I did on most mornings. I was all business.

Peter and I barely spoke while we prepped the restaurant for opening. He asked me a couple of times if I was all right, and I did my best to assure him that I was just preoccupied with family matters. I made a production of telling him about the conversation I'd had with my aunt the day before and that seemed to pacify him.

The Mahjong Matrons filed in promptly at nine and I brought their tea out and scurried into the back to call Calvin from my office. He didn't answer so I left a message asking him to call me back as soon as possible.

When I returned to the dining area, I saw that Esther had stopped by and was standing at the head of the Matrons' table. They were speaking in hushed tones.

As I approached the table, Helen caught sight of me and seemed to hush the others. I stood next to Esther and smiled. "Hi, Esther, what brings you by?"

Helen spoke before Esther had a chance to reply. "Will our food be ready soon? We are all very hungry this morning."

"Should only be another fifteen minutes or so," I said, turning my attention back to Esther. "Can I talk to you about something?"

"Yes, of course," Esther replied. She bowed her head politely to the Matrons before turning around and signaling me to follow her. She chose the same booth my aunt had chosen the day before.

I told her I'd be right back before hurrying into the kitchen to grab some tea for our table. I also checked on the status of the Matrons' food to see just how much time I would have before being interrupted. I'd guessed right and there looked to be about fifteen minutes left before everything was done, so I rushed back out into the dining area and sat across from Esther.

"I'm glad that you stopped by because I've been meaning to come see you at the store," I said while pouring her a cup of tea.

"Oh? Is everything okay?" Esther asked. She nodded a thanks as she slid the teacup closer to herself.

"Esther," I began again. "I was hoping you could tell me a little bit about Ruby and her ex-husband David Yang."

Her body went rigid. "Why would you want to know about this?" She turned and glanced across the aisle at the Matrons' table, but they all remained seemingly oblivious to our conversation.

I knew better though. I knew they were trying to listen in.

I shifted in my seat. "I know this is kind of awkward, because of your past history with Ruby, but I wanted to know a little bit more about her . . . what kind of person she is. And what exactly happened with her ex-husband."

She leaned forward. "Why? Are you getting into trouble again? You know that your mother will worry about this."

I didn't know how to answer that question. I knew that whatever I said would result in some type of lecture on how I should mind my own business. Esther was a firm believer in leaving the past in the past, and though she had provided information to me from time to time, I didn't know how far I could push the envelope. And that's when it hit me. I decided to take a different approach . . . one that involved her beliefs about the past.

"Well, I guess what I'm wondering is that if you're willing to leave the past behind you, then why do you refuse to sell any of her jewelry now?" I asked this as innocently as I could so Esther would know that there was no malice behind the question, just sheer curiosity.

She regarded me with confusion. "Her jewelry? What does this have to do with her ex-husband?"

"Well, uh, nothing really. I guess I was just wondering about him separately because I hadn't realized she was married before," I explained, laughing nervously. "You know how sometimes I get hyper after too much coffee . . ."

"I see."

I had a feeling that Esther could see right through my cover story, but she didn't say so, and decided to entertain my question.

She sipped her tea, focusing on the black lacquer tabletop. "I have forgiven Ruby for her mistakes, but I do not wish to bring her back in my life. Some people are too much trouble and not worth the headache."

I nodded. "I can understand that. It's just a shame, I guess. Her jewelry is so nice and it would look great in your shop. I know there were several pieces I would have liked to buy myself." I opted out of telling her that I'd bought earrings from Ruby for Aunt Grace since this would probably hurt her feelings, and she'd want to know why I hadn't bought them from her store.

My hands were starting to get clammy. I knew this whole line of questioning wasn't going to get me the information I wanted to know. What I really needed to know was what happened with Ruby's ex-husband, David Yang.

She checked her watch, shaking her jade bracelets out of the way. "I should return to the store now. I will need to open soon."

My pulse quickened. I needed an answer and I didn't know how to get it from her. There was only one thing left to try and it was a low blow, but I had to do it. "Do you think that my mother would know what happened with Ruby and David?"

Esther eyed me with suspicion. "Lana Lee, do you think I was born yesterday?"

I batted my lashes. "I don't know what you mean."

She huffed. "If I tell you this, will you promise to stop asking questions? Your mother is already unhappy."

I held up my right hand. "I promise that if you tell me what I want to know, I'll stop asking questions."

She tapped the side of her teacup, and then leaned over the table. "I am surprised that you do not already know."

"I know some details, yes," I admitted. "But I don't know the full story."

"David Yang is not a good man. He is selfish and difficult and he made Ruby act crazy."

"What do you mean, 'act crazy'?"

"David was hardworking, he loved money too much. He would work late almost every night, but Ruby did not believe this. She would think he was sleeping with other women, but could not prove it. One day, she could not take it anymore and tried to make them get in a car accident."

My eyes widened. "Really?"

Esther nodded. "This changed them. After that, he became mean and she became more crazy. She started to follow him to work and sit in the parking lot, waiting to catch him. Then they began to fight. He hit her a couple of times and then the real trouble began." She waved her hands around as she listed what happened next. "Fighting all the time, then divorce papers, then she went to his work again and told everybody what happened. He almost lost his job. Many of us did not approve of her acting this way, but we also felt sorry for her."

"I can understand why," I said, attempting to imagine what it would have been like for Ruby. No one knew what truly went on behind closed doors, and how bad things had gotten between the couple. What drew these emotions out of her to begin with? What part did David play in creating or reinforcing these insecurities? "So how did it get resolved?"

Esther sighed. "David paid her a lot of money to be quiet. She did not want the money at first, but her lawyer told her this was the best thing for her to do. She needed to move on and begin a new life. Now she is married to a new man and she seems to be happy."

Esther's story had left me with a mix of emotions I couldn't identify. The situation was definitely not black-and-white, and I felt myself settling into a muddled gray that made my head hurt. This wasn't what I had expected to hear from her. Then again, I didn't know exactly what I'd expected to hear.

"For everyone, it is best to leave the past in the past, Lana. I do not feel angry toward her, but I do not wish to bring this person back into my life," She stood up from the table. "I hope that she has found peace."

* * *

After Esther left, my mind was uncontrollable. I considered all the angles pertaining to this new information. Did it have any significance for the present situation? Ruby had been traumatized by her first marriage, and perhaps that had left her with a desire to take matters, between Sandra and Ronnie into her own hands. But it didn't necessarily mean she was involved in what happened to Ronnie Chow. It might just explain why she wasn't sad about his death. I know if it had been me in her shoes, I wouldn't have cried for the man either.

It was another slow day at the restaurant, so I lounged up front, only getting up once for a call-in takeout order.

Nancy was finally coming back to work today, and I waited at the hostess booth for her to walk through the door. She looked almost like her old self again, except for a few burn marks and scratches on her arm. She had a long scratch running the length of her chin. But other than that, her porcelain face remained intact.

She gave me a long hug as she greeted me at the podium. "I am so happy to be back," she said. "I was starting to go crazy sitting at home all the time."

"Well, we're glad to have you back," I said. "Now things can go back to normal around here." While she settled in, I filled her in on what had been happening around the restaurant and how Anna May would be going to work at the law firm in a few weeks.

After we were all caught up, Peter came meandering up front and tried his best to remain manly, though I could tell he was excited to see his mom back at work. I slipped into the back to give them some privacy.

I had a missed call on my cell phone from Calvin, but he'd left no message. I quickly called him back.

"Hey Lana," he said. "Thanks for calling me back. I have news for you."

"Oh yeah?" I sat up straighter in my chair.

"My uncle admitted to setting off the bomb that went off in the trash can last Friday."

My heart pounded. "He did?"

"Yeah, it was almost like he wanted to confess. He felt horrible about it because he knows people could have gotten hurt if something had gone wrong. But he did it so the cops would stop looking at my mom. He figured if he set off another bomb when no one from my family was around, they'd realize that my mom didn't do anything wrong and would turn their investigation elsewhere."

"Oh."

"I laid into him pretty hard after he confessed. I mean, totally reckless, you know?" Calvin sighed. "He knew what he was doing though . . . like, he knew that it wouldn't be too serious."

"Calvin . . ."

"Please don't tell on him, Lana. He knows what he did was wrong, but no one got hurt . . . you know? Plus, he told me he didn't have anything to do with my father's death, and I believe him. He said that no matter what a scumbag my dad was, he was still my father. He just wanted my mom to leave him and be happy. If I had known all of this, I would have stuck around more. Maybe if I'd helped my mom, she wouldn't have felt trapped."

"You can't blame yourself, Calvin."

"I know . . . just don't tell, okay?" he pleaded. "The thing is, if the cops know that my uncle did what he did, they're automatically going to think that he's guilty of setting the bomb that blew up my dad's truck. And that's going to stop them from figuring out who really did it. I think we both agree we don't want that to happen. Whoever did this can't get away with it."

He had a point there, and I wrestled with the decision. "Tell me about Winston. What did you learn about him?"

"Oh yeah, Winston," he said. "What happened with him is legit. He's pissed too. He said this is the second time that someone has messed with his truck. He lost a whole weekend of work this time around and had to pay for all these repairs to the fuel lines."

"Hm, interesting," I said.

"Lana, promise me. Promise you won't tell. At least, not yet, all right?"

"Okay, Calvin. I promise."

We hung up and I sat back in my chair. I had no idea what to do with this information. Was his uncle telling him the truth? Or had he fed Calvin half-truths to get him off his back? Maybe Gene knew that I was still asking around and wanted to throw me off his scent. How would I know for sure that he was being honest with his own nephew? And how would I know that Calvin was being honest with me?

My sister called just then and reminded me about dinner with my family. With the way my day had started, I'd completely forgotten. She warned me not to be late, and I promised that I wouldn't be.

I had to deal with my family first, and then once and for all, I would get to the bottom of this.

CHAPTER
29

"And the Oscar goes to . . ." Megan said, cupping her hands over her mouth and mimicking an announcer.

The workday had flown by, and now I was in front of my vanity, touching up my makeup for tonight's family dinner. Megan and Kikko were sprawled out on my bed, keeping me company while I rambled about all the information that had come my way the past two days.

"My improvisational skills are really coming together," I said, laughing at her theatrics. "I'm pretty sure that guy thinks I'm buying a food truck from him."

"Well, just be glad you didn't give him your information because he would be calling you day and night with deals of the century," she joked.

"For real." I sighed, putting on my bronzer. "I still don't understand this whole thing though. None of it makes any sense. Do you think that Gene is telling Calvin the truth?"

"I mean, it's possible," Megan said, leaning back and staring at the ceiling. "He knew exactly what he was doing. He has the training after all. And he admitted to it . . . almost like he wanted to take credit for skillfully setting a bomb that didn't hurt anyone."

"Wait . . . go back," I said, turning around to face her.

"I said that he skillfully—"

"No," I hopped up from my vanity stool. "No, you said he knew what he was doing."

"Yeah . . . military training and all that."

"The salesman at the dealership said that the person who asked him about the propane tanks wanted to know if an explosion would happen just like on TV."

"So?"

"So, that means the person who went there didn't know what would happen in real life. Someone with military training or background would know exactly what would happen and wouldn't need to ask if things happened like they do on . . ." I stopped.

"On TV."

"Yeah . . . exactly, just like on TV," I said, sitting back down and assessing myself in the mirror. All I had left to do was touch up my hair and I would be ready to leave. "I have to go," I said, bouncing up from my seat and rushing to the bathroom.

"Wait, what's going on?" Megan asked, following after me. "What did you just figure out?"

I looked at her reflection in the mirror. "We're looking for someone who was worried about a food truck explosion before any explosions had happened. Someone who asked questions about the 'safety' of food trucks because they couldn't decide if they should get one or not. And then they asked if it's just like on TV."

"Yeah . . ."

"Well, there is one person who comes to mind who fits the bill. Now all I have to do is prove it."

CHAPTER

30

It took all my mental strength to keep my foot from slamming fully down on the gas pedal. I was speeding along I-271 heading north and praying that there were no cops around. The sun was starting to set and there was only a half hour before I had to meet my family for dinner. All I wanted to do was check out something really quick and I didn't want to wait until tomorrow.

I pulled up in front of Ruby's house, leaving my car parked in the street. The light was on in the front window, and I was hoping that she was the only one that was home.

I rang the doorbell and saw a shadow move through the house. Ruby opened the door and peeked outside. "Oh Lana, what are you doing here?"

"Hi, Ruby, mind if I come in?" I asked.

She stepped aside so I could pass. "No, of course, please come in," she said.

I stepped inside and assessed the living room.

Her jewelry findings and tools were sprawled out on the table and it was clear that she had been working on some new pieces when I walked in.

"Would you like something to drink?" she asked, gesturing toward the kitchen.

"Sure, I'll have some tea if you have any."

"I'll just heat some water," she said and disappeared into the kitchen.

I glanced at the TV and noticed that it was another episode of *Burn Notice*.

A few minutes later, she returned, picked up the remote and put the TV on mute. "What brings you by?"

"I just wanted to ask you about Winston Leung again," I said. "Something doesn't track for me."

"Have you mentioned it to your boyfriend yet?" she asked. "I am confident he would be able to help us."

"See, the thing about Winston is that he was long gone when the food truck exploded. And he wasn't even at the night market when the second bomb went off." I didn't bother to fill her in on the fact I knew the second bomb was Gene's doing. Not for these purposes, anyway.

She forced a smile. "Well, Lana, that type of thing would be easy to do with a timer, I'm sure."

"How did you know there was a timer? The police never mentioned that to the public," I said.

Her eyes widened. "Yes, they must have said it in the news report. I remember hearing it."

"Detective O'Neil never released the particulars since the investigation is still on-going." I reminded her.

She laughed nervously, her eyes traveling to the muted TV. "I probably saw it on one of my shows then," she said, standing abruptly. "Would you excuse me? I think the tea is ready."

The pot wasn't whistling, but I didn't say anything. She needed a moment to collect herself, and so did I. What the heck was I doing here? Was I not thinking properly? What exactly had I thought I was going to do? Part of me thought that I was going to find out something crucial to take back to Adam or even Detective O'Neil, and part of me thought maybe I'd find evidence of some type in her house. But now that I was sitting here and she'd slipped about the timer, I had no idea what business I thought I had sitting in her house. I had potentially set myself up for some serious danger.

I thought about sneaking out the front door while she was in the kitchen, but before I could stand, she appeared in the doorway. She appeared calm and was all smiles. "Lana, would you mind coming into the kitchen? I have a few different teas you can choose from."

A pit formed in the bottom of my stomach. I smiled politely, attempting to not look anxious. I didn't want to be farther from an exit than I needed to be. "Whatever you pick is fine. I like any kind of tea."

"But there are so many kinds," she said, gesturing for me to follow her to the kitchen. "I would hardly know what to choose."

I didn't know what to do. I felt frozen in my seat. But I had to act natural, right? I couldn't let on that anything was wrong, so I needed to play along for the time being. I gave myself a quick pep talk and stood up, my legs shaking the slightest bit.

She stood waiting for me in the hallway next to a door that was ajar and obstructed a full view into the kitchen. The door had been closed the other times I'd come by, and I hadn't given it much thought, thinking that it was a closet door or perhaps a pantry.

But as I neared it, I noticed there were a set of stairs leading down. It was a basement door. The light was off, but I could see the top two steps in the light coming from the living room.

She smiled at me pleasantly. "There's so much tea to choose from, I hope you can find one that you like."

"I'm sure I will," I said, slowing down. She wouldn't let me pass her.

With the same smile securely plastered on her face, she grabbed the basement door, pulling it wide open with one hand and with her other hand reached out to grab my right shoulder. She dug her nails into my skin and then attempted to push me forward with all her strength.

I was so caught off guard, I lost my balance for a moment. But I fought against gravity and Ruby's push to right myself, causing my body to swing backward, falling into the door trim instead of down the stairs. My shoulder slammed against the door frame and I tried desperately to remove her hand from my arm. I wasn't steady in the least and I ended up swinging her with me as I pulled back, aiming my body toward the living room.

Her nails were digging so deeply into my arm, I thought for sure she would draw blood. I stumbled farther backward, trying to regain my balance, and continued to pull her along with me. I managed to grab onto the door frame with my left hand and with my right hand I pushed her again. She smacked into the open basement door, hitting the back of her head. It dazed her momentarily, and I took advantage of her confusion to shove her toward the basement steps with what strength I had. As I shut the basement door behind her, I saw her catch herself on the bannister before she could fall completely down the stairs.

I slammed the door shut, and realizing that it couldn't be locked from the outside, I pressed my body weight against the door. I held the knob with one hand as I heard footsteps mounting the stairs, and she began to twist it from the other side, trying to get out.

"Lana, what are you doing?" she screamed through the door. "Let me out of here, right now."

"No," I yelled back. "You were going to push me down the stairs."

"No I wasn't," she said, rattling the knob. "You misunderstand. Now let me out!"

My hands were starting to sweat again. I couldn't keep hold of the doorknob for much longer.

My cell phone was in my purse, which I had left by the chair in the front room. How was I going to call for help?

"Lana, let me out, we can talk about this," she said. She'd relaxed her attempts on the handle for a minute and was beating on the door with both fists instead.

"I can't do that, Ruby, sorry," I said, checking out my surroundings. The first thing I searched for was a wall phone that I could grab. But there wasn't one within reach if they did have one. The kitchen chair was too far away for me to touch without letting go of the door. But if I could somehow get it over near me, I could use it to jam the door shut and then grab my cell phone. I calculated the distance between me and the chair.

I swept my left leg out in the direction of the chair, but my legs were too short.

The teakettle started to whistle.

"Lana, let me out," she yelled again. She went back to twisting the doorknob and I continued to hold it tight as best I could.

I decided to try another tactic. "If I let you out, what are you going to do?" I asked. "Are you going to try to lock me in the basement again?"

"No," she said. "I wouldn't do that. I told you, you misunderstood."

I snorted a laugh. "That's a hard thing to misunderstand."

"Lana," she said, pounding on the door. "You must let me out."

"I know it was you, Ruby," I said to her calmly. "I know that you blew up Wonton on Wheels."

Silence on the other side of the door. I relaxed my body a little bit; my legs were starting to cramp up and so was my hand.

In a soft mumble, she said, "I had to do it. You wouldn't understand."

"Why?" I asked. The teakettle was still whistling and the sound was driving me nuts. My eyes traveled back to the dining room chair. While I had her talking and occupied, I could make a grab for the chair. I waited for her to start speaking again.

"Because, don't you see, Lana?" she began. "Ronnie was going to kill her eventually. I had to do it . . . she was never going to leave him. Then it would have been too late."

"So you went snooping around at the car dealership asking about food truck explosions and just decided that's how you wanted to go about this?"

"How did you know about that?" she asked.

"I went there looking for proof that Calvin was telling me the truth about his father buying another food truck. The salesman told me that someone else had been around asking about what could happen in the event of a food truck explosion. That got me thinking that someone like Gene or Calvin who have experience with that kind of thing wouldn't need to ask anyone."

"I wasn't sure what to do. I couldn't ask anybody if this could really happen or they would know that it was me. Please, you must understand what I had to do."

"There are other ways you could have handled it," I said. And then I made a run for the chair. As I was grabbing it, she must have heard me or maybe she saw the shadow from underneath the door, and when I turned back toward the door, the doorknob began to turn.

Holding on to the chair, I lunged for the door just as she opened it a crack. I slammed all my body weight against the door to keep it closed, hitting myself in the shin with the chair at the same time.

"Damn you!" she yelled, pounding on the door again. "Let me out!"

I took a few deep breaths and reminded myself that when this was over, I really needed to start working out. "I can't let you out," I said once I'd controlled my breathing. "You're just going to try and hurt me. I know how this goes."

"Lana, we're on the same side," she said. "I'm not going to hurt you. We're both women. Women stick together. Why do you think I was trying to help Sandra? She needed me!"

I had to get the chair propped against the door without her trying to push it at the same time. I pressed my hand against the door, holding it closed with all my weight as I tried to shimmy the chair in between my body and the door.

"Is that why you went after Winston? You were the one to cut his fuel lines, weren't you?" I asked, trying to keep her occupied. I finally had the chair in place. Now all I needed to do was slide it under the door handle.

"Yes, but he deserved it," she said. "He tried to hurt his wife several times. She may have gotten away, but maybe the next woman would not have been so lucky."

"Just like your first husband hurt you?" I asked.

She was quiet for a moment, and I took the opportunity to slide the chair into place. I didn't know how long it would hold, so I hurried and raced for my purse. She started to respond as I was coming back to guard the door.

"Yes, like my husband hurt me," she said softly.

"He is lucky that I let him go with his life. Winston is lucky too."

"I understand your pain, Ruby. I really do. I can't imagine what you've been through. But that is no excuse for what is happening now. No matter what you say, there are other ways." I pulled out my phone and dialed 911.

The dispatcher answered and asked my emergency.

"I need someone to come here," I said. "Right now."

"Where are you?"

I rattled off the address as fast as I could.

"Who are you talking to?" Ruby pounded on the door. "Let me out!"

"I'm sending a car out now. Are you in immediate danger, ma'am?"

"Yes! Please hurry!" I yelled into the phone.

I hung up without saying anything else and continued to press my weight against the door. I didn't trust the chair even though it seemed to be holding up pretty well so far.

"You might as well give up," I told her. "The police are on their way now."

She continued to bang on the door. "We're on the same side," she said. "You don't have to do this. I only wanted to save Sandra from herself. Can't you understand that?"

I didn't respond to her question because, in truth, I didn't know if I was capable of understanding such a sensitive topic; I had never been in a similar situation myself. Yes, I had been in danger a few times, but they were isolated events and nothing that would cause me to feel pushed to the edge.

However, what I did know was that I couldn't allow her to roam free after murdering someone whether she felt he had it coming or not.

The front door of the house started to open, and I assumed that it would be the police. But it wasn't, it was Ruby's husband, Don.

"What the . . ." He gawked at me. "What are you doing here?"

"Who's there?" Ruby yelled through the door. "Don, is that you?"

"Ruby?" He searched the room in confusion and rushed over once he realized where her voice was coming from. "Do you have my wife locked in the basement?"

"She was trying to push me in there," I explained to him. "Your wife is responsible for the food truck explosion and killing Ronnie Chow."

He scoffed at me. "Nonsense, get away from the door before I have you arrested." He pushed me harshly to the side, right into the kitchen. I lost my balance, falling squarely on my butt. "I've never heard anything so ridiculous in my life . . ."

As he removed the chair, Ruby pushed with all her strength at the door, knocking him back. He lost his balance and fell backward, slamming into the wall behind him.

Ruby's eyes were wild with panic and she took one look at her husband, and then at me before running through the front room. I saw her grab for something quickly off the front table before she hurried out the door.

"Ruby?" her husband yelled. "What are you doing? Where are you going?"

"I told you, she's guilty!" I said, trying to stand. I had fallen so hard my tailbone stung with pain and it was a struggle to get up.

We heard the start of an engine outside and both of us raced to the front door just as Ruby was taking off down the street.

However, she didn't make it far. The police had almost arrived and in her hurry to make a quick escape she ran head-on into a police cruiser.

The Mayfield Heights Police Department was not entirely happy with my story of what happened. I tried to convince them the best course of action was to call Detective O'Neil, but they assured me they weren't done with me just yet. Ruby's husband had caused quite a scene and was attempting to paint me as the bad guy.

I sat on the chair that I'd been holding the basement door closed with while the responding officer put in a call to the Cleveland Police Department to see if I was telling the truth.

While I was sitting there, my sister called. I was still clutching my cell phone and I was unsupervised at the moment, so I answered.

Before I could say hello, she started talking. "Lana, where the heck are you? You're already thirty minutes late. Mom is not happy with you for keeping us waiting."

"Yeah." I glanced at the police officer who was busy talking to someone I hoped was Detective

O'Neil. "I'm probably not going to make it. Go ahead and eat without me."

"Why aren't you coming? Where are you?"

The officer turned around to face me. "Ma'am, I'm going to need you to get off your phone for the time being."

Anna May must have heard him because she said, "Lana Lee, you better have a damn good reason why you can't make dinner tonight."

"Trust me, I do."

EPILOGUE

When Ruby was transferred to the Cleveland Police Department, she finally broke down and fully confessed to what she'd done to Ronnie and Wonton on Wheels. She'd gotten the idea from one of the crime shows she was so fond of watching and decided that Ronnie needed to be taught a lesson. Though she had not tried to clarify the fact to me during our little hostage situation, she did tell the police that she hadn't meant to kill him. But she wasn't exactly upset that it had turned out the way it did either. Her original intent had only been to severely harm him so that he could never lay a hand on Sandra again. Because the research she'd done on homemade explosives had been spotty and hurried, she hadn't realized the true impact her creation would have.

She also admitted her guilt regarding the tampering of Winston's food truck. As she'd mentioned in her confession to me, he reminded her very much of David Yang, and when she'd gotten wind that he had a domestic dispute on his record, she felt it was her job to dole out further punishment.

Ruby did not take responsibility for the second explosion, which the police couldn't understand. But since Calvin and I were the only ones who actually knew who the guilty party was, I had a feeling that crime would go unsolved. With everything their family had been through, I couldn't bring myself to rat out Calvin's uncle. A part of me felt guilty for holding on to the secret, but I reminded myself that despite its scaring the crap out of me, no one was actually physically hurt.

Calvin and Sandra decided to open a food truck together. And though Calvin still planned to help his uncle out at the repair shop, he wanted to spend as much time with his mother as he possibly could. Wonton on Wheels would live again.

As far as family matters went, my aunt and mother were able to make amends, and according to Anna May, the family dinner I missed out on was one of the best our family ever had. Of course, it would be the one I wasn't there for.

Once I relayed how I had been delayed at Ruby's house, my family gave me a pass for missing dinner. To make up for it, I had breakfast with them on the way to the airport.

I made sure to give my dad an extra big hug and thank him for being the patient man that he was and always had been. I was more than grateful to have a father like him instead of someone like Ronnie, and that feeling was even stronger now after everything I'd learned about the Chow family.

During breakfast when no one was paying attention, I slipped my aunt the earrings I had purchased from Ruby. We shared a nice moment that was just ours, much like the chat we'd had in the restaurant the other day. I knew that my aunt and I would always have this special bond and for that I was grateful.

When we dropped my aunt off at the airport for her flight, my mom wished her safe travels and told her to come back as soon as she could. And while I was happy to see the change in their relationship, I was still hoping a considerable amount of time would elapse before the next family reunion.

The *Plain Dealer* contacted me for a comment on my ordeal, but I politely turned them down. The less my name showed up in the paper, the better. My cover was already blown with half the Asian community already, no sense in adding to my notoriety.

Now, a week later, I stood at the edge of my bed with a suitcase open and filled to the brim with clothes that I probably wouldn't need. Adam and I had jointly agreed on the Poconos after all, and I was excited to get away, especially after the events of the past two weeks.

Just as I was zipping up my suitcase, Adam showed up in the doorway of my bedroom. He was dressed casually in a light linen dress shirt and cargo shorts.

I tilted my head and gave him a once-over. "Are those your legs?" I asked with a smirk. "And do you actually have flip-flops on?"

"Very funny, Lee," he said, stepping into my room. "We're going on vacation . . . shorts and flip-flops are vacation gear."

"Yes, but when is the last time your legs actually saw the light of day?" I joked.

"All right, that's enough." He rushed me and scooped me up, throwing me over his shoulder into a fireman's carry. "We'll see how funny things are from the trunk of the car."

Giggling, I pounded on his back with my fists. "Put me down."

"Not a chance, missy," he said, grabbing my suitcase with his free hand. "I'm getting you out of here without any more interruptions. And we're going to have a fun and relaxing time . . . come hell or high water."

He carried me through the apartment, refusing to put me down. Kikko waddled after us and I waved good-bye to her and to Megan as we passed.

A feeling of hope was beginning to come back to me, and I smiled as he whisked me out of the apartment and through the parking lot. Once again, it was good to be me.

Read on for an excerpt of

- - - - - - - - - - - - - - - - -

Egg
Drop
Dead

- - - - - - - - - - - - - - - - -

Available in March 2020

from St. Martin's Paperbacks

CHAPTER

1

- - - - - - - - - - - - - - - -

"I am not going to wear a qi-pao to Donna Feng's party, Mother!" I was standing in front of the mirror that hangs on my bedroom closet door while my mother, Betty Lee, held the Asian-style dress against my body, the plastic hanger pushing firmly into my neck.

"Why not?" my mother returned in somewhat of a whine. "You look *so* cute."

I think most of us can agree that women in their late 20s do not want to be labeled as "cute." And you could mark me on that list. Who am I? Lana Lee, nice to meet you. I'm your average—not so average—Asian American gal, recently turned twenty-eight, with not a clue about martial arts, math that goes beyond long division, or how to speak any dialect of Chinese. But, I can use chopsticks like a son of a gun. So that's something, right?

If you had to find me in a crowd, it wouldn't be a problem because fifty percent of my hair is currently pink. I love hamburgers and pizza almost as much as I love noodles, and if you asked me to cook you a proper Chinese meal, we'd both starve that night. That's why I manage my parent's Chinese restaurant instead of cook there. No one wants me behind a wok.

In recent weeks, we'd added a catering service to the family business to help bring in extra money. Summer months at the noodle shop could be slow, and we were dead smack in the middle of July.

Our first catering job was for Donna Feng, the owner of Asia Village—the shopping plaza my family's restaurant was part of. It was Donna's birthday and she wanted to have a fancy dinner party at her house. When she first proposed the idea, I of course jumped at the opportunity thinking that it would include food for maybe ten to fifteen of her closest friends and family.

However, that was not the case. It turned out she was thinking more along the lines of a small, intimate party of fifty. You know, because all of us have a close-knit group of fifty people. Regardless, I was up for the challenge and it was nothing Ho-Lee Noodle House couldn't handle.

I'd had a very specific dress in mind for the party, and it did not resemble this navy blue qi-pao covered in dragons and clouds that my mother had picked out. The black dress I had chosen with its high lace color and cap sleeves was feminine, sleek, and most of all, mature. It didn't make me feel like a ten-year-old dressing up in a costume.

My mother is a small Taiwanese woman with an

extreme desire to keep me at the age of seven, and this dress was evidence of that. She released the hanger's hold on my neck and waved the dress in front of me. "But this is so beautiful. If Mommy was younger, I would keep this for myself."

"Well Mother, as they say, age is just a number. It looks like it will fit you just fine." I smiled sweetly at her.

She scowled in return and laid the dress on my bed next to Kikkoman, my black pug, who had been watching our every move with intrigue. Kikko sniffed the silky material before letting out a groan that might be mistaken for human.

When my mother turned around to face me, she planted her dainty hands on her hips—as was her customary stance when speaking to me—and jutted her head forward with determination set in her dark brown eyes. "Everyone else who is working will wear the same dress. This will show high class."

"So, Peter's going to wear *that* dress?" I responded with a smirk.

My mother did not find it amusing. "You are not funny, Lana Lee."

I glanced back at the dress on my bed. "Neither is making me wear that dress."

"Why?" My mother asked. "Your sister is okay wearing this dress. She did not give Mommy such a hard time."

"That's because she's a kiss—"

"Hello!" A cheerful voice yelled from the living room.

"We're in here!" I shouted back.

It was my best friend and roommate, Megan Riley. And hopefully she could talk some sense into my mother. Kikko hopped down onto the floor and wiggled her curly tail as she went to greet Megan who was on her way to join us in my bedroom.

Her blonde hair was iron board straight, and she was dressed in a black t-shirt and skinny jeans, most likely coming home from a shift at the Zodiac, the bar where she works. Lately she had been working a mixture of random hours due to the short staff problems they were having. "Oh hey, Mama Lee," she said, giving my mother a hug. "It's nice to see you."

My mother looked up at her, squinting as she assessed her. "You look skinny."

"Ma, you always say that." She squeezed my mom's arm playfully, and turned to me. "What are you guys up to? Want to get some dinner or something?"

"You came just in time," I told her, grabbing the dress from my bed. "My mother wants me to wear this," I shook it at her. "Isn't it ridiculous?"

Megan took the dress from me and looked it over. "What's wrong with it?"

"Don't you think it's a bit cliché?"

"I think it's cute."

I threw my hands in the air. "Exactly."

My mother groaned.

Megan laughed and handed the dress back to me. "Stop being so stubborn, Lana. It's just one night."

"I'm not being stubborn."

Okay, in truth, on the must-knows about Lana Lee . . . stubborn makes the list.

* * *

The next evening, after much going back and forth with the dress I had purchased for myself versus the dress my mother required me to wear, I decided not to create unnecessary waves and give in to her request. So I dutifully put on the qi-pao and a pair of black, patent leather stiletto heels to add some edge and went on my way to Donna Feng's house in Westlake without another thought about it.

The wealthy widow lived with her two teenage daughters in a house that was big enough to host two full-size families. Without her husband, Thomas, around she found herself struggling to handle a lot of the affairs that come along with taking care of a house that size. Between raising two teens, the charity work she did within the Asian community, and her mild involvement with Asia Village she quickly found her hands full. So, instead of minimizing her responsibilities, she'd recently hired a maid, a live-in nanny, and a gardener to help with the various tasks around the house.

I pulled onto Donna's street and parked my car a few houses down behind my sister's car. We'd been instructed to allow more room for the guests to have better parking options.

It was approaching sunset and the humidity of the day had mostly dissipated. A light, refreshing breeze ruffled the leaves on trees ever so gently.

The dress was a little tight—probably from all the doughnuts I'd been eating recently—and I shimmied myself out of the car, thankful for the respectable slit down the side. As I walked along the sidewalk listening to my heels click-clack, I immediately regretted my choice of footwear.

My sister, Anna May and Peter Huang, our head chef, were in Donna's driveway unloading the food trays and dining accessories that we needed for the evening. Peter had borrowed his cousin's beat-up work van and it stuck out like a sore thumb in this ritzy neighborhood. I made a mental note that we might need a catering van if we were going to get serious about this side business.

Peter noticed me approaching and gave me a casual head nod. His normally ballcap-covered head was bare and his shaggy black hair looked to have been trimmed and slicked back. Also missing from his typical apparel were his beat-up combat boots that he wore in the kitchen at Ho-Lee Noodle House every day. In their place were polished, square-toed dress shoes. He noticed my assessment and spoke before I could say anything. "My mom said I had to, so don't give me a hard time, okay?"

"I wasn't planning on saying anything," I lied. "You look sharp."

"Thanks, I feel weird though. And they're so not cool to cook in. I told my mom they were going to get ruined, but she didn't care." He shrugged. "So whatever."

My sister batted his arm. "Stop saying you look weird, you actually look like a grown-up for once."

I regarded my sister with a quick assessment. Of course we looked the same in our matching qi-paos, but my sister had gone for classy and I'd gone for sassy. Her hair was impeccably done, a French bun, not a hair out of place. Classic pearl necklace and matching bracelet, French manicured nails and sensible kitten heels. Whereas my hair was French braided and swept up to the side in a messy sort of way with strands of pink left down to frame my face, thanks to Megan's ability to copy hairstyles from magazines. I'd chosen bold silver jewelry, chunky rings, cuff bracelet, sparkly chandelier earrings, and of course, these blasted stilettos.

As I thought about them, my sister's eyes landed on my feet and she snorted. "Lana, you're going to die in those shoes within the first hour."

"I'll be fine, let's hurry and get this stuff inside so Peter can move this van. I'm surprised Donna hasn't said anything about it yet."

As the three of us walked inside, I cringed as the toes of my shoes started to pinch. But you know how sometimes you focus on the smallest inconveniences of life, not realizing that things could be so much worse?

Yeah, it was going to be one of those times.

CHAPTER

2

- - - - - - - - - - - - - - -

Donna Feng is the kind of woman who makes a statement just by walking into a room. She is bold, she is coiffed, and she exudes the kind of confidence any woman would covet. I often found myself searching within for the same type of confident mentality.

It is on a rare occasion that you would find Donna in a state of flux. However, today she was in rare form. When we entered through the front door, we found Donna in the sitting room standing next to a slightly shorter woman in a sleek black suit, barking orders at a team of people in crisp white shirts and black dress pants. I had no idea who the people were, but my best guess told me they were here to help make Donna's party the best in the city.

Donna, though in a stunning dark gray A-line dress, appeared less than confident. Her fists were clenched at her sides, and I could see the anxiety in her eyes as the other woman talked.

"Okay people, guests will start to arrive shortly,

and everything has to be absolutely on point! I expect nothing less!" The woman clapped her hands together in quick succession. "Flower arrangements on all the tables, settings placed to perfection . . . if anything is out of place, put it in place. Now move!"

The workers left the room in single file.

My sister and I shared a look as we followed behind Peter. Donna caught the movement from the corner of her eye and clasped her hands together in excitement. "Oh Lana, darling," she cooed, ignoring both my sister and Peter. "You've arrived! Come in, come in. I'm so glad you're here!"

She greeted me and my sister with a hug and gave a respectful nod to Peter. "Lana, I'd love for you to meet my party planner. This is Yvette Howard, and she is absolutely brilliant at what she does. I don't know what I'd do without her."

The shorter woman stepped up and smiled brightly. She had the exact same air of confidence that Donna carried and I could see why Donna would choose her. "It's nice to meet you."

"Yvette," Donna said, putting an arm around me. "This is my caterer, Lana Lee, her sister, and their cook. Lana was so gracious as to handle all of the food prep, and since she's a family friend, you can see why I didn't need any help in that department."

Donna and I sort of bonded around the time of her husband's death a few months back, and ever since then she had seemingly taken more of a liking to me over my sister. She wasn't a huge fan of Peter because he happened to be the illegitimate son of her deceased husband. However, because of this, she did show him a level of respect. I knew that it was painful for her to see him since it was a reminder of her husband's infidelity, so considering the circumstances, I think she handled her encounters with him pretty well.

"That's wonderful," Yvette replied with fake enthusiasm. "It's really nice to meet all of you, but I want to go check on things on the back deck and make sure we're just about ready."

Donna patted Peter on the shoulder, and gestured to the kitchen entrance with her other hand. "Let's get you guys situated. You can set everything down in here. You'll have to excuse the mess, it's been absolutely chaotic all day. I can't seem to find any competent help except for Yvette, and the girls have been driving me nuts since the moment they got out of bed this morning."

Jill and Jessica Feng were Donna's twin teenager girls who were a bit of a handful these days. Both of them had decided it was a good time to go through their rebellious phase. I had a suspicion it had something to do with their father's death and everything that came out about Peter being their half-brother didn't help the situation.

No one talked about it either . . . including Peter. The girls never spent any time with Peter and he had never tried to offer getting to know them. Neither Donna, nor Peter's mother, Nancy, had ever encouraged it.

I set my armload of items down on the flawless marble countertop of the kitchen island and assessed the room. The stainless steel appliances were sparkling and definitely cleaner than anything you'd find in my apartment. The ceramic floors were equally clean and I'd bet money you could eat off of them if the situation called for it. "Donna, everything is immaculate as usual. You're worrying over nothing."

She released a heavy sigh, leaning against the island. "Everything just feels absolutely out of order. How's my hair?" she asked, quickly changing subjects.

"It looks great!" my sister chimed in from behind me. "And your dress is amazing."

"Thanks dear," she said smoothing out the lines near her waist. "Calvin Klein never lets me down, I can tell you that. And you girls look lovely as well." She assessed our matching qi-paos. "It was a great idea of your mother's to have the ladies wear matching outfits. Uniformity is a clear sign of classic professionalism."

I bit my tongue because I didn't agree. I thought it was an awful idea, but now wasn't the time to express my true feelings about my attire to the birthday girl. "Donna, why don't you go and relax for a little while and let us handle everything down here. I can get the door as the guests start to arrive. And Yvette seems to have everything else under control."

"Oh sure, I suppose you're right about that. I probably should check on the girls one last time as well. They invited a few of their little friends over and I want to make sure they understand the ground rules. After all, this is an adult party." As she started to walk away, she turned around to say, "Just send everybody out onto the back deck and I'll be down in a little while."

After she left the room, Peter, who had remained silent during the whole conversation, let out a low whistle. "Dude, someone needs to chill."

Easy for Peter to say; I'd seen him emote maybe a whole two times since the day we met. Although it was odd for Donna to act out like this.

"Give her a break," my sister said, swatting his arm. "Women get weird on their birthdays as they get older. Life is passing, things haven't happened, things have gone to the wayside, whatever. There's always something. And she's already a widow."

"Age is just a number," I said, knowing full well what would happen next. But there are those moments where I just can't help myself.

My sister rolled her eyes at me. "That's because you're not even thirty yet, Lana. Trust me. You're going to be singing a different tune in two years. Mark my words."

"Doubt it," I replied. "You've said this to me every year for how many years and I still don't agree."

"Lana, *I* am the big sister, so trust me. I know."

My sister is only three years older than me, but she acts like there's twenty years in between us. She is always warning me about this and that and how things are just all heading down from here.

On more than one occasion, I've been called an idealist, and truly, I think it's a blessing if anything. Yes, I'd like to believe in the good of life and humanity. Is that so wrong?

Instead of caving to the typical argument that follows between us on the subject, I decided to busy myself with the actual task at hand.

The bulk of the party would be outside in the backyard around the pool. My friends from the plaza, Kimmy Tran—who was also Peter's girlfriend—and Rina Su would also assist in serving food. The

menu was predominantly appetizers and we would
be those girls you see walking around with trays.
Yes, I was a tray girl. But also as manager of Ho-
Lee Noodle House, it was my job to make sure that
everything ran smoothly. My parents would be in at-
tendance at the party along with my grandmother,
but they were coming as guests. It was just the Lee
girls working tonight. Nancy had been exempt from
the evening because of the weirdness between her
and Donna. I thought at first that it might hurt her
feelings, but she was actually quite relieved. Her and
our other cook were at the noodle house keeping the
place running so we didn't have to close to cater the
party.

Peter went out to move the van, and my sister
got busy preparing the final tasks before the party
started. Not only because this was Donna's birthday
party, but it was our first catering gig and there would
be many prominent guests here that might want our
catering services for themselves in the future. I'd
had special menus and extra business cards printed
to hand out to guests if anyone asked. Nothing could
go wrong tonight. Absolutely nothing . . .

2842